Full Figured 7:

Carl Weber Presents

Full Figured 7:

Carl Weber Presents

Nikki Rashan

and

Ni'chelle Genovese

www.urbanbooks.net

Urban Books, LLC
97 N18th Street
Wyandanch, NY 11798

ISBN 13: 978-1-60162-394-2
ISBN 10: 1-60162-394-1

First Trade Paperback Printing November 2013
Printed in the United States of America

10 9 8 7 6 5 4 3 2 1

Distributed by Kensington Publishing Corp.
Submit Wholesale Orders to:
Kensington Publishing Corp.
C/O Penguin Group (USA) Inc.
Attention: Order Processing
405 Murray Hill Parkway
East Rutherford, NJ 07073-2316
Phone: 1-800-526-0275
Fax: 1-800-227-9604

Sugar on the Side

by

Nikki Rashan

Chapter 1

A Walk Down Sugar Lane

My momma named me Sugar. I was born in a south-side Chicago hospital at the end of August. It was 1981. Momma said it was her plan to name her first-born child the zodiac sign under which he or she was born, meaning, had I been born in February, I would have been walking around with folks calling me Aquarius or Pisces. Or Gemini or Cancer had I graced the world in June. But Momma, pregnant during a burning-hot summer, ate one scoop of vanilla ice cream twice a day to cool her sweating body in Chicago's mid-year heat. She decided to bypass her original plan and name me after the sugar cone she nibbled on every day with her ice cream. She told me she nibbled just as much on my sweet, fat baby cheeks for many months after I was born.

My momma's name was Noxzema. Yep, she was named after the famous cleansing cream, so it was no wonder she would have had no problem with a daughter named Virgo or a son named Sagittarius. As a child when my neighborhood friends would inquire, "What's yo' momma's name?" I would make something up. Some days she was Mary, some days she was Pam. She was any name except Noxzema. I lied to avoid the snickering and in-my-face laughter I would encounter had I told the truth. It would have been the same kind of laughter I had endured when kids learned my name was Sugar. I was always teased and called different versions of sweet treats like Tootsie Roll, Slo Poke, or Swedish Fish.

I don't think Momma realized the effects the name Sugar would have on me. It was as if she had had some sort of premonition for the sweet tooth I would develop as a youngster. Or maybe the name was a curse, who knew. Either way, I was sucking on Blow Pop after Blow Pop as a toddler, and devouring Hostess CupCakes and Twinkies in grammar school. I was never fat. I was pudgy at two and three, with a chubby, round face and protruding tummy. People told Momma I was adorable at that age. In fourth and fifth grades, I was chunky. Then people told Momma I had a pretty face but, "You better watch that baby's eatin'," they warned. My thighs rubbed together, my shirt rose over my belly, and I couldn't run as fast as the other kids could during recess. If my foot happened to make contact with the ball during a game of kickball, which didn't happen often, I would be hit "out" only halfway to first base. For that reason, I was usually picked last to be on a team during gym class and was the recipient of nonstop teasing from classmates about my poor athletic skills.

Life changed in 1994 when I discovered singing and sex at thirteen. At that time my once-round, shapeless body had transformed, deflating around my waist and inflating around my hips. My breasts grew full, my behind lifted and swelled, and my thighs remained thick, but suddenly curved the way Momma's did in the pictures I saw of her before she had me.

My friend Shonda had a Halloween house party that year. A group of about ten of us eighth graders was in her basement after all of us, too old for trick-or-treating, sat around eating the candy we had just collected going door-to-door in homemade costumes anyway. It had grown dark outside; the half-hidden sun no longer sent light through the basement well windows. Shonda liked it that way; she wanted it to feel like we were in a dimly lit nightclub like the ones we saw in the movies and on television. Some of the latest R&B slow jams played from the radio. Some of us hummed along to the songs, and a few coupled up and started slow dancing, shamelessly grinding hip to hip in front of everybody. A fresh song by Boyz II Men came on and Dante, a fourteen-year-old high school freshman I had known since we were young kids, asked me to dance.

Dante wasn't fly. He was hardly even cute with his oblong, stretched head that matched his straight and lean body. His arms easily wrapped around my waist, bringing me close; his body settled into the tenderness of the flesh of my hips and thighs.

"You lookin' good lately, Sugar," he whispered. His breath smelled of a chocolate and peanut candy bar.

"Thank you." I giggled. His hand moved up and down my spine.

"'I'll make love to you,'" he sang along with Nate, Wayna, Shawn, and Michael. "'If you want me to.'"

"I like this song," I told him suggestively. I had never been touched by a boy and even though I didn't love the way his body felt pressed into mine, Shonda had told me how good some of the boys made her feel when they laid on top of her. I questioned if I would ever be touched again if I didn't offer to Dante what I knew Shonda gave to boys.

"You wanna go to the closet?"

I looked toward the corner storage room to which Dante referred. I had never been inside the space, but imagined it to be a filthy, dusty area filled with old, unwanted items that hadn't yet been delivered to the Goodwill. Still, I eagerly told him yes.

Inside the cramped space, we nestled against a stack of used, down-filled winter coats. I knew what was about to happen and only a few minutes later I learned the moment was not how Shonda had described it. I hadn't experienced sparkles like she said she did. I had only felt pain and even if there hadn't been any discomfort, I hadn't liked the way Dante moved inside my body. I would forever remember my first sexual experience as unfulfilled and confusing. I was left with a cramped neck, stiffness in my hips, and no desire to allow another man inside of me. I had my clothes back on and was out of Shonda's house before Dante had a chance to ask me for another forgettable encounter.

Back at home in my room, I turned on my stereo and pumped up the volume to Aaliyah's "Back & Forth," a jam everyone had bumped in their cars and portable CD players that summer. Not only did we love the song for her innocent, whisper-like voice, but because Chicago's own R. Kelly had his hand in bringing her music to the world. I sang with her, louder and more powerful than her soft-spoken melody. Leaned against my wall with my eyes shut tight, I belted the words from somewhere so deep within I almost hadn't recognized the sound that came from my mouth. The energy was like a steady push upward, under my diaphragm and ribs, a rush that forced its way from the depths inside of me as if it had been waiting years to exit and reveal its power. The surge was intense, the stirring I felt ecstatic. I sang song after song until I became exhausted from the exertion of both physical and emotional energy. As soon as I collapsed on my bed, Momma opened my door, her eyes red and shiny with tears. She held me in her arms.

"It's all right, baby girl, it's all right."

I didn't have to tell her I just had sex for the first time, she knew. My momma's instincts had always been keen.

When I was younger and had snuck cookies or potato chips to bed at night, I'd be just about to munch on my first bite when she'd enter the room, snatch the snack out of my hand, and walk out of the room without a word. Then there was the time when I had tried to hide a bad test grade from her. See, my momma made me show her my homework every day and each Tuesday I would have a new math quiz to give her. I failed one test in the sixth grade and, ashamed, I folded the red-marked paper into a small square and hid it in the corner pocket of my backpack. When Momma asked about Tuesday's quiz, I told her Ms. Johnson hadn't been at school that day and the substitute didn't know we took quizzes on Tuesday. My eyes must have shifted or watered slightly, or Momma just knew better. Calmly, she asked for my backpack. Shuffling my feet against the worn brown carpeting throughout our house, I walked to my bedroom and retrieved the backpack. She went right to the zipped pocket and got my quiz. I stopped trying to fool Momma after that.

"Come on, take a bath," she instructed, and led me to the bathroom. She sat on the toilet while I rested in the warm water. She had even sprinkled in her special bath salts, the ones she used after long shifts on her feet at the hotel where she was a member of the housekeeping crew.

"I can't imagine tonight was a good night, not the way you came in singing like a cheatin' preacher's wife."

She asked for details, which I shared with her.

"Wash real good around there." She pointed to my young womanly parts. "We don't need none of that boy's little men trying to swim around your sea. I hope it's not too late." She put her hands together, closed her eyes, and looked like she said a silent prayer to God. "After this, watch yourself, Sugar. You're not a little girl anymore; you're a woman now. Men can tell once you've given it up to somebody, makes them think it's easier for them to get to you now, you hear? No daughter of mine is about to be prancin' up and down these streets with a fat belly. I'm not trying to bottle-feed any grandbabies at thirty-two. So if you want birth control, we'll get birth control. But that don't protect from everything."

I lowered myself farther under the water and blew bubbles while Momma watched. Finally, I told her, "I don't need birth control, I don't want to do it again. I didn't like it."

She chuckled. "Child, that's every woman's story 'til the next boy or man comes along and whispers something good in her ear. You have learn that not everybody is worthy of that special part of you. Even when he's telling you he's going to love you forever and can't nobody love you like he can, you make him prove it first."

I heard her words and tucked them deep inside to that same place where the fire had been sparked just a short time before. My feelings about boys and men were just as strong as the spirit behind my newfound passion. I equally despised one and loved the other.

"I want to sing," I told Momma.

"I heard you, Sugar. I haven't heard a voice like yours since the great Chaka Khan. It's strong. Brought me to tears. If you want to sing, I'll help you sing."

And just like that, Momma did. I sang at every neighborhood backyard barbecue. I sang for the women in the beauty shop where she got her hair done. Momma scoured newspapers and asked friends about any and every talent show in the Chicago area. Even though I wanted to sing music of younger stars like TLC, SWV, and Brandy, Momma told me my voice was too robust for their simple lyrics and style. She taught me the songs of some of her favorite artists like Stephanie Mills, Aretha Franklin, and Roberta Flack. She was convinced I could also sing the greats of Stevie Wonder, Donny Hathaway, and Luther Vandross.

Over the next six years, I focused on nothing other than singing and schoolwork. On weekends, I sang at weddings, birthday, and anniversary parties, and even opened for a few local performers before their concerts. Dante and every boy who approached me after performances were granted nothing more than a "thanks, but no thanks" to their offers to take me out. Music and singing had become the greatest love of my life next to Momma. Then I met Dani.

Dani waited for me at the side of the small stage where I had just performed "I'll Always Love You" by Taylor Dayne at her cousin's wedding. She held her hand to me and guided me down three steps to the floor. "Beautiful song by a beautiful lady," she complimented me.

At nineteen, I had matured to a tall five feet nine inches, a curvy mini diva in the making. I had never been and still wasn't a slim girl. Around that time people told me I reminded them of a hot, new full-figured singer named Jill Scott who had just hit the scene. My face remained full, though I had mastered the art of makeup and skillfully highlighted or contoured my cheekbones, forehead, and chin to minimize their fullness, and I dramatically emphasized my almond eyes and soft lips with color. My breasts, desirable at size FF, were perched high and were on constant display in low-cut tops. My waist curved with the assistance of lightweight girdles and accentuated my rounded waist and healthy thighs. I wasn't fat; I was sexy. Everyone told me so and no one could tell me otherwise. Momma had no issue with me using my sensuality to attract an audience; it kept the gigs coming. She was proud that I had such focus and determination and hadn't let Dante or any other salivating man deter me from my goal of becoming a famous singer.

"Thank you," I told Dani.

She was tall with an athletic build, short hair, and a remarkable smile. I recognized her as a talented former high school basketball star with promise at a Big Ten university. She had, however, gotten into trouble after getting caught smoking weed the summer before she was to leave for her freshman year. From what I heard, the university was willing to let the first slip slide, but after a second under-the-influence encounter with her recruiter, Dani's scholarship slid right from under her basketball-playing feet.

"Dani," she told me.

"Yes, I know," I responded.

"I told my cousin you were best singer Chicago has."

Silently I agreed. "You've heard me sing before?"

"Who hasn't? You've seen me play before?"

"Who hasn't?"

We both laughed. A second later Momma was at my side with my purse.

"Time to go, Sugar." She eyeballed Dani from her tapered haircut, shirt, and tie, down to her flat shoes. Dani was the opposite of everything I represented with me in my glamorous weave, spectacular makeup, fitted dress, and high heels.

"Hello," Dani said to Momma and extended her hand.

Momma took it graciously, never one to shun a fan, though the handshake was short, abruptly cut off when it seemed Dani was prepared to kiss the back of Momma's hand. She turned to me. "I'll be in the car. See you in *one minute,*" she emphasized.

"I see where you get your fire," Dani acknowledged after Momma walked away.

"She means no harm; she's just looking out for me."

"You ever let anyone else look out for you?"

I had already learned to seduce through music and
singing. It was easy to manipulate a fan into believing
he was my chosen one with a wink or blown kiss while I
sang a love song in his direction. It was all innocent to me
and shame on them for taking it seriously when the song
was over. With Dani there was no music and still the song
inside me stirred. I took a step closer and flirted with a
woman for the first time.

"You look out for me, I'll look out for you," I cooed in
her ear.

"Bet that," she said.

"Cool." I adjusted my purse from my hand to the bend
of my arm. "Good to know you're watching my back." I
winked at her and walked away. I felt her eyes against my
backside during my stroll out of the hall to the exit door. I
felt an excitement in my chest and between my legs that I
hadn't experienced before. Momma sensed it.

"We've worked hard at building up your name for you
to tear it down dealing with folks like that."

"Folks like what, Momma?"

"You know who I'm talking about, child. Them girls."

"What if I like 'them girls'?" I challenged, unsure if I did
or didn't, only knowing I had ignored all sexual yearnings
and cravings while developing my career and suddenly I
wanted to release my desires.

"You got to understand how this world works. People
will praise you one day and scorn you the next. I didn't
say nothing was wrong with women on women, but that's
private. That's grown-people, shut-the-door kinda business, you feel me? You've been a good girl all these years.
I ain't mad at you for finding interest somewhere. I was
wondering when it was going to happen. But if that's
where it's at, be smart and keep it quiet. Matter of fact, let
me handle it."

The next day Dani picked me up in her Buick LeSabre.

"No smoking and no drinking, Miss Thing," Momma instructed Dani, aware of Dani's drug history.

"I gave it up, ma'am. Learned my lesson. No worries, I'll take care of your daughter just fine."

"You better, she's precious." Momma watched us drive away from the living room window with her arms folded across her chest.

"Your moms is something else," Dani told me as we headed down Seventy-ninth Street. "According to her we can't go anywhere except back to my apartment. Is that cool with you?"

It may have been immoral for Momma to send me off to sleep with a woman. She would know that by the time I returned home that night I would have experienced my "second first"; my second time having sex, my first time with a woman. But that was Momma's way of looking out for me. If I was going to do it, I would do with her knowledge and with her blessing and control.

That afternoon Dani introduced me to my body. She showed me every place I hadn't known appreciated a kiss, a caress, a lick, and a squeeze. Dani was aggressive in her lovemaking, though patient with me, and seemed to delight in knowing I was a virgin to the experience she granted me.

Between bites to my thighs and sucks to my middle she told me, "I know why your moms named you Sugar." She licked deliciously. "You taste just like it."

Wednesdays were my least booked nights, so Momma scheduled my visits with Dani for those midweek evenings. For about six months I learned the talent of making love from Dani. I surrendered to her strength, she to my passion. We couldn't get enough of each other until one Wednesday morning Momma came to my bedroom to tell me I wouldn't be seeing Dani again.

"Why not?" I questioned. Of course Dani hadn't dumped me. Not me, not Sugar.

It seemed Dani had given up smoking weed, but had taken on the job of selling it instead. She had been arrested the night before and from what Momma learned, Dani would likely get jail time. Even if she didn't, Momma said my days with Dani had to cease.

"You're blowing up, Sugar. We can't let Dani blow out your fire. This could have been a bad situation and I'm sad to realize I could have messed things up for you. We have to be smarter. I need some help. Somebody to be my eyes when I can't see."

"You're always in control. I never thought I would ever hear you say something like that," I told Momma.

"Me either. But I can only do so much."

Momma still worked at the hotel and had become an assistant manager over the housekeeping staff. She booked my gigs on breaks and in between work hours, and when she couldn't attend an event with me, she sent my Aunt Jeanie as my guide.

"Let me figure something out," Momma said. "Until then, let's stay focused on your singing, hear me?"

With that said, for over a year I set aside my desires once again. The summer of 2002 I turned twenty-one and Momma threw me a grand party at the Ritz-Carlton downtown. The ballroom was filled with every local celebrity of Chicago, a few national B-list recording artists, and anyone with a name attached to the music industry. The crowd was rich and arrogant, and I devoured and digested every compliment I received. My head swelled.

The highlight moment of the evening was on me as the lights went down and the spotlight landed on my table. Momma handed me a microphone just as the music to Chaka Khan's "I'm Every Woman" started. I worked the crowd, walking from table to table belting out the lyrics better than Whitney Houston ever did. At least that's what I told myself and based on the crowd's response I believed it.

Toward the end of the night Momma was engaged in conversation with a well-dressed woman who exuded elegance in a soft masculine style. Like most of the people at the party, she oozed confidence, but from across the room I saw that she had what no one else in the room had been able to get: Momma's undivided attention. They stood close, the woman speaking pleasing words to Momma. I knew this because of Momma's soft expression, unlike the hardened look she gave snaky folks who tried to feed her bullshit. Several minutes later they began to walk toward me. For some reason my heartbeat quickened. The woman, dressed in a tailored white suit that fit every angle of her body perfectly, met my gaze fearlessly. She wasn't a knee-knocking fan seeking an autograph and she wasn't a celebrity herself. She was business. And she possessed something else, too. I saw it in her eyes.

"Sugar, this is Ace. Ace, Sugar," Momma introduced us. "I'd like the three of us to talk. We have a meeting tomorrow at noon."

Ace extended her hand to me and then held mine in both of hers. She didn't let go.

"I look forward to tomorrow." When she spoke, she smiled, her lips widening like a ballet dancer's grand jeté jump: graceful, fascinating, and beautiful.

"I as well," I responded.

Momma eyed me intently. Ace released my hand with a nod of her head, turned from us, and exited the ballroom, apparently satisfied that she accomplished what she had come for: she had a meeting with me.

Chapter 2

Sugarcoated Lie

"Back up off me, Franco," I growled through a mastered fake smile as Franco and I posed on the red carpet at an awards dinner devoted to honoring leaders in the Chicago community. I was a 2013 recipient for the hours of service I contributed to a local nonprofit organization by providing free vocal lessons and coaching to girls and boys ranging from ages twelve to seventeen. The program was in its third year and we had a waiting list of kids wanting to be taught by me.

When Ace first brought the idea to my attention, I questioned why I would want to spend my time and energy on young kids with hopeless dreams of superstardom. I mean, if I, Sugar, who was once described as "the voice that's been missing from music" hadn't yet sold millions of records around the world, what made these young kids think they had a chance? Don't get me wrong, my singing career had been one to envy and one that only a few achieved.

When Momma and I met with Ace the day after my twenty-first birthday, we had signed a manager-and-client contract by the end of the day. Ace took over the lead of my singing career, but consulted with Momma on most aspects. They both would then advise me. The one thing Ace didn't seek Momma's input on was her personal intentions with me. And I didn't need Momma's consultation on that either. I knew I wanted Ace from the second she pulled out my chair for me at the fancy brunch inside the Ritz-Carlton that morning.

She had reserved a private table where we could talk business. We sat next to one another, Momma opposite us. Ace talked smooth, but not fast. She wasn't a slick-talking salesperson, and still we quickly realized she understood the business and had contacts throughout the music industry. She warned us that we would face challenges on the road to superstardom, and would cross many who didn't have my best interests at heart, but instead their own intentions at the forefront. It would be her job to weed those folks out. She had then turned and leaned toward me and told me, "I'll take care of you." We started sleeping together a week later. She had been my private lover for eleven years.

Momma didn't disapprove; she was happy I had somebody in my life. However, about a minute after she learned of our love affair, she summoned a meeting with me and Ace to discuss how we would handle our relationship in the public eye. I was young with a promising career ahead of me and falling in love at the same time. My joy overflowed I was prepared to share all of me with the world, which included the fact that I was in love with a woman. Ace and Momma aggressively disagreed. They protested my willingness to out myself as a lesbian singer, and asked that I name famous singers and musicians who were openly gay. There were few relevant R&B singers I could list, recalling that even the obvious celebrity lesbians remained hushed and in the closet about their private lives. I conceded, eager to boost my career to its ultimate level, and finally I agreed with Momma and Ace that everyone needed to know my name for my singing talents, not because I was gay.

For years, I dodged questions during interviews about who I shared my love life with, and insisted my sole focus was my career and I had no time for dating. When people would approach me, Ace, or Momma about achieving the honor of taking me out on a date, we shared the same story: I had no room in my schedule to date anyone. No one knew Ace was my boo and I was hers.

I was mesmerized by Ace. She fascinated me with her business savvy. Sometimes I would sit in her office pretending to sit quietly on the couch writing song lyrics when really all I wanted to do was listen to her business calls and be in her presence. I was Ace's primary client, as I should have been. Her focus was on making me the "next greatest of all time," she said. Ace secured backup singing gigs for me with some of America's top recording R&B artists. Within five years I had been to nearly every state in the country and my passport had more stamps than a young Chicago child could imagine he or she would ever have. In every show in which I sang backup, I was generally granted a two-minute solo while the headliner went backstage for a wardrobe change. I would take that opportunity to step front stage and create a memorable experience for the thousands of people for whom we performed. I wasn't born to be a background singer so in those spotlight moments I would shame the headliner with my vocal skills, bringing about applause just as loud, if not louder, than that for the headliner. It was only a matter of time before I finally recorded my first single.

It was 2008 when I recorded "He's the One," a sultry track about a woman declaring her place in her man's life. The message of the song was to let all the women after her man know that she was his woman. The song was a local hit and even though I sang about a man, I had written the lyrics myself based on my relationship with Ace. Thing was, everyone on the outside thought someone else was the love of my life. When, actually, behind closed doors Ace gave me all the love I needed.

When we traveled together, we always booked two rooms, usually adjoining. After the release of the single, we were in Indianapolis for a performance at the Black Expo that July. Ace's assistant had been unable to secure adjoining rooms and instead we were booked on separate floors in the hotel. Ace spent the night in my room and the following morning we ordered room service almost two hours before I had a scheduled interview in my suite with a local journalist. After breakfast, Ace prepared to leave to go shower and dress in her room. The plan was she would meet me back in my suite for the interview. Daringly, we shared a kiss that lingered even once Ace opened the door of my room. As she backed out of the doorway, we finally parted.

"Oh, can you set the tray outside?" I asked quickly, and dashed back inside to retrieve it.

Just as I handed her the tray, topped with empty plates and glasses for two, the journalist arrived at the door. He was a short, curious man, a well-known music critic in the city. The right side of his mouth smirked upward as he caught Ace dressed in the slacks she wore to last night's show, her blouse barely buttoned and her blazer hanging casually over her forearm. Moreover, there I stood in my bathrobe. Ace set the tray on the floor outside the door, then closed the door in my face, leaving her to deal with the journalist.

A part of me panicked, another part felt relief. Finally! Maybe Ace and I would be able to reveal what we meant to one another. I had grown weary of denying my love for her and couldn't understand why she had continued to hide the love she had for me. Whenever I pressed her about coming out, she had shut the conversation down by telling me the time wasn't right. I didn't understand anymore. Didn't she realize how many people would love to have claimed me as their own? Didn't she know that there were many who begged for the opportunity to drape me on their arm? She didn't know many people wished I would sing love songs into their ear every night like the ones I did to her?

Ace called five minutes after she left my room to inform me that the interview would no longer take place in my suite, but instead in one of the small conference rooms near the hotel lobby. She told the journalist that I had been ill the previous night with possible food poisoning, and because I had been ferociously throwing up, she stayed with me overnight. The story was weak and phony and I doubted the journalist bought it. But I had no doubt that Ace shared it in such a manner that convinced the journalist that despite whatever he thought he saw, he didn't see. The interview was a breeze and the write-up he published was phenomenal.

After that incident, Ace suggested we hire a front man, someone to pose as the newfound love of my life to deflect any questions that might surface about my continued singlehood and lack of a special person in my life. I was angry with her, insulted that she continued to only love me privately. I was also frustrated that she felt my fan base would vanish if they knew I loved another woman. How could she feel that way when so many of my fans were gay themselves? Still she insisted I have a fake boyfriend in my life and shortly after that's when Franco entered the picture.

Franco was the closeted boyfriend of Derek, a longtime friend of Ace's. Franco and Derek had been an invisible couple for over ten years, with Franco frightened to come out of the closet because of his family's religious background and affiliations. From what I learned, he had front women of his own from time to time, women he would occasionally bring to church or to a family Christmas gathering in order to deceive his family by pretending to be straight.

His partner, Derek, a shy and quiet engineer, was complacent with the arrangement. I heard that they both were shocked to learn that Ace and I were in a relationship, with Franco excited to share some of my limelight.

The announcement of our relationship arrived when Franco accompanied me to a show in Cleveland about two months after my close call with Ace. I brought Franco onstage just before the end of the show, serenaded him with a love song, and introduced him to the audience as my baby. Five years later, he was still "my man."

"Girl, you know you like when I feel on your booty," he teased through a smile at the camera and lowered his hand below my waist. He swiftly ran his palm over my full behind. Franco, more than I, reveled in his role in our fictional relationship, and played it up in front of the cameras whenever he could. We both continued to smile and pose until we reached the end of the red carpet. He grabbed my hand and led me inside the ballroom.

Ace and Momma were already seated at our table in front of the stage. Ace recognized the tension in my expression, which tended to reveal itself more and more whenever Franco and I had to make an appearance. Almost every piece of my life was perfect: I was an amazing singer with a fan base that reached around the world. Although I hadn't been an overnight sensation like an *American Idol* winner, I had earned my status the old-fashioned way by working hard. I was a star with a career that was still growing and yet the biggest part of me was a secret. I was tired of it and mad at Ace for encouraging the façade.

After I was presented with my award, I began my acceptance speech. "I'm honored to help young ladies like Maria," I said. Maria, one of my students in the program, sat at our table that evening. I had grown to love all my young novices, or gems, as I called them. They worshipped me and I owed them some affection in return for their loyalty. "I'm grateful for the chance to help our Chicago youth fulfill their dreams," I continued. "If it weren't for my mother and all she sacrificed for me, I wouldn't be where I am today. I'm happy to return the favor."

I paused and directed my attention to my table. "Momma, thank you. Thank you for all that you are in my life and for honoring my dreams like they were your own. Franco, you're an unbelievable man with an enormous heart. Thank you for allowing me inside." I looked to Ace. "I can't leave the stage without a deep thanks to my manager, Ace. Words can barely express how fortunate I am to have you guide my career. Not only are you an advocate for this program, you endorse me in all that I am. I pray that you and I continue this amazing partnership so we can show the world that with dedication and commitment, a person really can have it all. I love you."

The room erupted in applause when I wiped a tear from my eye. Ace, Momma, and Franco played it cool and clapped along. When I returned to the table I hugged Maria, and then wrapped my arms around Momma in a tight embrace. Ace stood and gently hugged me, careful not to press her body close to mine. "I'll meet you in your limo when this is over," she whispered in my ear, and passed me off to Franco. Arrogantly, he placed his hands at my waist and when I leaned in to offer him my cheek, which was our agreed-upon signature public display of affection, he instead reached for my chin and brought my face and mouth to his lips. For the first time in five years, he kissed my lips, and he did so in front of a room of hundreds of onlookers. My automatic response was to pull back. But I didn't. I took Franco's unexpected act of aggressiveness and used it against Ace. She was, after all, the one who put us together. I kissed Franco back and the slight waver of his lips showed that even he was surprised. We ended the kiss with a big smack and smiles. I settled back into my seat between Ace and Franco and took a sip of wine.

Using my peripheral vision I saw Ace's eyes scold me, both for my speech and for the kiss with Franco. Her tan skin flushed, the heat from her body warm next to me. I didn't even look at her. Maybe Franco's surprise gimmick was just what she needed to finally realize she wasn't the only one who wanted my sweet sugar kisses.

Chapter 3

Give Me Some Sugar

"Get out," Ace instructed Franco when she got inside my limo. We had driven only two blocks before the limo pulled over to the side of the road and parked. Ace's limo had been following mine.

"What?" he asked with a fake perplexed expression.

"I'll deal with you later," Ace responded, not answering his question, her voice aggravated.

"Can I get in your limo? How am I supposed to get home?" he wanted to know.

"Call a cab. Or call Derek, your man, remember?" she asked with emphasis on "your man."

"Yeah, yeah, girl, I know I got a man. Y'all have a good night now." Franco got out of the limo and straightened his suit and tie before closing the door. Ace then instructed the driver to head to her address.

I tried to pretend like I hadn't heard their exchange. I was engrossed with my phone and my Twitter account. I was a Twitter fanatic and utilized the tool to connect with my fans. Ace encouraged it and said any celebrity who didn't take advantage of the easy access and communication with their fans didn't really want to be famous. She made sure I tweeted at least once if not multiple times a day. I had just tweeted a message: Sugar @SugarChi-town My gems, I love you all!

"What was that about?" she questioned.

I put my phone down, pulled out my MAC compact, and dabbed my nose with powder. "What are you referring to?"

"Your speech. Beautiful, but risky, Sugar, and you know it."

"I didn't say anything that wasn't true," I told her, placing the compact back in my purse and turning to face her. "What are you so nervous about? That those people back in that ballroom know I'm in love with you?"

"They might with the way you said you loved me staring all lovesick in my direction."

"I don't hear you complaining when I tell you that I love you while you're laid on top of me, so what's the problem?" I asked, even though I already knew.

"You know what the problem is."

"You really think my fans will love me less if they knew the truth?"

"Yes, now they would. It would be worse coming out now since you've been flaunting Franco around for years as your man. You'll come off confused and unstable."

"First, Franco was your idea and had I come out before him, that wouldn't even be a problem," I retorted. "Second, how many women discover themselves later in life? I could be one of them. 'Singer Falls in Love With Woman, Comes Out as Lesbian.' Can't you see the headline? People will eat it up. It's only halfway true, but at least I don't have to live in secret all the time. *We* don't have to live in secret all the time," I added.

Ace shook her head adamantly. "We can't, we're too close to you reaching the superstardom you've worked so hard for," she tried to convince me.

"I'm already a superstar," I reminded her. "But at what sacrifice? What if I go on to sell millions of records? Does it even matter if I can't celebrate it with the woman I love? If I have to kiss you behind closed doors after kissing Franco in front of everyone else? Is it worth it?"

"Aren't you willing to do whatever it takes to make it? What happened to the eager girl I met on her twenty-first birthday?"

"I'm right here but I'm no longer twenty-one," I reminded her. "Eleven years ago I was happy to stay undercover with you. I didn't know it was going to go this far, lying and acting like I have a man. Now I've lost myself in this whole mess." I looked out of the window at the darkened streets. "I'm tired, Ace. I'm tired of pretending to be something I'm not. I shouldn't have to either. I'm Sugar; plenty of women would be happy to have me on their arm."

"Don't go there with me," she warned. "Not after all I've done for you."

I looked at her again. "You get paid for it, my dear, so don't go acting like I owe you shit. You're so sure coming out will ruin my career, but I'm willing to take that chance. I've toured the world, hung with more celebrities than most people can imagine, and my bank account is quite comfortable. If it all ended today, I'd still be happy if I still had you."

I hoped Ace would feel the sincerity of my words. I hoped she would realize how much she meant to me by knowing I was willing to sacrifice nearly twenty years of work for her.

"We can't," Ace insisted.

"No, *you* can't. What's the problem, you scared for people to know you're a dyke? You think people can't look at you and figure that out?"

Ace was wearing a black tuxedo, and though it was soft, contoured, and feminine, it was her constant signature style at special events and occasions. She always had on pants and a jacket. Her hair had remained short since I met her; she alternated various cuts dependent upon the "in" look at the time. Ace's face was beautiful; her eyes were a shade of green, a random trait inherited somewhere in her family lineage. Even in her late thirties, her skin remained flawless. She focused on drawing attention to her lips and her smile, her most captivating feature, with dramatic shades of lipstick from deep browns to reds to pale shades of nude; they all looked great on her. Yet with her gentlewoman exterior, there was no mistaking Ace as a lesbian. Perhaps stereotypical to suggest, but it may have been the aggressive and confident nature with which she carried herself and handled those she encountered. She wore the pants, literally and figuratively, and could be a stubborn bitch when handling business. I guessed that was the reason I had succumbed to the status of our relationship for so long; I was the star, but had surrendered to her authority.

"It doesn't matter to me what people think, it's what they know," Ace told me. "People can speculate all day long about me, you, Franco, trying to figure out if the whole shebang is false. But if they don't know, if they don't have proof, then to me we can always chuck it off as haters trying to mess up your game. It's career suicide for both of us if we come out as a couple."

"Cool, all right. Well it's time for me to start making some decisions, then. I can start tonguing Franco on the red carpet, because I saw how much you loved that. I can start playing the role better than you thought I could. Or maybe it's time for me to move on," I threatened.

"You won't," Ace challenged.

"Guess you'll have to wait and see, now won't you?"

The limo pulled up to Ace's condominium on the north end of downtown Chicago. For convenience, I lived in another condominium only five blocks away. The closeness made it easy for us to spend evenings at the other's place.

I didn't budge when the driver opened my door. "Aren't you coming?" Ace asked.

"Absolutely not."

"Driver," Ace said. The driver closed the door and stood positioned outside the limo. "Come on, Sugar, don't be like this," she pleaded.

"I'm for real; if you don't want to share me with the world, why should I keep sharing myself with you in hiding? I'm better than that," I declared.

"You're better than most people, which is why I'm trying to give you the best possible career, can't you see that?"

"What about love? Is this the best love you can give me, where no one else can see?"

Ace dodged the question and detoured to my weakness: my body. "Come on, you look so sexy tonight. I want you," she whispered. She took a chance and leaned to kiss my ear. I was sure she was confident the driver couldn't witness our interaction through the midnight black tinted glass. "Give me some of your sugar," she begged, her voice soft and desiring me.

My body immediately responded. Sex with Ace was just as exhilarating as the electricity I felt when singing on stage in front of thousands. She fed my ego like an obsessed fan, raving at how much she loved every curve of my body. During lovemaking, Ace's sole purpose was my enjoyment; she required little if any attention, seemingly satisfied to have the opportunity to please me, like a devoted groupie, content just to be in my presence. Why couldn't she worship me the same otherwise?

"No," I decided to the discontent of the throbbing I felt below. "Not tonight."

Ace jerked back, surprised. "You've never turned me down," she stated factually.

"It's a new day, Ace. You either want all of me, or nothing at all."

She groaned angrily. "Call me in the morning once you've come to your right mind." She tapped the window, the driver opened the door, and she got out. Back inside, the driver lowered the glass separating me from him.

"Home, ma'am?"

"Not yet," I told him. "Take me to Boystown."

He tipped his head at me and the glass rose again. My body was hot and my ego deflated. I needed a fix and what better cure than for a celebrity to show up unannounced at the club where all the gay boys adored me like the leader of a cult. If I was lucky, maybe there would be a female worshipper mingling with the boys, one who wouldn't mind a spoonful of my sugar tonight.

Chapter 4

Sugar Kiss

On the dance floor I was surrounded by sweaty, top-less men gyrating their bodies to the overpowering bass pounding through the massive speakers throughout the club. Pink, blue, and white lights flashed across the floor in unison with the fast-paced thumps of the music. Bare-foot, with my heels in my hand, I moved with the crowd, feeling the vibrations from my toes to my fingertips.

I had been to many gay clubs during my years of per-forming, mostly for paid guest appearances and when I traveled to perform at small venues across the country, and other times with some of the male backup singers I befriended on the road. Per Ace's instructions, I never left the VIP section and was not allowed to mingle with the patrons other than for an autograph. Ace would have had a fit if she saw me now, with one pretty boy grind-ing innocently against my ass while I pumped my hips against another hottie in front of me. When the DJ played the club-mix version of "He's the One," the crowd went wild, screaming my name over and over. "Sugar, Sugar, Sugar!" My crushed ego was repaired.

After my song went off, I squeezed through the party-goers to the crowded bar, with people stepping back and parting like the Red Sea to make room for me. Before I could order, a lemon drop martini was placed before me. "We read it's your favorite," the male bartender told me with a wink of his blue eyes rimmed with black eyeliner. Though I was overwhelmed with thirst, I sipped the drink delicately, ladylike, like a diva should.

A moment later, an eccentric-looking woman emerged from the dance floor and walked up to me. She wore a vest with no shirt, ankle-length skinny jeans, and high-top Converse. Her hair, a spiked Mohawk, was damp with sweat. She was about five feet two inches, skinny, and as unwomanly as a prepubescent sixth grader.

"I sing," she told me as her introduction.

I'd be rich if I had a dime for every time I heard that. "What do you sing?" I asked.

"I'm the lead singer in an all-girl band called Beau. We sing at small clubs in Chicago. Have you heard of us?" she asked, hopeful, her already oversized eyes bulging with anticipation while she waited for my response.

"No, darling, I haven't."

"Well, we'd be honored for you to come to one of our performances."

If I had another dime for that statement too, I'd have made the Forbes richest people list. "Do you have a card? A Web site? I'll see what I can do," I lied.

"Sure. The site is 'Beau Luv 4 U.' That's b-e-a-u l-u-v, number four, letter u."

I sipped my drink. "Sure, sure, I'll look you up." I turned my back to her and faced the bar. The bartender stopped preparing a drink in the middle of pouring shots of vodka into a glass to check and see if I needed assistance.

"You good, Miss Sugar?" he asked, and eyed the young-looking girl.

"Right now I am, thank you," I answered. "Don't stray too far," I added.

"Maybe you'd like to meet another member of the group," the little one suggested, continuing her conversation.

I turned around again. "What's your name, honey?" I asked.

"I call myself Rock in the group; my real name is Sandy."

"Okay, Rock. Sandy. Who else do you have here?" I asked, hoping for a quick meet and greet so I could move on with enjoying the rest of the night. I loved my fans, but not always up close and personal, and not the ones who didn't know how to take a hint that their time with me was up.

Rock Sandy waved her hand to someone across the club. I couldn't tell exactly who through the thick throng of bodies. Then I saw a woman appear to my right. She had the same off-the-wall style as Rock Sandy, but expressed her irregular look with a provocative edge. She wore knee-high riding boots over bare legs that led to a short, fitted clingy dress that hugged her body. A heavy belted chain hung at her waist, with an extended piece that connected and looped around the top of her boots. Her makeup was as extreme as some of the drag queens in the place, dark and exaggerated around the eyes. Her hair, a massive untamed 'fro of curls, frizzed into a bobbing halo around her head.

"This is Trendy, our guitarist and bass player," Rock Sandy told me. "Trendy, I need not tell you who this is."

She held her hand out to me. I shook it. "A pleasure," we said to each other simultaneously. Rock Sandy walked away.

"Would you like a drink?" I asked her, flipping my usual role of accepting a drink and making an offer instead.

"Thank you, but no. I'm driving tonight," she explained.

"How decent of you," I commented and took a sip of my martini. "So, is Trendy your real name or your band name?" I asked. "I'm pretty sure it's got to be your band name."

"My real name is Nisha. I go by Trendy in the group."

"Nisha, I like that."

Nisha blushed.

"I like Trendy, too. Do you have a preference?"

"For you, please call me Nisha."

"Okay then, Nisha, how long have you been playing?"

Nisha leaned her back against the bar, and rested her elbows against the counter. Her bracelets danced circles around her wrists. "Since I was about eleven."

"And how many years have passed since you were eleven?" I asked, curious to know her age.

She smiled. "Twelve years."

I did the math. "Twenty-three, okay. So young—"

"I'm legal," she said.

"Yes, that you are," I replied, eyeing the way the muscles in her thighs flexed when she adjusted her weight from her right leg to her left.

"But I've been following you for as long as I can remember. When I was about ten I saw you perform at a fair. Your voice is stunning. I've followed you since. You've been so influential to us singers and musicians in Chicago. We love you," she told me.

Of course you love me. "I'm flattered," I responded honestly.

Nisha turned around and leaned face forward against the bar, her palms resting at the edge of the counter. "I have to say, I never thought I'd see you here, in this club, outside of the VIP section and alone I might add." Her eyes were curious.

I finished my drink and placed it on the counter. The bartender promptly took the glass and replaced it with a freshly made martini. "Well, every now and then a change of scenery is good for the soul."

Nisha, young and smart, was not complacent with my explanation. "That's true. But here?" She looked around the place filled with openly gay individuals. "I bet there are a million other options you had, but you came here. Isn't that something?" She leaned her head to the side and awaited my answer.

"I love music, all kinds of music, and I wanted to dance tonight," I continued to explain. "And I love people, all kinds of people, and I wanted to meet some tonight," I explained.

"Interesting," Nisha said, her eyes resting on mine. The color of her eyes was as deep, dark, and intense as her makeup. "I hope you've satisfied your goal for the evening."

"I believe I have," I told her. "Are you sure you wouldn't like a drink? I can have my driver take you home if needed," I invited, realizing it was probably unwise to ask a stranger into my limo with me. But if anything happened to me after I left the club, there would be at least a hundred witnesses who would have seen Nisha leave with me.

Nisha didn't object to my second request and ordered a brandy with Coke. "Thank you." She took a long swig.

Nisha and I continued our conversation. She told me the history of Beau and how long the group had been together, explaining that she and Rock Sandy had been friends since high school when they created the band, which had grown to six members. She and Rock Sandy considered themselves the leaders of the band, and on their own secured the band's gigs. "Someday we will need management if we want to reach the level of success we seek," she told me.

"That's true; the right manager will help get you where you want to be. That's been my experience."

"I know. I've read all your interviews and you always give thanks and praise to your manager," Nisha acknowledged.

I nodded my head and told Nisha the short version of how Ace helped blossom my career. A story she already knew from her readings.

"You two have been together a long time," she commented.

I nodded. "A long time indeed. But, enough talk about me," I said, something I had never in my life said before. "Would you like to dance?"

"Me?" Nisha questioned.

"Of course, you. You're not here just to hold up this bar, are you?" I teased.

"No, not at all." She quickly swallowed the remainder of her drink. "Let's go." Without asking, Nisha took my hand in hers and led me to the middle of the floor, where we immediately became the center of attention. The high-energy music still pumped through the speakers and we danced fervently to the beat.

After twenty minutes of nonstop movement, I was tired and sweaty. I asked Nisha if she was ready to leave. She told me that she was, and she would be right out after she gave Rock Sandy her keys. I waited in the limo for a few minutes, which granted me the chance to touch up my makeup. Within five minutes the driver opened the door for Nisha. She settled comfortably into the leather seat across from me.

"Where do you live?" I asked.

"Not far, a little bit west of here," she told me and gave me the address, which I gave to the driver. "Thank you for the ride. I appreciate it."

"No problem."

"Um, Rock told me she invited you to a performance. I'd love for you to come as a special guest. A special guest of mine if that's okay. When your schedule permits of course."

"I think I can make time for that. I'll check your site for dates and coordinate it with my schedule."

Nisha blushed again. Her brown skin had had a flushed, flustered reddish undertone since we said hello. "You know, Sugar, I am a true fan of yours. I hope you don't mind if I ask for your autograph." She smiled gently.

"Absolutely. Come." I patted the empty space next to me. Hunched and bent forward, Nisha crept across the limo and sat at my side. She began to riffle through her purse until she pulled out a small pad of paper and pen.

"I use this pad to write lyrics that spontaneously come to mind. Even though we sing mostly covers, every so often we perform our own songs, too," she said proudly.

"I carry paper around for the same reason," I responded, and took her pad of paper from her. On the inside flap I wrote, "Nisha, it's been a pleasure," then signed my name in its signature form with a large, oversized "S." Next, I placed my mouth on the paper and left an imprint of perfectly shaped puckered lips.

"Wow," Nisha said, startled by the affectionate gesture. She puckered her lips and softly kissed the paper where I left my imprint. "A sugar kiss. Thank you."

I didn't say anything, only smiled at her. We rode quietly the remainder of the ride.

"I don't know how many times I can say thank you," she said when we arrived at her apartment building.

"You're welcome, Nisha. Really, it's no big deal."

"I'll see you?" she asked cautiously.

"You will," I told her and then tapped on the glass. The driver opened Nisha's door.

"Good night, Sugar," she said before stepping out of the limo. We waited until she was inside her apartment building and the door closed behind her.

"Home, ma'am?" the tired driver asked for the second time once back inside.

"Yes, home."

"Long night for you," he stated.

"Yes, a long night with a perfect ending," I responded as the glass separated us once again.

I pulled out my phone and clicked on my Twitter app. Sugar @SugarChitown Had a great time tonight. Thx guys and gals. Sending sweet sugar kisses to u!

Chapter 5

Sugar Momma

"This is what happens when you don't listen," Ace said angrily, slapping a newspaper against her desk. I had just walked into her office and closed the door behind me when she erupted. "You can't disobey me, Sugar, not like this."

"What are you talking about?" I quizzed, annoyed by her attitude toward me.

"This." She threw the newspaper at me after I sat in one of the chairs in front of her desk.

I picked up the paper, a local publication circulated primarily on the north side of Chicago. At the bottom of the front page were two photos of me at the club a few nights prior. The headline above the photographs read Sugar Delight with a short summary that chronicled my evening, including how long I had stayed on the dance floor, with added focus on the dance I shared with Nisha. A portion of the article read: "Sugar and Nisha, a member of the local band Beau, shared a drink at the bar before they hit the dance floor. The two were seen departing the club in the same limousine."

I shrugged my shoulders and casually placed the newspaper on Ace's desk. "My gay fans will be pleased."

Ace was vexed. The nostrils of her narrow nose flared. "Do you know how this looks?"

I shrugged again. "It's all true so there's nothing to be mad at," I responded, unconcerned.

"This is not the kind of attention you want to bring to yourself," Ace contended. "And who in the hell is this Nisha?" Ace demanded to know.

I smiled mischievously. "She's someone I met that night. Lovely young lady. A bass player."

"So after you turn me down and act like you're going home, you decide to stray off to a gay club and pick up another woman?"

"First, I never told you I was going home. I only said I wasn't going home with you. Second, I didn't pick her up. We talked and we danced, that's it."

"That's not it; you let her inside your limo. What's up with that?"

"I offered her a ride home."

"Why?"

"Because I was enjoying her company and wanted to extend it as long as possible."

Ace was quiet, and then laughed. "I get it, Sugar, I get it. You're trying to teach me a lesson, make me jealous maybe? This is not the way to go about it. Not by giving the media something to gossip about. We just talked about this. You know better."

"I know better than what? To hang out at a gay club? Why not? *I am gay.*"

"I'll tell you why. I was going to wait until I had more details to share this with you, but I may as well go on and share it with you now. We are so close to signing a deal for you to sing a duet with your favorite male singer, and you know who I'm referring to. He wants *you*, Sugar. Out of all the popular female artists out here, he wants you. If this goes well, who knows what this can lead to for you?" She leaned forward. "We can't chance any lesbian rumors about you, Sugar. Who's going to listen to a lesbian sing a love song to her man?"

"Are you serious?" I screamed, unable to contain my excitement. I jumped up and sat on Ace's desk in front of her. "E doesn't want Alicia, or J-Hud or Beyoncé?"

Ace placed her hands on my thighs and squeezed. "He wants you, baby, you. We fly to L.A. next week."

"Ace, this is a dream come true!" I squealed.

"It is. And that's why I need you to lay off all these emotions you've been going through. I understand we're hiding our love, but that's the nature of the game. As long as I stay true to you and you stay true to me, I don't see what the problem is. You just sit back and let me take care of you like I'm supposed to. It's not only my job but it's my desire. I love you and only want the best for you. Let me handle this. Let me handle us. I got you," she said convincingly.

I got up and walked to the window. Ace's office was on the thirty-fifth floor of a downtown tower with a beautiful view of Lake Michigan. I stared into the water, deep in thought. For over ten years Ace had been my leading lady. In business, she had steered me in every right direction. There had not been one deal gone bad and not one person who had taken advantage of me, not under Ace's guidance. She made sure I had the best of everything in every aspect of my life, including in the bedroom. Aside from keeping our love a secret, she had pleased me in every way.

"You know these emotions I'm going through aren't new. I've wanted to come out for years and I won't live like this forever," I told her without turning from the window. "But, I'll back off for now, Ace, until this record deal is confirmed. If you're right about the success of this collaboration, I'll lay low. I still won't promise you I'll stay quiet forever. I still feel like I'm trading my soul for a hit record and a paycheck."

Ace walked and stood behind me. "Half the industry has secrets and skeletons, you're not alone, and you know that."

"I don't care about everybody else, that's what you don't get," I reminded her. "This is about my life, my heart."

She put her arms around my waist and pressed her body against mine. "Shhh . . . Okay, okay. I hear you, baby. Just know I'll do whatever it takes to keep you happy." I turned to face her and she read my pleading expression. "Okay, not everything," she clarified. "Is there anything I can do for you right now to put a smile on your pretty face?"

If she wasn't going to satisfy my heart, she could at least satisfy my closet instead. "There's a new pair of red bottoms I've been craving," I told her.

"You got it."

"And a Tiffany ring."

"No problem. Anything else?"

"Yes, there is."

"What is it?"

I reached for the handle attached to the blinds. I closed them and then walked to the couch at the end of Ace's office. I slid off my shoes, unzipped my skirt, and lowered it over my hips to the floor. My panties were next. I stroked myself.

"Come here, momma, let me give you some sugar."

Chapter 6

Sugar Temptation

Sugar @SugarChitown I'm back, y'all! L.A. was the sheezy! Come out tonight to check out the single.

"I've been waiting for you to come to one of our performances," Nisha told me while I sat at a table between Ace and Franco. "I haven't seen your face in the crowd yet. Guess I got anxious to see you again."

We were at a sophisticated lounge just south of downtown at the listening party for a first play of the single I recorded with E in L.A. The song, "Feel My Love," was a sexy mid-tempo track about the tenderness of lovemaking between a man and a woman. The label and everyone involved with the project was certain the single would be a success. We had just played the track to the crowd's listening pleasure and praise. Now guests were mingling, sipping on drinks, and eating appetizers until it was time for the meet and greet.

Nisha again expressed her unique style with black suede heels, purple and black striped leggings, and a sheer, sleeveless top. Her hair was combed into several long twists that were piled high into a bun at the crown of her head. Her lips and cheeks were colored in the same deep purple as her leggings, her eyes heavy with black shadow.

"Nisha, hello, good to see you." I stood and reached for her hand, which she embraced between hers, a gesture

Ace had done upon our first meeting. I remembered it vividly, as I had shared with Ace that it had been a turn-on when she cupped my hand between hers. Nisha and I looked at one another, a subtle affectionate exchange between us. Finally, Ace stood as well.

"Well, well, this is headline-making Nisha. Nice to meet you." They shook hands. "I'm Ace, Sugar's manager."

"Yes, I know. It's a pleasure," Nisha replied.

"And this is Franco." Ace gestured to Franco, who had remained seated with an absurd grin on his face. "Sugar's boyfriend," Ace added.

Franco stood and grabbed Nisha's hand. "So nice to meet you," he said, his voice deeper than his natural tenor. He had practiced using a lower tone when he spoke in his role as my man.

Nisha smirked. "Franco, I've seen you in pictures with Sugar. Great to meet you as well."

We all stood awkwardly. "Are you alone? Would you like to join us?" Ace offered.

"I'm not alone but I'd like to join you, yes, thank you." Nisha sat in the empty chair at Franco's side.

"I read that you're a member of a band," Ace casually said to Nisha, like that was all she knew about her. Like she hadn't gone online and read all she could find about Nisha and Beau, surprised and irritated that she hadn't heard of their music already. And like she hadn't mentioned her name and questioned my motives with her every time she got a little perturbed with me about my desire to come out, which I still brought up daily even though I had lied and said I'd give it a temporary rest.

"Yes, yes, I am. My friend and I started the band in high school, we grew the members to six, and we've been playing together for several years now."

"Where do you all play?" Ace inquired.

"Oh, mostly little spots around the city." Nisha listed a few venues.

"I know the owners of all those places. Actually, I have connections with the owners of most venues throughout the entire city," Ace bragged.

I observed the way she leaned toward Nisha with an imaginary fishpole like Nisha was fish she wanted to bait. I tried to decipher Ace's angle.

Nisha was intrigued. "That's awesome. We sure could use someone like you in our corner. I mean, look at what you've done for Sugar." Nisha looked me in the eyes. "She's amazing."

"That she is," Ace agreed. She pulled out her business cardholder and handed Nisha a card. "I'd like for you to give me a call. Let's talk."

Franco and I exchanged a brief, curious glance before I devoured Ace with an intense stare.

"Really?" Nisha was elated.

"Yes, really." Ace smiled, and glanced in my direction. Her expression spoke nothing.

"Again, thank you, thank you, both."

"You're welcome," Ace replied. "So tell us, what do you think of 'Feel My Love'? It's hot, isn't it?"

"Yeah, it's hot, you did those lyrics right, Sugar. You're going to have all us fans dreaming about you at night. That is, if we're not already."

"Well of course I want my fans to have sweet dreams about me," I said to her.

Franco put his arm around me and gave my shoulder a squeeze. "Lucky me, I'm the only one whose dream is a reality." He kissed my cheek and nuzzled his nose in my ear.

Ace laughed. Nisha smiled. I kicked him under the table.

"Will there be a video?" Nisha asked.

"Yes, we filmed it last week," Ace told Nisha. "It's going to debut on BET in a couple weeks. In the video, Sugar's fans will get to see a side of her they've never seen."

"How so?" Nisha asked.

Ace nodded to Franco. "I'm in the video," Franco proudly announced. "The video is just as hot as the song," he told Nisha.

The video had been shot in an ocean-side mansion in L.A. E and I shot scenes singing together in various luxurious rooms throughout the house and on the private beach. Separately, E sang his verses to a sexy, Brazilian woman while making love to her in the master bedroom. I was told that when the lights and cameras went off and the crew left the room, E and the woman remained in bed.

Franco and I shot in the morning on a balcony with the ocean as our backdrop. We wore only silk robes with Franco's body grinding against mine in the front and from the back while I sang to him about how his body made me feel. Ace had stood on the opposite end of the balcony and watched the entire shoot. She told me that Franco and I looked good. I didn't speak to her for the rest of that day.

"So do we get a taste of your lovemaking skills in the video?" she asked me.

"Wouldn't you like to know?" I teased.

Ace shot me a dangerous look. I was walking that line I had promised I would stay away from and she was displeased. I didn't know what it was about Nisha and why I couldn't help but flirt with her. I had sworn to Ace that I wouldn't do anything to reveal my secret until the single became a success, but a part of me refused to submit. I was Sugar; I still had a mind of my own and a right to do and say whatever I wanted to. Even if that was by flirting with someone else right in front of her. She might have been offended, but I was offended every time she insisted I front Franco as my man.

"When's your next performance?" I asked. "With the single it's been a busy time but I definitely want to see you perform."

"I'll set up a date for us to go when Nisha calls me," Ace interjected.

I wanted to remind Ace that I could go attend any concert I wanted to without her help or approval. "Be sure you call soon, then," I advised Nisha instead.

Ace stood. She had had enough. "Nisha, we'll talk soon." She eyed Nisha in a way that let her know her visit to our table was over.

Nisha stood as well. "Wonderful to meet you, Ace and Franco. Good night, Sugar."

"Enjoy the rest of your evening," I told her.

Nisha walked away, her hips swaying sweetly, and disappeared into the crowd.

Franco slapped his hand on the table to snap my attention away from Nisha's ass. "Sugar, I get this is a fairy tale bullshit relationship and everything, but you can't be playing me in front of people. I refuse to look like a fool," he said to me and then looked to Ace. "And, I think y'all have some tweaks to work out. What the hell is up with the two of you? It's clear that girl is fancying Sugar and you go setting up meetings with her?"

Ace leaned forward. "Franco, let me set this straight for you again, because you seem to keep thinking this is about you, and it's not. You need to stay in your lane. You're Sugar's man, that's it. You don't even have to speak for all I care; just sit back, smile, and look at her just as smitten as her fans. You also don't need to concern yourself with how I handle Sugar."

"Excuse me, how you *handle* Sugar?" I interjected.

"Yes, how I handle you," she stated confidently. "We're on the right track, your dreams are about to manifest, and you keep testing the waters with that baby you call yourself flirting with."

"I can do whatever I please," I responded defiantly.

"Sugar, you promised," Ace reminded me.

"I know what I said and don't worry about it. Nobody is going to question anything when that video drops. Nobody will have any idea you and I are fucking behind the camera."

"That's enough," Ace said, her words angry. Suddenly she smiled at someone approaching our table. "Hey, Randy, how are you?" She stood to greet one of the managers of the top-rated R&B station in Chicago.

"Great, Ace. Just wanted to stop by and wish you and Sugar congratulations on the track. We're looking forward to having you in the studio tomorrow morning when we play it for the first time."

I stood to "air kiss" both of Randy's cheeks. "I can't wait, it's always a blast. And I love that you treat me like a queen," I said with a fake English accent and toss of my layered weave.

Randy chuckled. "You are the queen, Sugar. Will you be having the usual?"

"You know it. Green tea with lemon and honey. Thank you, love."

He kissed my hand and then departed.

Ace resumed the conversation where she had left off. "Like I was saying, I don't want to keep having this conversation. Drop it."

"Well you just brought it back up, honey," I informed her.

"Because I'm trying to put an end to this once and for all."

"I know exactly how to put an end to it."

She shook her head. "Not happening."

"Never? You think I'm about to spend the rest of my life trapped in your closet? *That's* what's not happening."

"Just let it go, Sugar. I'm tired of this. You're ruining what should be a wonderful night."

"No, I'm not. I'm good, babe. You're the one getting flustered. I simply stated my truth. No matter how big this single is, no matter if I sign a multimillion dollar contract next week, you better believe someday the world will know exactly who Sugar is and what I represent. And you better believe they will love me just the same."

"You don't know that."

"And you don't know they won't. Well I'm not worried. It won't be nearly as controversial as you think. It's not as if I'm out here singing love songs to Jesus. I'm Sugar, not a gospel singer coming out of the closet. And you really think people will start dragging your name through the mud if they learn we're a couple?"

"It looks bad for business."

"Is that right? So now I'm bad for business?"

"I shouldn't be in a relationship with a client."

"Why not? People do it all the time."

"Sure, if they were already a couple first. But I sought your representation first. It won't look right on my part."

"Well lie and say we were already a couple, then. That's a lie I'm willing to uphold forever if it means we can be out and proud."

"No," she replied.

"What is it, Ace? You can't possibly be that damn paranoid. I've seen you in action; you know how to smooth over any situation and mold it just how you want it. You can't keep hiding behind the same line that this is bad for our careers. It's got to be more than that."

Franco interrupted. "Ladies, my ladies, cool this shit for a minute. I'm going to get a drink."

I directed my anger at him. "You know we don't get our own drinks," I spat. "What would Sugar's man look like at the bar?"

"I bet the same way you looked at the bar that night in the club," he responded with sarcasm, his voice its usual higher pitch. "We all saw the pictures."

"Different occasion. Tonight is my night and none of us goes to the bar. We get served," I reminded him.

"Well really I just wanted to get from between the two of you, but since you wanna act like I don't have two legs to walk on . . ." He snapped his fingers at the server passing by, who then came to our table.

"What can I do for you?" She sounded bothered and hurried.

"First of all, my glass should never get to empty before I get another drink," Franco snapped, deep into his snobby husband-of-a-celebrity role.

Ace would agree with Franco's statement, as she was also annoyed whenever our service was less than ten, but she never lashed out at staff. If we experienced poor service at a restaurant or hotel, she would place a call to the owner or manager the following day to inform him or her of what occurred, and to ensure that if we ever returned to their venue our service would be impeccable.

"With that said, Don Julio on the rocks," Franco told the server. He turned to me. "Sugar?"

"I'll have another," I said, holding up my near-empty martini glass.

"You do know what she was drinking, don't you?" Franco challenged.

Franco didn't faze the server, a young woman dressed in black slacks and a black blouse. In that upscale environment, likely she dealt with obnoxious patrons often. "Yes, Sugarman, I do remember." She walked away from Franco.

He was about to respond to her backside when Ace stopped him. "Stop being an ass, Franco," she told him. "I'll make the call tomorrow," she said to me.

After my second drink, I spent the rest of the night signing autographs and taking pictures with fans. During the entire time, Nisha and Rock Sandy sat at a table across the room and watched my every move. Finally, as the crowd dispersed and about a dozen guests remained, Nisha returned to my side.

"May I have a photograph to go with that kiss?" she asked. Her eyes twinkled under the influence. "I framed it."

Next to me, Ace inhaled sharply. It was barely audible, but I noticed it.

"Absolutely," I told Nisha.

I began to realize Nisha wasn't fooled by the façade. Though I hadn't said or done anything directly to identify my true sexuality, she wasn't as ignorant of the truth as Ace wanted her to be. She may not have known Ace was my woman, but I was convinced she knew Franco wasn't my man.

We stood close to one another, the fronts of our bodies touching, our heads to the side in order to face the camera. Her left hand rested at the top hump of my behind. A slight dip lower and she would have been on the verge of caressing it. I smiled at the thought and pressed my breasts against her body.

"Mmm," she murmured in response.

The photographer snapped the photo. We blinked with the flash. He checked the photo on his digital camera.

"Another, ladies. Keep your eyes open this time." He laughed.

We leaned even closer, our pudgy cheeks touching from wide smiles. That time our eyes remained open.

"Beautiful," the photographer told us.

Before she removed her arm from around my hip, Nisha looked to Franco, who was busy on his phone, then back to me. She whispered softly, "I won't tell."

"You won't tell what?" I asked innocently.

She sighed with a soft smile. "Come on, Sugar."

One thing my momma always told me was to listen to my gut. Although I had tolerated Ace's judgment about keeping my sexuality a secret, and committed to silence at least until the single hit the charts, I trusted what my gut told me about Nisha and felt the time had come to set myself free. Whatever happened as a result, Ace could clean up the mess if she was still my manager. And if she was still my lover, too.

"Thank you for keeping my secret, I appreciate that. But soon enough I'll reveal to the world just who I am."

She smiled. "Anything I can do to help?"

I thought for a moment and had a crazy idea. "I do believe you can. I'll let you know when it's time."

"I'll be waiting." She turned around and nodded to Rock Sandy, who had been waiting several feet away. They were about to leave. "Before I go, I have to tell you." She paused and took a step forward. "You are definitely the sweetest temptation I know."

"Likewise, honey, likewise."

Sugar @SugarChitown What a night! You ready to Feel My Love? Soon . . .

Chapter 7

Sugar High

The single was a hit. My fans adored it. Radio stations played it on regular rotation. Because the song was a collaboration and not my record, I didn't tour with E to promote the album, but he gave me a shout-out at every interview. More than ever, the industry wanted a little more of Sugar, the voice on the hottest track to hit the airwaves all year long. There was already talking of a Grammy nomination.

I already knew my voice was the shit. The success of the record confirmed it. I was a natural born singer. There was no need for extras like Auto-Tune to correct imperfections because I didn't have any. Everywhere I went in Chicago, someone, usually multiple people, stopped and asked for my autograph. They wanted to take pictures of me and with me on their camera phones and iPads. They all wanted to know what it had been like to record with such an established star:

"What's E like in person?"

"What was it like in L.A.?"

"Did everyone drive Bentleys and live in mansions on the hill?"

"Are you going to leave us for L.A.?" they would ask.

"I love Chitown, my roots are here," I would tell them. "I don't plan to leave unless I get too big for y'all," I would add.

"Well Oprah didn't leave us," they would tell me, disappointed that I might someday depart from the Windy City to the West Coast.

"That's Oprah. I'm Sugar, darling."

The few drops of humbleness I had managed to maintain before the record were gone, had vanished. I was a star and expected to be treated like a star. I had already wanted five-star treatment wherever I went and, now, no matter how exceptional the service I received, I expected more. I expected my food to be prepared faster than everyone else's. When I entered a salon or spa, I dared there be a delay or wait time and expected immediate attention, even if that meant someone else lost an appointment.

I redecorated my condo. Not that it hadn't been elegantly furnished; it was already fly with a cheetah-print theme throughout from the rug in the living room to the seat covers in the dining area to the comforter on my bed. I upgraded to a custom-made Italian leather living room set, complete with a sofa, love seat, coffee table, and ottomans. My queen-sized bed was donated and a California king canopy bed rested in its place. I also bought a 2013 Range Rover.

I hired an assistant, something I should have done years before. Her name was Yoshi, a thirty-seven-year-old, pint-sized Asian woman who had tired of a boring career as an receptionist in a doctor's office and wanted to experience what it felt like to be among the famous, which I was. Yoshi made calls, ran errands, and cleaned up after me. She became the first contact anyone had with me, including Ace and Momma sometimes. If I was busy relaxing in my Jacuzzi tub, Yoshi would tell them I was unavailable and would get back to them at my earliest convenience. Yoshi craved responsibility, and wanted to do whatever I asked of her. She was the perfect devotee.

In my opinion, Ace wasn't dealing with my success as well as she should have been. She told me I was being extravagant with my spending and pretentious in attitude.

"You're on an ego trip, Sugar. Calm down," she advised.

"What are you telling me to calm down for? You're my manager. And you're my woman. You're supposed to be my number one hype woman. You should be proud of me. I shouldn't have to be happy for myself by myself," I retorted.

"I am happy for you. I've been wanting this success for you for a long time. You deserve it. Just don't let it go to your head too much. You still have to treat people right, especially the ones who helped get you to where you are. Your fans. And me."

I couldn't deny Ace had been the architect behind the level of success I had reached. Over the years, she had been the one wheeling and dealing contracts and hustling through negotiations. But I was the one who people loved. It was my voice on the record and on the radio. It was me in the music video. It was me who signed autographs and starred in photo shoots. I believed in my heart I wouldn't be where I was without Ace. I was also convinced I could continue without her.

For years, we had kept my true self hidden in order to get the world to love me. Now that the fans had affirmed their adoration of me, there was nothing that would stop them from loving me. I was positive about that and ready to squash the doubts she had been standing by all those years. I was going to prove that everyone would still love me, with a secret plan I had concocted without Ace's knowledge. She wasn't going to control that part of my life anymore. After the world found out who Sugar really was, Ace could decide if she wanted to stay or if she wanted to go.

Chapter 8

Sugar Rush

Momma didn't like Nisha. I was sure she didn't like her mostly because Ace didn't care for her. I learned the only reason Ace had offered to meet with Nisha was to keep an eye on her to determine what her plan was with me. Momma had told me any woman who wanted to get close to me and my manager was up to no good. What Momma and Ace didn't know what that Nisha and I were up to no good together.

Momma was at my side in Ace's office with me when Ace's assistant called to tell her that Nisha had arrived.

"You have to be careful who you allow in your circle of friends at this point, Sugar," Momma cautioned before Nisha opened the door.

"I got this, you two don't need to worry," I told them both.

I sat on Ace's couch dressed in tight leather skinny pants and an Ed Hardy shirt, with my weave pulled into a high ponytail. My makeup, as usual, was flawless. It was nine a.m. on a Monday morning and I was picture-perfect. Momma sat next to me, comfortable in dress slacks, a blouse, and heels. At fifty-one, she didn't look a day over forty. Money and natural beauty had done us both well. We remained seated in the back of the office, observers to the meeting between Ace and Nisha.

Nisha walked into the office, fresh and less intense than usual. She wore washed-out, light blue skinny jeans, a T-shirt bearing the face of the great Angela Davis, and peep-toe ankle boots in the middle of July. Her hair was smoothed into a bun at the nape of her neck and she wore minimal makeup. Her appearance was common for an artist; we didn't need to wear a business suit. That was left for the agents and managers, like the cream-colored business suit Ace had on that morning. As strained as our relationship had become, I always found her attractive and delicious when I saw her, as I did that morning.

"Good morning, everyone," Nisha said, acknowledging me, Momma, and Ace. She didn't seem surprised that there were extra guests at the meeting. She walked back and shook both my and Momma's hands. She then shook Ace's hand and took a seat in one of the chairs in front of Ace's desk.

"How are you this morning?" Ace asked. She generally opened business meetings with casual talk, trying to learn a bit of history about the person who sat opposite her.

"I'm doing well, thank you. Rock and I were up into the early morning hours writing a song. I'm working on very little sleep but, nonetheless, energized and happy to be here," Nisha answered.

"That's good. As I'm sure you know, there are sacrifices artists must make in order to succeed and survive in this business, sleep being one of the biggest, but easiest, sacrifices. There are others."

"I'm used to missing out on sleep, that's not a big deal. Anything beyond that must be negotiated." Nisha smiled.

"Time away from family is a hard one for most," Ace said. "Do you have family? Or someone special in your life who you'd miss on the road?"

Nisha adjusted in her seat. "My parents are in Chicago, living on the far south side. I'm the oldest of four. My siblings are much younger, still in high school and grade school."

"And are you close with them?"

"Not exactly," Nisha responded.

"Do you mind if I ask why not?" Ace inquired, though I recognized the confident tone in her voice. She already knew the answer and was about to make a point.

"We're not close because of my sexuality," Nisha answered honestly. "They don't agree with my being a lesbian. I'm not close to my sisters and brother either. My parents don't want me around them. So being away from my family wouldn't be a big deal; we're separated as it is."

Ace nodded. "I'm sorry to hear that. You do then already understand that even in this day and age, with as much progress that's been made for gays and lesbians, that there are many who still don't and won't condone it?"

"Yes, I understand that firsthand."

"I'm glad to hear that," Ace couldn't resist and glanced at me. I gave her no response in return. She had no idea I already knew Nisha's life story. She had shared it with me during the many conversations we had been having on the phone.

"And someone special? Are you in a relationship?"

"There's a woman I have interest in, yes. Time will tell where it goes."

Ace met eyes again with me briefly. I looked away.

"Your band? Are the members all lesbian?"

"No, they're not. Just me and Rock. But you know, some of the others are curious, but don't identify as lesbian. They predominately date men but a couple of them may sleep with a woman every now and then," Nisha told Ace. "That's how we roll."

"I see. How do you plan to handle your sexuality as your band becomes more popular? Ideally, how would you see yourself portrayed?"

Nisha readjusted in her seat. "Well, I want to be known first for my skills on the bass and guitar. That's my talent and that's my passion."

"That's exactly what people should know you for, your musicality," Ace asserted loudly. "What about your private life? I assume you're openly gay."

"Why do you assume that?" Nisha questioned.

"The story of your family's shun. Your being at the gay club."

Nisha turned around and looked at me. "Sugar was at the gay club." She turned back to Ace. "She's not openly gay."

Ace was angered. Whatever angle she thought she would use against Nisha was about to backfire if she was suddenly forced to respond to questions about my sexuality, which Nisha already knew but challenged Ace anyway. I was curious how Ace would respond. If the statement had come from any person other than Nisha, Ace would have laughed and agreed that of course I wasn't gay and had visited the club just for a good time out with my fans. If she indirectly responded to Nisha, it would seem that she was avoiding an answer, which might be an admission of guilt whether Nisha knew anything or not.

Ace peered at me, an intimidating look that stated she had had enough of me. She wasn't going to make herself look bad by answering the question. "Sugar, you can probably respond to this one yourself."

Momma reviewed me suspiciously. Momma and Ace were still in cahoots when it came to keeping my lesbianism a secret. "I have lots of gay fans, Nisha, as you know. I was in the mood for partying that night and that's where I went. It's not that I hadn't been to gay clubs before. I had been to many. That night it was unplanned, that's the only thing. Just think, if I hadn't gone that night, we all wouldn't be fortunate enough to be sitting here in this meeting right now. I'm glad I followed my instincts that night."

Ace resumed control of the conversation before Nisha could press that I hadn't actually responded to what she had indirectly asked: was I gay? Maybe she had decided to leave it alone since she knew the answer anyway.

"Nisha, as you know, there were pictures of you and Sugar published in a newspaper from that night."

"Yes, I know."

"It's easy for celebrity rumors to spread like wildfire. They have to be careful with every move they make because everyone is watching. It would have been easy for a bunch of gay rumors to erupt about that night. Fortunately, Sugar has me." Ace peeked at me. "It was easy enough to explain why she was there that night for the reason she just told you. Sugar and I have had this conversation many times and she knows that people can speculate all day long about whatever they want. It doesn't matter what they think they know, as long as they can't prove anything. That's where I come in. It's my job to do what's in my client's best interests at all times. So before you and I go any further, I need to know exactly how you want to represent yourself to the public."

"I'm not sure I understand exactly what you mean."

"Well, people like labels. Fans will want to know who you are, what you represent, who your friends are, who you sleep with. It's none of their business but they think it is. So, again, what is it that you want them to know? Do you want to be an out music artist? Or do you want to keep your private life private?"

"I'm not trying to hide who I am," Nisha told Ace.

"Meaning you're okay with being identified as a lesbian?"

"That's what I am, of course. There's nothing to be ashamed about. I've lost my family because I was honest with them. There's no way I'm about to lie and pretend to be something else for people I don't even know."

Momma exhaled loudly. Inside I smiled and agreed with Nisha.

"I see." Ace leaned back in her chair, quietly thinking. "Sugar knows that I had an idea to put her and Beau together in an effort to bring some recognition to Beau. At the same time, I have to be mindful of exactly who I'm connecting her to and what they represent as well. It has to benefit her first and foremost."

"I understand that," Nisha said.

"Sugar has a performance coming up in a couple weeks. I'm sure you know about it; it's at the Weekend In the Park event. If Beau is willing to sing a few of your R&B covers, we can arrange to have you open up for her. Depending on how that evening goes, we may or may not have another meeting."

Perfect, I thought. Ace was helping to set up my plan without even knowing it.

"Seriously?" Nisha asked, seemingly surprised when I knew that she wasn't. "I'll run it by Rock but I have no doubt she'll be in agreement. This is an honor."

"Call me after you talk to Rock and I'll fill you in on the details if this is a go."

"Thanks, Ace."

"Also, please understand that there are no promises here. This is a favor. It's a trial to see if this might work for all of us."

"Understood."

Ace rose from her chair. Nisha did the same. "Great, then. I'll expect to hear from you no later than tomorrow," Ace stated.

"Absolutely." Nisha spun around and said good-bye to Momma and me before she left the office.

"I'm not trying to tell you how to do your job, but are you sure this is best for Sugar?" Momma asked Ace.

"It's one show. It can't do any harm to see how Sugar's fans respond to Beau. I followed up with a few of the venues they've played in and I hear the turnout is fairly small, but consistent. And patrons tend to feel satisfied. From what I've been told, Nisha is a great musician and Rock has a wonderful voice. I'll pick the songs they will sing that night to make sure it blends with Sugar's show."

I let them talk without interruption. Neither of them knew that by the end of that night, my career would never be the same.

Sugar @SugarChitown So much on the horizon, fans! Stay tuned.

Chapter 9

Sugar Free

"Sugar, are you sure you want to do this?" Nisha asked when we spoke on the phone about a week after her meeting with Ace.

Nisha had spoken with Rock Sandy about opening for me at my concert in the park. Rock Sandy agreed to the performance without question and both acquiesced to Ace's request to sing popular number one R&B jams during their show. Ace believed that if the crowd recognized all of the songs, and the songs were performed well, then concertgoers would respond positively to them. They were set to sing five songs, closing with Beyoncé's "Irreplaceable." I found it odd and funny that Ace selected that song considering the plans I had for the night of the show.

"Yes, I'm sure. It's time. Why, are you getting nervous?"

"Me? No, not at all. I just don't have as much at risk as you. You have a single out that's hot. This will create publicity for the record, either good or bad. You're going to have a shitload of questions to answer. How honest are you willing to be?"

"I'll tell whatever I need to in order to come clean."

"That includes Franco? Have you thought about what this means for him when people learn he was just a front?"

I shrugged even though she couldn't see the gesture. "He should have known someday it would come to an end."

"And what about Ace?" she questioned softly.

"She's going to be upset, no doubt. But she'll come around eventually. I've got to show her that my fans will love me no matter who I love for myself. I'll let her decide if she wants to stay on as my manager."

"After all your years together, you're willing to take that chance?"

"I am."

"What about the other aspect of your relationship?"

"What do you mean?"

Nisha sighed and laughed gently. "No need to pretend, Sugar, I'm not blind or stupid. It's written all over both your faces. It's obvious there's more to your relationship than just manager and client."

I hadn't confessed my relationship with Ace to Nisha. All she knew to that point was that Franco had been hired to front as my man to conceal my true sexual identity. She hadn't been told that Ace wasn't only the conspirator of the false image, but the main party to the entire affair.

"What is it that you're suggesting, Nisha?" I asked anyway, curious how that young thing had figured it out.

"Well, you've told me all about the charade you all have been putting up so no one finds out you're a lesbian. But not once have you mentioned who you've dated over the years or how your girlfriends felt about having to be kept a secret. Not that you have to; maybe you feel it's none of my business. But you've told me so much already, I can't see why you'd keep that a secret. Unless Ace *is* the secret."

I weighed whether to tell her the truth. There was no concrete reason not to, especially with as much knowledge as she already had. I was willing and ready to out myself, but for some reason, respect I supposed, I still wanted to protect Ace. She should have been proud to claim me as her own, and if she wasn't prepared to share that with the world, then that would be her loss and Nisha's gain.

"Ace has been the love of my life since the day I laid eyes on her," I confessed to Nisha.

"So you were about to let me walk into this fire without telling me the entire story, were you?" she questioned.

"I was," I admitted. "Because I knew that Ace wouldn't come to you anyway. It would let her secret out. For Ace, her best-kept secret is the truth behind this lie."

"I have to tell you, Sugar, the world might be shocked to learn about you being gay, not so much with Ace. It's pretty clear she's into chicks."

"I know, and I've told her that over and over. And still she insists neither of us can come out of the closet. Even if people suspect it, we shouldn't confirm it."

"Well back to my original question. You're sure you want to do this? This is going to kill your relationship with Ace," Nisha stated.

"She's going to be hurt. Or mad. Probably both," I realized. "It's time for me to take the wheel on my personal life. As much as I love Ace, I won't keep hiding who I am. Not anymore. I felt this way before the success of this latest record and even more so now that I've blown up."

"It could backfire. You assume the best thing is to come clean and believe that everyone who loved you before will continue to love you. That's not always the case. I speak from experience."

I understood where Nisha was coming from and knew that she spoke about her experience with her family. I wanted to tell Nisha I was sorry for what happened with her parents, but remind her that I was Sugar with millions of fans around the world; I wasn't worried.

"I get what you're saying, honey, but I don't have time to worry about who doesn't love me after this. That's their problem, not mine."

"Even if there's bad press from what we're about to do?"

"All press is good press as they say."

"Okay, just making sure. I should have known you had already considered all angles."

I considered the possibility that Nisha was getting cold feet herself. "You're not worried about the response you'll get, are you?" I asked. I could easily find someone to replace her.

"Nah, I'm good. After what I've been through with my family, there's not much anyone else can say that will affect me. Plus"—she breathed heavily into the phone—"I'm happy to be the chosen one."

"The timing couldn't have been more perfect for us to meet. You know, dear, I don't know if Ace planned to take you and Beau on as a client, but what we're about to be will guarantee that she won't."

"That's cool," Nisha said. "If Ace even hinted to wanting to keep me gagged and tied up in the closet, I wasn't going to sign with her anyway. I'm happy playing little bars in Chicago if that's what it takes to be me."

"I hear you. I wish I had had the same backbone you do when I was your age. But, better late than never. It's time for Sugar to set herself free."

We talked for a while longer, confirming every detail of our plan before we got off the phone. Then I showered, flat ironed my hair, applied makeup, and put on a sexy, summer maxi dress. I placed oversized, dark sunglasses on my face and a large brimmed beach-style hat. I was prepared to take a quick and quiet five-block walk to Ace's condo, incognito, unless a fan recognized me. Which happened more and more everywhere I went in Chicago.

Outside I took in the early evening warmth; the sun had gradually begun its slow journey to the west. I walked and softly hummed "All is Fair in Love," a Stevie Wonder oldie, its lyrics appropriate for my and Ace's upcoming fate. I loved Ace without a doubt, but I was ready to end it since she wasn't willing to live the life I wanted to live with her.

At a corner two blocks from her condo, I stood at a stoplight, irritated that the light hadn't changed upon my approach. A drop-top Sebring slowed and paused in front of me, though it had the green light. The car was filled with two guys and two excited girls. "Sugar? Sugar! Is that you?" they yelled.

I tipped my sunglasses down and peeked at them over the rim. I smiled and then put my finger over my mouth in a "shh" gesture. I didn't want to cause a ruckus in the middle of the street because a superstar stood on the corner. They respected my wish, honked their horn, and screamed, "We love you!" before driving off. *Of course you do. And you will still love me after next week.*

At Ace's condo I used my keys to let myself inside the building and I rode the elevator to tenth floor, where she had a corner unit on the southeast end that faced downtown. Inside she stood at the bar, her back to me, the floor-to-ceiling window displaying Chicago's skyline in front of her. She was casual, dressed in army green loose-fitting linen pants and a white tank top. A small tattoo of a music note rested on her shoulder blade. The muscle in her left arm curved slightly when she reached for a bottle of Belvedere vodka. She poured it over ice in two small glasses and added a lemon wedge to each. Finally, she turned around and walked toward me standing in the foyer of the open room.

I was taken back to her first approach to me eleven years ago. Even with the strain between us, she walked confidently, just as she had then, until she was right in front of me, her body against mine. She kissed my lips. "Hello," she said, and handed me a glass.

For a moment I felt bad for what I was about to do to our relationship. Ace had only done what she said was my best interest in mind by sheltering my sexuality and our relationship. She had spent years catering to my every other need and in a week I was about to throw it all away.

"Hey," I said to her, then took a sip of the potent libation as we both sat on her couch.

We had a busy week ahead of us. The next morning Ace was leaving for a three-day business trip to New York. I had several interviews lined up and classes to teach at the community center. I didn't know how much time we would have together before next Sunday's performance and I was hot for her. I wanted her between my thighs and because I didn't know if it was going to be our last time intimate with one another, I wanted to make it the best time.

I reached for her breasts, which were small, just enough to fit inside the palms of my hands. I rubbed and squeezed gently. I stroked her pointed nipples through the tank top. Ace continued to sip on her drink, her eyes on me. It was uncommon for me to initiate pleasure to her. All she had ever wanted to do was please me and only rarely was I allowed to be the aggressor on her. She didn't protest. I kissed her, drinking in the vodka on her breath. Slowly she lowered herself until she lay flat on the couch, and I was on top.

With my left hand I loosened the tie around the waist of her pants and slid my hand inside. She was aroused, her body told me so. I played with her lips, and she got wetter. I found her small pleasure spot and played with it. Her body ground against mine. I looked down on her, her eyes closed, her body twitching with pleasure. Until . . .

She stopped, her eyes suddenly opened wide. She grabbed my face between her hands and kissed me hard. She pushed me back until she was on top, back in control where she wanted to be. She dove under my dress and pushed my legs open. I wore no panties and she wasted no time. Ace once told me she had tasted no one like me before. She said the thick flesh at my middle was the juiciest and sweetest she ever had. She ate like she was ravenous.

We moved to her bedroom where we spent the rest of the evening wrapped around each other. She loved when I spread my legs and rocked my middle against hers, her flesh slippery and overpowered by the thickness of mine. She liked getting lost in my ass, my cheeks smothering her face while she licked from one end to the other. We indulged in every position imaginable, until rest commanded and took over our bodies.

In the morning, we lay facing one another when the alarm sounded at six a.m. We said little, as we had the night before. It was probably for the best as there wasn't much to say that wouldn't wind us into an argument. She recommended her driver take me home but I insisted I wanted to walk again.

On the early morning stroll back to my condo, energetic and focused joggers strode past me without acknowledgment. At the stoplight, drivers were busy sipping on coffee or touching up makeup in their rearview mirrors to notice me. No one paid any attention to the woman in a yellow wrinkled dress standing at the corner waiting for the light to change. Everyone was absorbed in his or her own Monday morning busyness. That was fine; I would have hated for paparazzi to have caught a photo of me in that state. No, I had to be perfect when the camera lens landed on me, just as I planned to be on Saturday.

Sugar @SugarChitown Rise & shine lovelies! Make sure you're fresh & camera ready today!

Chapter 10

Sugar Craving

The park was packed with concertgoers strewn about the lawn, most of them on blankets with picnic baskets and wine. Many had spent the day at the festival visiting art exhibits, eating famous Chicago foods like Italian beef sandwiches, listening to poetry, and shopping at the stands throughout the area. As the evening came upon us, the grounds became more crowded as they prepared for me, the headline of the entire weekend's events.

Prestin, one of the organizers behind the event, had been working closely with Ace in preparation for my performance. It had taken little convincing of Prestin for her to allow Beau to open for me. Ace had told me that Prestin, a lesbian herself, had already heard of Beau and wanted to support them in any way she could. I knew of Prestin; we had crossed paths occasionally at various happenings over the years, and I recalled feeling envious of her and her girlfriend's openness with their relationship. They walked red carpets together and were unashamed to show affection. From what I had read about Prestin, she had been single and loving every minute of her lifestyle until Jaye, a stunning beauty, captured and held her attention. She had been off the market since. I had wondered why Ace didn't feel we could have the same kind of open, successful relationship that they shared.

The night before, Prestin had been at the stage for my and Beau's rehearsal. She strutted the stage and venue gracefully in enviable stilettos.

"Everything good for you, Sugar?" she had asked after I ran through a couple of songs.

"I'd like more moments when the stage is darkened and there's one spotlight just on me. Ace, you know which songs I'm referring to and when I want that to happen," I told both Ace and Prestin. "Can you two work that out?"

"You got it," Ace had replied. Prestin took notes on the paper attached to the clipboard she had in her hands while Ace gave her specific instructions. I hoped they had gotten it correct, as it was of the utmost importance that the lighting was accurate.

"Is there anything I can get for you?" Prestin asked me. She had stopped by my dressing room backstage as I began to prepare for my performance. She had on yet another pair of glorious stilettos.

"More tea," I told her just as I sat in the chair while LaTrice, one of my hairstylists, began to part my weave. LaTrice was one of the best weave stylists I knew, but the girl was hood and spoke in Chicago's Southern-style dialect. I had kept her around only for her phenomenal hairstyling skills.

"So what we doin' tonight?" LaTrice asked, already fingering through my hair, grabbing portions, and mocking certain up-do and down styles.

"Curls galore," I told her. For my performance, I had selected an emerald green sequined gown and wanted to appear as glamorous as the great Diana Ross. "The bigger, the better."

LaTrice obliged and began to section off my hair.

"So you just blowin' up, girl," LaTrice said before she took a hot rod to my hair.

"I know," I agreed.

"I heard a DJ the other day say that 'Feel My Love' is as classic and timeless and Rick and Teena's 'Fire And Desire.' I was like, that's my girl!"

"Say what?" I replied, excited but not surprised by the compliment and comparison.

"Yes, girl, he said there was gon' be some babies made to your jam. I can't even lie, I done played it a couple times myself with my man. We be gettin' it on to you, Sugar, how you like that?" She cracked up.

"I would expect nothing less." We both laughed.

"So what you got next? Bet all the record execs callin' you now. You won't be singing backup no more, that's for sure." She finished a few curls. "This what you want?"

I fluffed the curls, which were brown with blond highlights mixed in. "Yep, this is it. About what's next, you'll find out tonight."

"Aw shucks, you 'bout to announce your world tour or something?"

"Not yet. Just sit back, enjoy the show, and don't leave before the lights go up," I told her.

"Cool. I ain't leaving anyway. My man is already out there with a spot up front, girl."

"All right now, that's how to do it."

There was a knock on the door before Prestin reentered with my tea. She placed it on the counter in front of me. "I was just running some of the details about the after party to Ace. We have the two of you and Franco set up front of the VIP section. Is there anyone else to be added to the list? Ace wanted me to confirm with you."

LaTrice looked at me anxiously through the mirror. I ignored her quiet begging and thought of Nisha and the rest of the members of Beau. "No, no one else. Thanks, Prestin."

"Sure thing. Just let Ace know if anything else comes up."

"I will."

She spotted my dress hanging in the corner of the room. "That's hot. Perfect for a diva. You'll be looking good, Sugar." She winked and smiled, then left the room.

"Girl, she looked like she was about to eat you up. She a lesbo or somethin'?"

"First, she was not looking hungry in my direction. And second, yes, she is, why?"

"Just wonderin', girl, just wonderin'. Every time I turn around somebody new done turned lesbo."

"Well I don't think she turned into a lesbian, LaTrice. Nobody turns gay; they are or they aren't."

"I'm just sayin', girl, half my old friends laying up with other women these days and that's after years of slurping on dicks." She stopped suddenly. "Oops, excuse me, I'm sorry, I ain't trying to be unprofessional. But anyway, God didn't make it for girls to be laid up with other girls. It ain't right, the Bible said so."

"What exactly does the Bible say?" I wanted to know.

"Girl, it's some scriptures in there talking about homosexuality being wrong. Ask anybody."

"I am. I'm asking you."

"Well I can't quote none of 'em right now, but I know that's what it says in there."

"Have you read the Bible, LaTrice?"

"Hell naw, I ain't read no Bible."

I shook my head. "Then how do you know what it says, and particularly that it says homosexuality is wrong?"

"Because that's what everybody says. My momma and my daddy said it is. And every preacher does, too. It's an abomination."

I tested her. "An abomination? What does that mean?"

LaTrice rested the curling iron at her hip while she stared up at the ceiling. "It just means that it's a sin. God don't like it."

"An abomination is something vile or disgusting and I disagree that gays are disgusting," I countered angrily.

"Why you acting mad, Sugar? My bad; you got somebody gay in your family or somethin'?"

"I'm just tired of hearing folks talk like all gay people are on a fast train to hell. Tell me, do you and your man plan on getting married?"

She held up her left hand and waved it so I could see it in the mirror. "He ain't put a ring on it yet."

"Well I do believe the Bible says something about fornication as well, doesn't it?"

"Forni-what?"

"My point exactly. Never mind, LaTrice. Don't ever try to debate anyone on this topic; just stick to what you do best: hair. I have to rest my voice now," I told her and closed my eyes until she finished my hair.

"I'll see you out there," she said as she packed up her tools. I nodded but didn't speak. She left.

I didn't trust most people to do my makeup so on most occasions I did it myself. After LaTrice left, Yoshi entered the room with my makeup kits. I had just begun to highlight my face when there was a knock on the door.

"Enter," I said.

The door opened slowly and in walked Nisha. Immediately I asked Yoshi to return to the hallway. Nisha closed the door behind her and stood next to me, her body leaned against the counter. I could smell her musky perfume. She wore cut-off, ripped jean shorts that revealed long, sexy legs. She ran her hands down the denim material and over her skin. I wondered how her hands would feel rubbing on my skin later that night.

"We're about to hit the stage," she said. "I wanted to see you one last time before."

"To see if I've changed my mind?"

She nodded, her 'fro bobbing with her head.

"I haven't changed my mind. The show will go on. And remember, this is only the prelude."

She smiled, relaxed. "All right. I'll see you in a bit."

"Go on out there and get them ready for me."

"I can do that. Now you finish getting fine so you can be ready for me later," she teased.

"I can't wait." We smiled at one another and she left.

When I began to apply my foundation several minutes later, I heard the music begin. Ace came in shortly after.

"Hey," she said.

"Hey," I said back. Our conversations had been so short and stilted since the morning she left for New York. We had talked on the phone a couple of times, and sent text messages, but only about the show, nothing of any substance and nothing related to us.

"Their set is about twenty minutes. You'll hit the stage about fifteen minutes after that. Need anything?"

"I'll need help into my dress when I finish my makeup, but Yoshi can do that if you have something to tend to."

She took a seat in the chair behind me. "Nope, just you."

I wondered if Ace wanted to make sure I didn't leave to go watch Beau perform. I bet she wanted to keep the same eye on me with Nisha as she wanted to keep on Nisha with me.

Her phone held her attention while I continued with my makeup. She glanced up only once while I applied my false lashes. "You look pretty," she said, and returned to her screen.

Finally, I stood and removed my robe. "I'm ready."

She put her phone on the table, got the dress, and removed it from the hanger. She unzipped it slowly, carefully, and opened it for me to step inside. I faced her, my hands on her shoulders, and placed my right foot and then left inside the dress. She pulled it up and on to my size-sixteen body. I turned around so she could zip the dress, her fingertips cold against my skin.

"Shoes?" she asked.

I pointed to my Gucci carry-on.

"Sit." I sat back in my chair while Ace knelt before me and placed a new pair of jeweled shoes on my feet. She stood back and observed me like a work of art. "Master-piece," she said.

"Thank you, Ace."

"You ready?"

"I was born ready, you know that," I told her.

"You're right about that," she agreed. We left the dressing room and walked to the side of the stage. Prestin handed me a microphone.

"How was Beau?" I asked Prestin.

"They did their thing. The crowd loved them," she said enthusiastically.

The MC, a radio disc jockey, announced to the hyped crowd that it was time for Sugar. I closed my eyes and said a brief prayer, which was routine before every per-formance. *Blessings over this entire space, Father.*

The crowd cheered louder as the music to my first song, "He's the One," began to play.

"Get 'em," Ace told me.

Prestin said, "Go on, girl."

I took a deep breath, licked my teeth, and stepped from behind the curtain on the left side of the stage. The spot-light focused on me. I waved to the crowd and clapped my hands in the air in honor of me right along with them. Then I dove right into the song, which required little movement, just me at the middle of the stage. I sang passionately, recalling the urgency and yearning behind the words when I had written them so many years prior. I had hoped Ace would not only listen to the lyrics, but hear the desire behind each word. I wanted everyone to know that she was "my one" and I was hers. Still she had kept our love hidden between the sheets. During the song I looked back to her once. She stood still as she usually did when I performed, composed and business-like. Instinctively, I pointed right at her and sang the words "she's the one," instead of "he's the one." Her expression hardened. I turned back to the crowd. Many of the concertgoers near the front of the stage strained to see just who I had directed my love to.

After the song, I spoke to the crowd and thanked them for coming out to see me and for all of their warm support of "Feel My Love." They cheered loud when I mentioned the song and some yelled over the noise at me, asking if I'd be performing the song. I had to tell them that E wasn't there to perform the song with me, but then I turned to the piano player behind me who played a few notes from the song. Then I sang my verse, making love to myself in my green dress. I ran my hands up and down my body, over my breasts, up my face, and into my hair. I gave them a visual Sugar orgasm and they seemed to cum right along with me. I looked down to see LaTrice and her man grinding with me and the beat. When the song ended I asked everyone, "Was it as good for you as it was for me?"

They all yelled, "Yeah!"

I continued the show by performing a few of my favorite covers, including "Do Me, Baby," "Let's Get It On," and "Inside My Love" by Minnie Riperton. Almost every song I selected for that night had a sexual undertone. That was intentional and would lead to the climax of the evening.

Sweat rolled down my skin underneath my gown and it shined against the edge of my hairline. As I was preparing for the final song, I asked for a towel. Prestin, tall, slim, and sexy in those heels, walked onto the stage and handed a small white cloth to me.

"Thank you, lovely. Isn't she beautiful, y'all?" I asked the crowd. They clapped and whistled in agreement.

"Before I leave here tonight, I want to give you all a special treat. You want to hear something new?" They cheered. "This is something I've been working on with a very talented young lady. We wanted to give you a little something extra tonight. Is that all right?" More applause. "You already met her earlier tonight, so without further ado, I'd like to bring Trendy back to the stage."

I took a few steps back to watch Nisha walk toward me from the right side of the stage, opposite from Prestin and Ace, who remained behind the curtain. Nisha carried a stool in one hand and a guitar in her other. She had changed out of the eccentric outfit she wore during Beau's performance and now had on a short and simple nude sleeveless dress with matching nude heels. She had tamed her curly 'fro into a beautiful, kempt high bun. She was sexy and chic and still edgy with her guitar in hand. The crowd went wild.

I glanced to my left at Ace, who appeared ready to explode with anxiety and fury. Her face was an angry and perplexed frown, her lips tight and pressed hard against each other. I turned from her and proceeded with the first step of me and Nisha's two-part plan.

Nisha walked the stool to the front of the stage and gestured for me to take a seat.

"How beautiful is Trendy?" I asked the audience as I walked toward and then sat comfortably on the stool, my heels resting on the wooden ledge at the base. Nisha stood close at my side.

"You know, there are only a handful of times in our lives when we meet someone who completely changes the direction of our lives. Well, Trendy is one of those people for me." I looked up to her and she turned to face me. "It's hard to believe we met only a couple of months ago but I can say that my life will never be the same." To the audience I said, "Trendy and I wrote a song together that we'd like to play for you tonight. The song is called 'From Behind.'" I nodded to Nisha and she began a delicate strum on her guitar. I watched her fingers caress and pluck the strings, then closed my eyes and pictured her fingers strumming the middle of my body a few hours into the future.

I began to sing the sensitive lyrics about a genuine love affair—a love so strong it defied time; a connection so real it created an experience neither of them had ever had before. From behind closed doors their love was enviable. But that's where it remained, for their eyes only. Next to me Nisha played while I would occasionally peek at her lovingly.

The chorus explained that their love was good, but misunderstood. They could never have forever if they swore to keep it behind the door.

The second verse I sang with more passion. It spoke about a lust so intense it made the body weak at one touch, one glance. When they made love it was hot like fire, intoxicating, and blissful. They sexed in every position: standing, sitting, missionary, and from behind. During that part of the song Trendy faced me, her guitar rested against her middle. She stared at me while she played with a delicate, slow grind of her hips. Sitting, I leaned toward her body, my face meeting her fingers as she plucked strings. I held the mic in my right hand and with my left I stroked the side of her hip. I sang to her about how good her body felt against mine, intertwined, so divine I could no longer resign to stay confined behind the door. She bit her bottom lip. I caressed her firm ass cheek and gave it a smack before she took a step backward.

I repeated the chorus again before the melody slowed and then stopped. Acoustically, I sang that I loved her too deeply not to love her freely. And even though it would hurt us both, I had to let her go. With my eyes shut and moist with tears, I sang the chorus one last time. When I opened my eyes, the only light from the stage rested on me, with Nisha dim in the darkness next to me.

The audience exploded in applause. I heard lots of whistling and a few women yell, "All right now!" I stood and bowed to the crowd. I walked to both the left and right ends of the stage and bowed and blew kisses to everyone. I met Nisha back in the middle, where we hugged tightly and then waved before we prepared to exit.

"For those of you who aren't ready to call it a night, don't forget the after party," I reminded everyone as they began to pack up their picnic items. I gave them the name and address of the venue. "See you there!" Nisha and I turned our backs to the crowd and prepared to greet Ace side-stage. We looked at one another before we rounded the curtain. Behind the velvety black material stood Ace with her arms crossed over her chest.

"I need to have a talk with my client," Ace said to Nisha, while looking at me. "Dressing room. Now." She turned and started to walk toward the room at the end of the hall.

"Guess you didn't run that by her first, huh, Sugar?" Prestin questioned, somewhat amused with a half smirk.

"It was a surprise," I answered. "What, she didn't love it?" I asked with sarcasm.

"No, I can't say she looked like she loved it. I did; it was pretty hot if you ask me." She looked back and forth between me and Nisha. "Pretty believable," she commented. "If I didn't know any better . . ." She stared at us without finishing her sentence.

"Prestin, darling, just what is it that you might know if you didn't know better?"

"I might say that there's even more sweetness to Sugar than what meets the eye."

I smiled.

"I've been around a long time. I've seen it all, you know," she continued.

"Well I say keep your eyes open, my beautiful Prestin, because from now on, what you see *is* what you're going to get." I winked at her.

Prestin laughed. "Okay, then, I'll be watching." She turned to Nisha. "Great show tonight. I'll be looking to connect with you and Beau again."

"I'd love that," Nisha said.

"Okay, let me wrap things up here. You had better get back there before Ace comes looking for you. I'll see you at the party."

She then got quiet while listening to someone speak through the headset over her head. She nodded silently at that person's words, and then said, "I'll be right there." She walked away.

"Let me get over to Ace," I told Nisha. She reached for my hand.

"Her feelings are most likely hurt already," she said.

"Maybe. Mine have been hurting for eleven years. It's time to put that to an end."

"I feel you, Sugar. I'm still in. But, if anything changes after you talk to Ace, I'll understand."

"It won't. I'll see you at the party, pretty girl."

She blushed underneath her already-flushed skin. "Okay." She turned in the opposite direction from where I headed.

Outside the dressing room, Yoshi leaned against the concrete wall, biting her short nails. She seemed shaken and I assumed Ace had angrily ordered her out of the room.

"I'll only be a moment," I told her.

Inside my dressing room Ace sat in the chair where I sat earlier while LaTrice did my hair. She swiveled back and forth in small half circles in the seat, agitated, her right pointer finger tapping rapidly against the leather arm of the chair.

"What the fuck was that about?" she demanded.

"The song with Nisha?" I asked as if I was uncertain.

"Yes, that fuckin' song."

"You know exactly what it's about. It's about me hiding behind Franco's ass and your rules all these years. I'm done."

"You're ready to fuck up everything I've done for you for a little girl?"

"What? This isn't about Nisha. This is about me and you and years of pretending and fronting to be a person I'm not. We had this conversation repeatedly well before either of us knew Nisha existed. This ain't about her."

"It sure as hell looked like it is out there."

"You jealous?" I snickered.

Ace stood up. "You can't play me like a fool in front of hundreds of people, Sugar."

I took a step closer and we stood face to face. "That's where you're wrong, honey. You don't have to worry about that since nobody even knows about us. Who's going to know you've been played?"

She didn't answer that question. "Look, cut this shit out right now. We have business coming up and I can't have you fucking it up with this crazy shit."

"Stop, Ace, just stop. You keep dangling music deals over my head like I'll keep dropping to your knees and bowing down to whatever you say. Well check this out, you can't control me anymore. Not in our relationship and not as my manager. You keep forgetting who everybody is cheering for. Me, not you. I'm running this from now on."

She leaned against the vanity table. "Is that what you think?"

"That's what I know," I responded confidently.

"Yeah, whatever, we'll see about that."

"Yep, watch." Before she could continue the conversation, I walked to the door and opened it for Yoshi to come back in.

"Yoshi, please pack up my things," I requested of her. She scurried inside and gathered my makeup cases and belongings scattered throughout the room. Ace's demeanor had relaxed after Yoshi reentered the room.

"I'll see you shortly," Ace said to me, a reminder that we had adjoining rooms at a chic, luxury boutique hotel a few blocks from the venue where the after party was being held.

"Yep." I didn't say anything additional and Ace left the room.

"Yoshi, unzip me please."

As she assisted me out of my gown, she asked, "Everything okay, Miss Sugar?" When I hired Yoshi, I requested that she call me Miss Sugar. I felt I deserved that kind of respect every time she spoke to me. "You seem bothered."

"I'm fine," I answered her, though it was none of her business that I had secretly begun to feel guilty for what I was about to do to Ace. Our private relationship was about to end in the most hurtful, controversial way. She'd be quietly humiliated, as I had been for eleven years whenever she pretended not to love me. I shook the guilt off and told myself that regardless of how high she had lifted my career, my love was worth more than dollar signs and applause. I'd prove to her that I could have it all: money, fame, and love, even if the love was not from her.

Chapter 11

Sugar Spy

"I heard about your stunt tonight," Franco said to me over the phone as I sat on the love seat in the bedroom of my suite.

"It was a beautiful song. I hate you missed it," I responded. "Maybe another time. I'm sure we'll perform it again."

"Sugar, you know you about to mess up a good thing," he warned.

"What good thing? Us? You've got to be kidding me."

"You're playing with everybody's lives right now, not just your own. How am I supposed to explain to my family why my girlfriend is on stage groping on a woman? Are you thinking about anybody but yourself?"

"Don't you know I've made you what you are? Nobody would even know your name if it wasn't next to mine. Show a little gratitude here. This ain't about you," I reminded him. "It's easy enough to tell your family we broke up. Explain it how you explained breakups with all your other front women."

"What?" He sounded panicked. "You're trying to end our relationship?"

"The show is over, darling. It's almost time to take your final bow."

"Does Ace know about this?"

"Ace doesn't need to know every step I take because this isn't about her either, it's about me."

"I'm calling Ace," he said like a baby.

"Stop acting like a pussy, Franco. What is Ace going to do, come give me a whoopin'? She is not my momma; I already have one."

"You on something, Sugar. Stop acting like the world revolves around you."

"But it does, darling, don't forget that." I hung up. "Yoshi!" I called. She opened the French doors and rushed inside from the living room space. "Bring my garment bag so we can choose an outfit."

Yoshi left and then returned with the large bag filled with at least seven different outfit selections. I wondered if she ever tired of my fetch-and-retrieve requests. Judging by her endless desire to please, I had to assume not. She hung the bag on the clothing rack that we had requested for the room. I fingered through the clothes and tried to decide which outfit would look best on camera that night. I dismissed Yoshi from the room again and dialed Nisha's number.

"What are you wearing this evening, my dear?" I asked after she answered. "We must complement one another."

"What would you like me to wear? This is your moment."

"You must be sexy. But that comes natural, doesn't it?" We both laughed. "It'll be hot if we're both in skirts. You wear something short and fitted with those glorious legs hanging out. High heels. Low-cut top, lots of jewelry. I want your hair wild, but your face has to be visible."

"Easy. That's most of my wardrobe you described. What about you?"

"I need you to have easy access." I picked through a few dresses and settled on a red wrap dress. Nisha could easily open it or lift it, which she preferred. "I have the perfect dress. We're set. I'll see you there."

"Cool."

"Yoshi!" I called for her again. She came back with her long, jet black hair flapping against her back. "Steam this dress for me, won't you? I'm about to take a shower."

"All of your necessities are in there for you already."

"Thank you." I entered the master bath with its marble countertop, jet tub, and separate glass shower. I turned on the water, tucked my hair under a shower cap and stepped inside and underneath the hot water. I let the water run over my body and rinse away the salty sweat from my performance. Then, I took my loofah and drenched it with a creamy, perfumed body wash that cleansed and softened my skin. My body was smooth and exfoliated when I exited the shower, and wrapped in a fluffy towel. I rubbed lotion of the same brand and scent into my damp skin while I lay on the bed. I summoned Yoshi again.

"My back," I told her. She rubbed the cream over my back.

"Anything else?"

"I'll let you know, thank you."

She nodded and left.

I put my iPhone on the dock that sat on the nightstand next to the bed, and played tunes from an R&B playlist I had created and filled with both old-school and current hits. While I reapplied my makeup, I sang along with the music, sounding better than the artists who recorded the music. I used liquid black eyeliner to draw extreme lines around my slanted eyes. Over them I applied winged false lashes that angled up and outward, lifting my eyes like a geisha. I applied fire engine red lipstick. Yoshi helped me into my dress and brought me a Prada clutch to carry. Lastly, I put on the platform red bottoms Ace had recently bought me. How would she feel when she saw them wrapped around Nisha's waist?

When I was ready, I called Ace from the living quarters. I told her I was heading down to my limo. She told me she'd be five minutes behind me. Yoshi accompanied me on the elevator ride down from the twelfth floor. "Is there anything else before you go?" she asked before the door attendant opened the door for me.

"Be sure the room to the adjoining suite is locked. That's all. Be back tomorrow morning at nine."

"Yes, Miss Sugar. Have a great night."

I smiled deviously. "I sure plan to."

I was shocked when I got inside my limo. "What the fuck, Franco? What are you doing here?"

"Escorting you to the party as I always do," he said calmly. "Why should tonight be any different?"

"Because it's a new day. Like I told you earlier, it's curtain time for you."

"Well I'm in it 'til it's over," he said. He was a spotlight whore.

"Suit yourself. This is your last limo ride anyway."

He reached for the bottle of champagne that sat in a bucket across from us. "Well I'm about to make the best of it." He poured himself a glass and had finished it by the time we finished the short ride to the venue. "It's been real," he said, seeming to surrender to the demise of our fake relationship and to whatever his unknown future held for him. "What do I need to do? Make it look like we got into a fight or something?"

"No, baby, I got this already. You just keep your mouth shut the rest of the night."

He adjusted his tie. "Your wish is my command, Most High."

"Finally you got it right."

Franco leaned forward and kissed my cheek. "In all seriousness, you're the shit, Sugar. I kind of admire you for tonight. I have to admit I'm sort of tired of running around in hiding my damn self. Whatever happens next, we're cool."

I doubted he would feel that way in a few days but I chose not to share that with him. "See you on the other side," I said.

We exited the limo and smiled for a couple of photographers who stood outside the club. We didn't pose or hug or act like a couple as usual; we walked in side by side with an understanding that it would be our last walk together. Upon entering the large, upscale space, we were immediately taken upstairs to the VIP section by one of the security guards. Prestin met us there.

"Sugar, Franco, this way." We were seated at a half moon–shaped table that overlooked the dance floor and bars below. Prestin waved to a young girl who looked like a model in training. She was about six feet tall, skinny, with golden blond hair and radiant blue eyes. "This is Amy. She's here to serve you in any way possible."

Amy smiled. "I'm a huge fan," she told me. "What can I get for you?"

"Lemon drop martini for Sugar and a margarita with Patrón for me," Franco ordered for both of us. Amy left to place our orders with the bartender.

"I'm around all evening; be sure to let me know if you need anything," Prestin told us. "I'm not sure if you've ever met my wife, Jaye. She'll be here soon and I want to be sure to introduce you," she said directly to me.

"I'd love to," I answered honestly. Maybe we could all be friends when this was over.

Shortly after Franco and I took the first sips of our drinks, I watched Ace enter the club, looking delicious dressed in her usual attire, a tan business suit with a blue camisole underneath. She made her way through the growing crowd until she greeted Prestin. Prestin walked her to the staircase that led up to the VIP section. A minute later she took a seat at my side.

"You look beautiful," she complimented me. Though her attitude was still stiff, she was kind upon her greeting.

"So do you," I replied.

"What about me?" Franco asked.

"Metrosexually handsome as always," Ace told him.

Amy came to our table to take Ace's order. "Grey Goose on the rocks."

We sat in silence for a while until a few more individuals came upstairs, including several up-and-coming artists who Ace knew. They came to our table, congratulated me on the success of the single, and set up meetings to connect with Ace. Soon the seven tables in the VIP section were filled with musicians, singers, and rappers, their managers, party promoters, and a few wanna-bes who had gotten on the list somehow. Bottles of champagne were popping at every table and the party had begun.

Times like that were part of the reason I loved being a celebrity. We got to party hard, usually free, and were treated like royalty. A few people lit blunts and freely smoked while the rest of us inhaled deeply, appreciative of the contact. The DJ played mostly R&B, rap, and house music. I stood out of my chair, high and buzzed, dancing with the beat and ready for Nisha. My heart beat faster when I saw her dancing on the floor beneath me. She was with another Beau member they called X, moving with the beat of the music. She looked up to me, winked, and held up a peace sign. Only she and I knew exactly what she meant.

Two minutes later I grabbed my Prada purse and told Ace and Franco I would be back. Ace was unusually drunk, comfortable in her element surrounded by others in the industry. This is what we did: we worked hard and partied even harder.

"Yeah, okay," she replied and went back to her conversation with a large man in a black T-shirt and jeans.

Franco hadn't even noticed. He was too occupied in a talk with a gentleman who was obviously gay. Maybe he'd finally come out of the closet too, I thought.

At the bottom of the staircase next to the guard who protected VIP I met eyes with Nisha. She tilted her head sideways to the right. I looked in that direction and saw Prestin watching me. Rather than pretend like I wasn't trying to escape the club unnoticed, I nodded my head at her and smiled. She placed a finger over her mouth, grinned, and then gestured for me to follow her. Nisha shook her head side to side to Rock Sandy, and then followed as well and we walked down a hall past the restrooms and around a corner to an exit door at the rear.

"If you're looking for privacy, there's a small office to the left." Prestin pointed to a door a few feet away. "If you want to leave, right this way. Be careful, the alley is dark. I can have one of the guards escort you if needed."

Without knowing it herself, Prestin had become the perfect accomplice to our plan. "We'll stay right here if that's all right. Can you be sure no one gets back here? We'd like some quiet time," I said with a big smile.

Prestin fanned her face with a wave of her hand. "You got it. Enjoy, ladies." She walked away, clicking the floor in yet another pair of stilettos.

Nisha and I stared at one another. "You got it?" I asked her.

"Yes." She reached in her purse and pulled out a camera. We looked around and found a stack of boxes that we could place the camera on top of. Nisha worked the camera, setting the timer and adjusting the focus to night vision. We moved the boxes toward the end of the corner that led back to the club. "Does this seem like the right place?" She spoke loudly enough for me to hear, as she was closer to the music, yet hushed so as to not draw attention toward us. I leaned against the wall.

"How does that look?" I asked.

She peeked through the camera and then moved the camera slightly to the right. "Okay." She walked back to me, twisting her fingers together, her hands slightly shaking.

"Are you nervous?"

"A little. I'm not nervous about the outcome of this; I'm a little anxious about being with you. I want this to be a memorable experience for you."

I eyed Nisha from head to toe, my buzz still on high. "I'm already pleased. I'm sure I'll be satisfied, too."

Her shoulders relaxed. "Let's do this. We have about twenty seconds before the first one."

I stayed my position against the wall and asked her to come forward. "Put your palms against the wall, your arms over my shoulders. Like this." She did. We positioned our bodies in perfect view of the camera hidden at the end of the hall. I licked my lips. "Now come here."

Nisha leaned forward cautiously and slowly, until our mouths touched. "You ready?" she asked, her lips brushing against mine. I warmed. Only the third woman to ever touch my body and I was instantly ready.

"Yes." I kissed her lips slowly, grazing mine against her small, puckered mouth. I heard the first click of the camera. I opened my mouth and invited her inside. Our tongues met and united for the first time. The camera clicked, capturing our exchange through the dim hallway. Nisha removed her hands from the walls and ran the fingertips of both hands down my neck and over my dress. She caressed the sides of my large breasts. We continued to kiss until she lowered her mouth to my neck. I tilted my head sideways. Click. She kissed and licked my neck like it was a sweet lollipop.

"Sugar," she breathed against my skin. With her right hand she caressed my thigh. Click. Nisha pressed her body against mine. Click. Finally, she opened the slit of my dress and slid her hand inside. I was ready and wanted her more than I thought I did. Her fingers tapped against the outside of my silk panties, musically, as if she was searching for the perfect note. She found it with the rub of my hood.

"Oh shit," I said automatically. I was no longer aware of the clicks of the camera. All I wanted was her fingers inside of me. I parted my legs, and she lowered the left side of my panties. I stepped one foot out, the panties resting at the bottom of my right ankle. She was careful to position herself so no part of my intimate flesh showed. She rubbed her masterful fingers against my lips and my clit, until she slid two fingers inside. Up and down I rode her, my focus solely on the pleasure I felt between my legs. Nisha nibbled and bit my skin as she fucked me. For several minutes she stroked in and out until I felt my muscles begin to contract.

She felt it too. "Yes, baby," she said heavily. I lifted my left leg and wrapped it around Nisha's waist, opening myself so she could go deeper. I ran my fingers through her curly, wild mane while I climaxed, her hair tight between my clenched hands. I bit my lip to conceal the sounds of pleasure that attempted to escape from my lips. We remained in that position for several moments, until the heightened sensations retreated and my body temperature lowered to a warm and soothing simmer.

I placed my leg back onto the floor and Nisha released her fingers from my flesh. She nibbled on my nose tenderly.

"Did you get what you wanted?" she asked slyly.

"Exactly what I wanted and then some," I replied.

She lowered her head and smiled. I lifted her chin with my fingers. "Thank you for doing this."

She took one hand and placed it under her skirt and inside her panties. She was slippery wet. "It was my pleasure, believe me." We both laughed.

I pulled my panties up and over my moist skin and straightened my dress as best as I could. Nisha patted her hair and smoothed her skirt as well. We walked to the camera, Nisha took the memory card out, gave it to me, and placed the camera back inside her bag. Then we edged to the end of the hallway before the bend that would take us back toward the club. I peeked around the corner and saw a large bouncer with his back to me. He stood near the women's bathroom, blocking anyone from walking past it, which would have led them directly to us. I cleared my throat loudly. He turned around, saw me and he held up one fat finger for me to wait. A couple of minutes later a group of women exited the ladies' room. Without turning around again, he walked forward and disappeared into the club.

Nisha and I dipped into the empty bathroom. In the mirror I saw that my hair was flattened in the back, my makeup smeared beneath my eyes, and I had small spots of sweat that seeped through the thin material of my dress. Quickly I fluffed my weave, powdered my face, and reapplied lipstick. I grabbed a bunch of paper towels and inside the stall I wiped myself and dabbed my stomach and chest until it was dry. Nisha reapplied lipstick and touched up her makeup also.

"Think anyone will know?" she asked, her lips curved into a sexy smile.

"I do believe we're glowing," I told her.

Back in the hallway I debated whether I wanted to go back to the VIP section, or leave to upload and view the pictures. I needed to look through them and choose the best one for the final piece of our plan.

"Are you about to leave?" Nisha asked.

I was hesitant to go back upstairs to Ace and sit next to her like I hadn't just allowed another woman to have me. I'd have to go pretend like I hadn't just cum all over Nisha's fingers in a darkened hallway with a couple hundred people partying and dancing in the next room. And after the picture was revealed, she would realize that was what I had gone to do when I left her side for twenty-five minutes. I knew I had been ruthless with her feelings and the plan, but was I that cruel and cold-hearted?

Still, I walked to the edge of the staircase that led to the VIP section. I peeked up at Ace, who sat comfortably surrounded by her peers, a few men I recognized as the managers of some local rap artists. The guys chugged back beers while Ace sucked on another drink. She leaned back in her chair, her legs open and sitting quite unlady-like, apparently oblivious to the fact that I was still gone. I turned back around.

"I'm going to escape through the back exit," I told Nisha.

"Okay. Sandy is inside somewhere waiting for me. Call me when you've taken a look and picked a photo. Can I see which one first?"

"Of course, my dear. I know we both want to look good for our big reveal."

We took a step back and kissed one more time, smearing the lipstick we had just reapplied. Nisha wrapped her arms around my body, caressed my ass, and squeezed.

"Mmm. I could get high off of you," she whispered.

I tapped the vein in her arm. "Whenever you need a hit, I'm here."

"I think I'm always strung out," she told me.

"A little sugar injection will do that to you." I winked at her. "I'll call you in the morning." I walked quickly to the back of the hallway, passing the place where only minutes before I had an amazing orgasm. I smiled. I opened the exit door and looked around. The alley was dark and smelled of warm garbage and liquor. The front of the club was about forty feet away. I stepped outside and ran in that direction, forgetting that I hadn't called the driver to meet me in the front. When I reached the sidewalk, I saw that there was a line that extended almost to the exact place in which I stood. I tried to turn my back and walk away but it was too late.

"Sugar?" someone called to me. "Sugar?" the person yelled louder.

I exhaled, put on my biggest, fakest smile, and turned around. Almost everyone in the line also turned around to face me at the same time. For the next fifteen minutes I signed autographs and took pictures with fans. Many asked why I was leaving the party so early. My excuse was the usual, because I wasn't feeling well. The nosey ones wanted to know why I was coming out of a dark alley and not escorted by security or at least a friend. I laughed off their questions and said sometimes celebrities have to make quick and quiet escapes. "It was unsuccessful tonight," I joked with them. After a few final photos, my limo pulled up and I told everyone I had to go. The driver opened my door and just as he was closing it, I heard my name again. "Sugar! Sugar, wait!"

"Close it," I muttered to him, which he did swiftly.

"Home, please," I told him. I didn't want to go back to the hotel and chance Ace knocking on my door. I sent Yoshi a message: I'm not returning to the room. Bring items to my condo at ten a.m. That way I'd have an opportunity to upload the pics, go through them, and get them ready for delivery the next day. I smiled smugly to myself. Yes, it was time for everyone to see just what Sugar was all about.

Chapter 12

Sugar Freak

"I can't find it," I shrieked into the phone. I was sitting in my kitchen sipping on a shot of gin with a trembling left hand.

"Wait, what? What do you mean you can't find it?" Nisha asked, sounding close to the same panic-stricken state I was in.

"What I mean is I can't find the fucking memory card. It's not in my clutch."

"Okay, okay, I can't breathe," she said. I heard her inhale and exhale loudly several times. "I remember giving you the card. What happened after you left the club?"

"I went out the back exit but then I got noticed by everybody standing outside, that's what happened. I ended up out there for fifteen damn minutes signing autographs."

"Where was the card?"

"It should have been in my clutch where I put it," I told her. "I've turned it upside down looking for it. It's not in there. I don't know what to do. This wasn't the plan." I shook my head furiously, trying to figure out how our scheme had suddenly gone wrong.

After I confessed to Nisha that Ace was more than just my manager but my partner as well, I also expressed to her my frustrations over the years of having to live in secret. I told her about the many arguments Ace and I had had because she refused to let me come out, and that she was also unwilling to publicly admit that she and I were in a relationship. I told her that I had had enough living in secrecy. Nisha and I then conspired together to reveal my secret in an explosive manner, one that would be unforgettable and create the coming-out headline I desired. We schemed to fake the release of one of the photos of her and me caught together intimately. The entertainment industry would eat it up. We lived in a time when information was instantaneous and we knew that the release of one or two photos would light up the Internet. We didn't worry about our reputations; celebrities were caught in compromising positions all the time and survived, if not thrived, afterward.

"Look at Kim," Nisha had said. "She was Paris' flunky before that sex video came out. Look at her now; she's one of the most famous people in the world. That could and should be you, Sugar."

We had planned to meet in the bathroom and then escape the club with Rock Sandy. From there we were to go to Nisha's truck, a Ford Escape, which had been parked on a quiet street a few blocks from the club. Rock Sandy was the planned photographer, and on camera would catch us kissing and groping one another in the vehicle. We were to be so absorbed in our passion that we didn't even notice we were being photographed. With that being the original plan, we weren't sure if Rock Sandy would have captured Nisha finger fucking me. We didn't want to publish that picture anyway; that was just for our own pleasure. We would have cropped the photos, and at least images of our bodies wrapped around one another would be all the evidence needed to blast to the world that I was gay.

When Prestin offered us a hideaway space with security protection on top of it, the plan became simple. It would have been easy enough to act like a sneaky photographer caught us in a compromising position. We had both been pleased that the scheme seemed to have come together so smoothly. Until the plan fell fast through the cracks with the loss of the memory card.

"It's got to be somewhere. You checked the limo?"

"I've checked everywhere, Nisha, it's gone. This is so fucked up." I shook my head.

"What are we going to do? If someone else gets their hands on those pictures . . ." She left the sentence unfinished.

"I know, I'm supposed to be in control. Shit, this wasn't supposed to happen."

"All we can do now is wait," she concluded.

"Wait for what?" I asked, exasperated. "I can't sit here knowing those pictures are out somewhere, probably on somebody else's computer right now."

"We don't have any other choice but to wait for them to show up, and I don't mean show up by someone turning the card in to the lost and found. I think we're going to get Internet coverage and the headlines you wanted, just not the way we planned." Nisha's voice cracked.

"I'm sorry," I said softly. "I didn't expect this to happen."

"I know you didn't but you have to know I never would have done this if I thought someone else would get their hands on those pictures. What if they send them to my family? My parents? My brother and sisters? I thought there would be just one picture posted, Sugar, just one of us kissing or something. Fucking you was just going to be the added bonus. What if they're all revealed? One big-ass slideshow of us fucking in a goddamn hallway? What if that happens? Then what?" She started to cry.

"Calm down, Nisha, calm down. I won't let that happen."

"How do you know? You can't promise me that."

She was right, I couldn't, and I couldn't tell her I hadn't already visualized the entire slideshow myself and felt sick when I pictured Momma's face when she saw the photos.

"You're right, I can't promise that, but I'll do my best to protect both of us," I told her.

I heard light sniffles over the phone as she continued to cry softly. "I have to go. Please call me if you hear anything."

"I will." We hung up and I set the phone on the island in the kitchen.

It was eight a.m. and for six hours since I had gotten home I had mentally repeated my steps from the hallway to the bathroom, back to the hallway, into the alley, and outside of the club. I had gone over it a hundred times in my mind and still I hadn't been able to figure out what happened to the memory card. My clutch had been closed the entire time except for when I touched up my makeup and for five seconds when I opened it to get a pen to sign autographs. *Except for those five seconds,* I repeated to myself. Had the memory card fallen out and I hadn't noticed?

I went into my bedroom and lay across the bed. I closed my eyes and tried to force my memory back to the moment when I opened my clutch, reached inside for my favorite pen, and closed it again. If I focused hard enough maybe I would recall seeing the small black chip fall to the ground without my having noticed it. I couldn't force the memory, no matter how hard I tried. I fell asleep, exhausted from not having slept at all.

About an hour later I heard the front door open and a minute later Yoshi entered the room. "Miss Sugar?" Slowly I sat up. "I brought your things." She had two bags over her small shoulders and two in each hand. She set them down in the corner of my room, then left and came right back. She handed my phone to me. "It's buzzing like crazy in there."

I looked at my phone and saw ten missed calls from Ace, fifteen from Nisha, and hundreds of Twitter notifications. I unlocked the screen and opened my Twitter account. My body froze when I saw it: a tweet from ThatGirl @lonestar5115 to Sugar @SugarChitown with one of the photos from the previous night. One that looked like it was right in the midst of my orgasm with my mouth open in the shape of an O with my expression an elated frown, and Nisha's hand hidden underneath my dress. The look on her face was aggressive; she seemed satisfied to have brought me such intense pleasure. **Sugar's A Freak!** the person had typed. I didn't move. I couldn't move. I was in total shock.

"Miss Sugar?" Yoshi came to my side. She saw the picture on my screen and gasped. She said something in another language, and then delicately she removed the phone from my hand and set it to my side.

How did this happen? I questioned while Yoshi left the room and returned with a bottle of water. "Be careful what you wish for, you just might get it," Momma once told me. I got it. The front door opened again and startled me out of my terrified state. Ace. She stormed into the bedroom.

"Get out," she yelled to Yoshi and slammed the door behind Yoshi after she ran out of the room. Ace had on lightweight pajama bottoms and a tank. It looked like she rolled out of bed and ran the five blocks between our condos.

Ace held up her phone with the picture of me and Nisha on display. "What the fuck is this shit?" she asked, each word slow and angry, her eyes dark with anger.

I hadn't had time to digest what had just happened, nor had time to gather my composure before I had to respond to Ace's fury. "You fuckin' this little bitch now?" she went on. "Eleven years I devoted to you and this is the gratitude I get?"

Ace's reaction was exactly as I had anticipated. Only I hadn't had the time to prepare for it as I thought I would. I thought I would know exactly what picture would be published online and when it would occur. I was supposed to know which Web site would blast the photo first and I would have control over the headline. I would have had time to put together a well-prepared response. I had none of that.

I didn't know if I should tell her the truth of what happened. That it had been my plan to leak photos to the press as my big coming-out story, but instead I lost the pictures and someone else beat me at my own game. If my original plan had worked out, I never would have revealed the truth behind the story and confessed that Nisha and I had concocted the entire scheme ourselves. I was at a loss as to how to handle the situation.

"Have you seen these comments?" she questioned. "People are calling you everything from a dyke to a ho to an immoral freak."

I didn't want to believe her. I was Sugar; everybody was supposed to love me regardless of my sexuality, and regardless of how they found out about it.

"Why, Sugar, why would you do this?"

Because I wanted to be free.

Ace snapped her fingers in my face. "Don't get silent on me now. Not only have you ruined your career, you messed up any chances of us ever being an open couple."

I grunted, suddenly out of my trance. "Don't you dare try to say some shit like that to me now, Ace," I snarled at her. "If you couldn't commit to me openly after eleven years, don't act like it was coming. Not now. Not now that you have this to use as an excuse. I'm not that stupid," I reminded her.

"Well it sure as hell isn't happening now. When was this, last night? You went and fucked that little bitch last night? Is that why you never came back? You weren't in your room, either. As a matter of fact . . ." Ace started roaming around my room, checking under the bed, the bathroom and the walk-in closet. "Is that skank bitch here? Where is she at?"

"She's not here, Ace. And stop calling her a bitch."

Ace rubbed her hands through her short hair. "How could you do this to me?"

"Do what to you? Give myself to somebody else? Somebody who's not afraid to show the public how she feels about me? You've been hiding me for too long. It's over."

"So this is how you tell me it's over, with it blasted all over the Internet?"

I laughed at her. "As far as everyone else knows, I cheated on Franco, not you, remember? Nobody knows it's over but me and you, just the way you set it up. Nobody will ever know your woman was fucking somebody else right under your nose."

Ace stepped forward like she wanted to charge toward me but thought better of it. "This is the stupidest shit you could have done right now."

"Whatever. I've been telling you for years that I wasn't going to do this forever."

"A few months ago you said you'd lay low. What happened to that?"

"I changed my mind."

"Yeah, ever since you met baby girl."

I rolled my eyes at Ace. "With or without Nisha, I was not going to stay suffocated by our secret. She came in handy at the right time."

"What's your plan, Sugar? Because I'm out of this. I'm done. You have to clean up this shit on your own."

"No problem, I can do that. I'm Sugar, I'm capable of many things as you can see," I said smugly, but on the inside uncertain how in the world I'd straighten up the mess I had made.

She stepped forward and pointed in my face. "Keep my name out of your explanation. Whatever story you come up with about being a lesbian, don't say shit about any type of relationship between us," she warned.

Even though I hadn't expected her to say she'd be okay if anyone knew we had a relationship after the photo was released, I was once again hurt that she continued to be so adamant that no one find out about us.

"What is it, Ace?" I demanded. "Are you ashamed of me? You can't keep lying trying to convince me you're that scared to come out of the closet. Your door is not that tight and it sure as hell ain't even locked; everybody knows you're a dyke."

Ace rubbed her temples with her fingertips and didn't answer.

"What is it?" I continued. "Is it because I'm not one of those skinny bitches you represent running around the stage half naked? Is that it? You don't want anyone to know you're in love with a big girl?"

She didn't answer. Instead of denying my allegation as a crazy statement, she looked at me, guilty, and then stared at the floor. I couldn't believe it.

"Wow." My eyes began to water. "So that's it? How can that be? All these years you blamed it on being closeted and trying to protect my career when really you were was ashamed of my size?"

"You don't understand, Sugar," she said weakly.

"You're right, no, I don't understand. Why would you even pursue me then? You could have had any of them skinny girls. Why me?"

"Because I wanted you. I love a healthy-sized woman. I love your body and all your curves. You excite me. I love you, Sugar, you've got to know that."

Angry tears fell from my eyes. "No, you can't love me," I realized. "Love isn't embarrassed. Love isn't ashamed."

"Image is everything in this business," she attempted to explain. "I'm around young, beautiful women all the time. But I chose you. I've been faithful to you all this time."

"Well you should have been fucking them little bitches if that's what this has been about this whole time. I can't believe you. I'm good enough to fuck, just as long as nobody know about it? Unbelievable."

"I didn't say that," she protested.

"You don't have to, you've shown me that." I opened my robe and exposed my nude body to her. "You're not deserving of all this. You talk about me not playing you like a fool when you've been playing me for eleven years. How convenient to have a client you could make money off of and secretly sleep with at the same time."

"It's not like that, Sugar. It's not as simple as you're making it sound."

I closed my robe again. "It is that simple, my dear. I was your paycheck and your pussy. Well that's over now."

"Sugar—" she started.

I cut her off. "I don't want to hear any more fake-ass excuses. I hope you now see that there are women who will appreciate me for *all* that I am."

"You think that girl cares about you?" she spoke loudly again. "All she wants is a record deal and her name in lights. She has nothing to lose and everything to gain by attaching herself to you. Do you know what you've just done for her and for Beau? People will be lined up for tickets to their next concert. You, all you've done is created a scandal behind your name. It's not the same."

"Nisha didn't use me," I defended on both of our behalf.

"She may not have intentionally, but she'll be the one who comes out on top reaping the benefits."

"You don't know her the way that I do," I stated. "She did this for me."

Ace was confused. "Wait, what do you mean she did this for you?"

I hadn't meant to let that slip. "Nothing."

"Yes, you meant something by that. Wait a minute, you two planned this shit? You took those photos on purpose?" she asked, stunned.

"What if we did? What's it to you? You don't give a shit about me anyway."

"I care about everything that happens to you, believe it or not. But this? Who plants pictures? You sound desperate as hell for fame."

"I'm already famous, let's not forget that," I corrected her. "I want to be free, Ace. That's all I've ever wanted just as much as I've wanted to sing."

"This is how you go about it, taking pictures of yourself against the wall with some other woman?"

"Hey, whatever it takes, darling. I'll show you that people will love me for my talent no matter who I love and sleep with."

"Who you sleep with matters, trust me, I know. People would rather believe in the fairy tale they created for you, whether it's real or not."

"You would say that. Well, just because you want to give in to whatever image you want and think you need to portray doesn't mean I have to keep it up with you."

"This stunt you just pulled will ruin the image we've worked so hard to create," she pressed on.

"Well I'm sorry to have wasted so much of your time and energy," I responded bitterly. "I'm done, Ace. Give me my damn keys."

She swung her keys around her first finger. "You're making a huge mistake," she warned.

"No, I'm not, you'll see."

Ace removed my keys from her ring and tossed them onto my bed. "This is it?"

I shrugged. "It is what it is." I got up, retrieved her keys from my purse, and threw them at her. They hit her in the chest and fell to the floor.

Livid, she scooped them up and threw them across the room. They landed somewhere deep in my closet. She eyed me furiously before she turned around and left the room.

I slumped back onto my bed, closed my eyes, and fought back more tears that warmed my eyelids. Eventually I picked up my phone, which had been buzzing during my entire argument with Ace. There were twenty-five new Twitter notifications and three more missed calls from Nisha.

"Yoshi!"

She rushed back into the room. Yoshi ran everywhere. "Yes, Miss Sugar?"

"Make me a mimosa." She darted out of the room again.

I called Nisha back. "Sugar, have you seen this?" she screamed in my ear after the phone rang once.

"The tweet, yes, I saw it."

"Who is this person? Do you know?"

"I have no idea."

"What do you think they will do with the rest of the pictures?"

"I have no idea," I repeated.

"How are you going to respond?"

"I—"

"You have no idea, right? Wake up, Sugar, we have to fix this."

"I know and I will. I need a minute to think."

"Has Ace seen it yet?"

"She has. She just left here," I told Nisha.

"Uh-oh." She sounded more understanding of my short responses and listlessness. "What did she say?"

"She's pissed off to say the least. Mad as hell at me, at you, and that we took the pictures on purpose."

"You told her? Why?" she asked, surprised.

"It slipped, I didn't mean to. I don't care that she knows anyway. She's just happy her precious little secret isn't out."

"That she's a lesbian?"

"Partly."

"What do you mean?"

I moaned sadly. "This episode revealed the fact that she hasn't kept our relationship a secret because she's closeted. She didn't want anyone to know about us because I'm plus sized."

Nisha was silent for at least thirty seconds. "What?"

"You heard me correctly. She's ashamed of me. Embarrassed of me because I'm not a skinny girl."

"I'm so sorry, Sugar," she apologized for Ace's hurtful actions.

"Yeah. It would have been easier to accept her being closeted rather than knowing she was embarrassed to call me her woman."

"You're beautiful, Sugar, exactly as you are. I mean that sincerely," she offered delicately.

"Not according to Ace you don't."

"What do you mean?"

"She said you used me. That you agreed to this situation to get your own headline for your benefit."

"Oh hell no, she didn't. That's not true, I hope you know that. I did this because I'm not ashamed of who I am and you shouldn't be either. I did it for you, to help you. Only for you."

"You mean that?" I asked, almost unsure what the truth was anymore. Ace had cleverly lied and concealed her truth with me for over eleven years. Why should I believe a young woman I barely knew?

"I do," she responded sincerely.

"Come over. Let's figure this thing out. We have to get control back over the situation."

"Cool. What's your address?" I gave it to her. "I'll see you in an hour."

I finished my mimosa in two swallows and called Yoshi to run me a bath. For twenty minutes I rested in the hot water and tried to pretend that I hadn't spent eleven years loving someone who was embarrassed to have me as her woman. No one had ever made me feel bad about my weight. Momma never had made me feel insecure or concerned about my size. Even when I wanted to sing during a time when all the young female artists were wearing shirts revealing flat, firm stomachs, Momma never encouraged me to lose weight. She was confident in my singing and trusted my singing would garner me the success I deserved.

When I met Ace she hadn't seemed the least bit concerned or bothered by my weight. In fact, she came off as if she adored my body. When we were together, she praised my shape, every curve and every inch of my skin she explored and devoured. Ace wasn't in the closet as a lesbian, she was shallow, and paranoid someone would know she had found intimacy with someone who didn't resemble the standard-package woman she believed others felt she should have been with.

Hadn't she been there over the years to observe how much people loved me, even with my few added pounds? Even if she was ashamed to have me on her arm, I couldn't believe she didn't realize how many other women, like Nisha, would be honored to call me their woman.

Maybe that was part of her issue, too. If she had allowed me to come out, I would have had the opportunity to meet other women, maybe even one who would be willing to share my love openly and willingly. She had protected my secret for her own private benefit. While I knew that our relationship was coming to an end, I hadn't expected to walk away with a wounded ego.

I got out of the tub and put on a flowered sundress that Yoshi had set out for me. I pulled my hair back into a ponytail and applied light makeup. My phone continued to vibrate because I hadn't gotten the nerve to read the comments and messages that overwhelmed my Twitter account. Just when I had forced the courage to pick up my phone and click on the Twitter app, the intercom buzzed from the living room. Nisha had arrived. I put the phone down again.

"Two mimosas, Yoshi," I said when I entered the living room. "After you get the door, please."

I walked to the balcony and opened the door. It was a drizzly summer morning and the warm, moist air swarmed the room. I took a seat on the couch. Nisha entered a couple of minutes later dressed in white shorts, a black tank, and Nike sandals.

"Hey, Sugar." She bent down and gave me a kiss on my cheek. She sat next to me and rested her chin in the palm of her left hand. Her skin was bare, fresh with no makeup. Without the intense eyeliner, lashes and shadow she looked even more youthful, not like the sexy, provocative guitar and bass player when she performed.

She held up her phone to me. "It hasn't stopped ringing."

"Mine either."

"I first saw the picture because I follow you and saw a notification. Soon after someone figured out it's me in the picture and attached me to it. Have you read the comments?"

"Not yet."

"It's not as bad as you may think," she told me.

"It's not? Ace made it sound like I've lost all my fans."

"No, not at all. I mean, everybody is shocked and wondering what the hell is going on with you. Of course some people are ragging on you being a sinner and saying they're going to unfollow you and not buy your music. For the most part, though, you have a large support system. Your fans are chiming in telling people to shut the hell up and mind their business. They're mad at the person who released the picture, saying it was an invasion of your privacy. And you have the support of most of the gay and lesbian community in Chicago. They're all talking about it, happy to welcome you into the family."

Of course Ace hadn't mentioned any of the positive comments; she only wanted me to believe I had made a mistake by coming out, as nontraditional as the process had been.

"What about you? Have your heard from your parents?"

She looked away. "No, I haven't. I guess I don't expect to either. Even if they find out about it they won't call. I was panicking about it earlier, but the more I thought about it I think I realized that's kind of a done deal, you know?"

"I understand. I'm sorry."

"It's cool. I'm a grown woman and make my own decisions. I don't need anyone's approval, definitely not theirs. They raised me and provided for me, but if they can't love me for me as I am now, that's on them." She looked me in the eyes. "Same with Ace. She may have guided your career and helped get you to where you are, but if she can't appreciate and love you for all of you, her loss, Sugar, not yours. Doesn't she know how many women would be proud to claim you as their own?"

"My sentiments exactly. I told her that all the time." We laughed.

"So how are we going to handle this?" she asked.

"We need some help," I told her. "I can respond to Twitter comments all day but that's not going to resolve this. We need radio, we need newspaper. We need some-one with connections before this gets too out of control. Especially since we don't have control or access to any of the photos ourselves, this person can do whatever they want with them. We have to get out here and make some kind of statement to take away some of their power in this situation."

"You can't call into a radio station on your own? You know all the DJs in the city. They'll accept your call any-time, especially now. Their ratings will shoot through the roof."

"That's true," I agreed. "But we need an ally. Someone else with a name and clout to stand in our corner." That person instantly came to mind. "Prestin."

"Do you know her like that?" Nisha asked.

"Not on a personal, friendship level, no. But she's high profile, a lesbian, active in the community and connected with people all over the city. And based on how she helped us out last night, I don't doubt she'll help us today."

I got up and retrieved my iPad from my bedroom. Yoshi set our mimosas on the table when I returned. I pointed to the guest room and like an obedient pet Yo-shi went to it and closed the door behind her. Finally, I checked my Twitter account and viewed the hundreds of comments beneath the photo of me that showed the world my cum face.

Like Nisha had told me, a few people had condemned me to hell:

God don't like ugly! @SugarChitown
@SugarChitown Nasty! Immoral!

Many were supportive:

We love you! @SugarChitown
Haters will hate, do you! @SugarChitown
@SugarChitown Love your music, don't care
about nothing else!

As expected, there were sexual remarks as well to both
me and Nisha:

Damn, can I get some of that @SugarChitown @
TrendyBeau312
Fuckin sexy as hell! Get that sugar, girl! @Sugar-
Chitown @TrendyBeau312

I continued to scan and read while Nisha watched over
my shoulder. "Look!" she pointed to the screen. "Is that
Prestin?"

The tweet was from @PrestinMgmtGroup: Sugar is
beautiful Chicago talent. She has our support. @Sugar-
Chitown

"Yes, that's her."

"You're right, Sugar, she has your back. Call her," Nisha said with a bit of hopefulness.

I found Prestin's Web site online and called the number listed in the contact section. An enthusiastic woman
named Cheryl answered the call and, after I asked to
speak with Prestin, told me that Prestin was in a meeting.
I gave her my name and number for Prestin to call me
back.

"Um . . ." She paused a moment. "Is this Sugar the
singer?"

"Yes, it is," I responded cautiously, unsure what Cheryl might have had to say next.

"Oh my God, girl, this is crazy. Forgive my unprofessionalism right now but I'm one of your biggest fans. I was at the concert last night. It was great. That song at the end was hot, girl. I've been to all your Chicago shows."

I smiled. "Thank you, Cheryl, I appreciate your support."

She whispered next. "I also want to say I saw the photo this morning. Hotness is all I can say." She giggled. "Don't even sweat it; your true fans won't leave you."

"That's what I'm hoping."

"We got your back. Oh, wait, Prestin's door just opened. Good talking to you. Hold on a minute, please." She placed me on hold. A couple of minutes later Prestin picked up.

"Sugar, good morning. Are your ears ringing this morning? Your name is on everyone's lips today. How are you holding up, hon?"

"I've had better days," I answered, mostly referring to the rejection I felt by Ace and, partially, because of the concern surrounding the unknown whereabouts of the photos.

"Yes, I'm sure it's not one of your best days. What can I do for you? I'll do anything I can to help."

"That's why I'm calling. Nisha . . . Trendy is here with me. We need some guidance. Can I put you on speaker?"

"Of course."

I hit the speaker icon and set the phone on the coffee table in front of us.

"Mind if I ask why Ace isn't helping?"

I stared into the phone and spoke. "We, um, we severed ties this morning. Irreconcilable differences."

"I'm not one to pry, Sugar, but if you need my help, it helps me to know the truth," Prestin urged.

"All I can say is our relationship, in every aspect, has ended."

"Ace was more than your manager?"

Was there a reason I should protect her? "Yes," I admitted. I felt a little weight lift off my shoulders. "She's been my partner for years."

"I figured that. Everyone figured that."

Nisha hit me on the leg like "I told you so."

"Really? I'm learning that it wasn't a secret like we thought it was."

"Chemistry," Prestin stated. "It can't be hidden. I've known Ace a long time on a casual level, but everyone knows she's a lesbian. Most people assumed you two wanted to keep your relationship private. But when Franco showed it we knew there had to be more to the story. I'm not even going to ask for details about that. Judging by that picture and what I've witnessed on my own, I'm guessing Trendy has a little something to do with the breakup," she suggested accurately.

"She plays a role, absolutely."

"What would you like me to do?"

"We're not sure how to respond to the picture," I told Prestin. "It's all over Twitter and who knows where else it might wind up."

"Yes, ladies, about that picture. I may be the only other person besides the two of you who knows exactly when and where that picture was taken."

"You're correct."

"And I don't believe anyone else was back there to take that photo," she continued.

"Correct again."

"You wanted this photo leaked," she concluded accurately.

"We took them ourselves," I confessed. "We wanted the photos to be seen, but not like this, though. I lost the memory card and obviously someone else got their hands on it."

"Ah, I see. Damn. I don't know if you'll ever get your hands back on those photos, Sugar. Why would you do this?"

"I wanted to come out and I wanted to come out in an unforgettable way," I explained.

"You love the spotlight, don't you?"

"I do. I was made for it. I'm convinced my fans won't desert me because of this. I have to prove to Ace that they won't," I added.

"Next time you have a wild idea like this, come to me first. You and Trendy put the camera down." She laughed. "Seriously, this is a lesson learned I'm sure. The first thing we need to do is address it in some kind of statement. Let me make some phone calls, and how about you and Trendy meet me here at two?"

"We'll be there. Thanks, Prestin."

"Anything for family. See you soon."

Chapter 13

Sugar Fix

Later that afternoon Nisha and I were seated in Prestin's office located in the west loop of Chicago. It was a small and sleek space, with Cheryl, the pleasant receptionist, seated behind a desk in the waiting area. There were two rooms that made up the rest of the space: one was Prestin's office and the other a small meeting room.

When Nisha and I arrived, Cheryl had jumped anxiously out of her seat and ran to us both with hugs like long-lost friends or relatives. She then had Nisha take a photo of me and her, and then me take a photo of her and Nisha. "I won't tweet them 'til you say I can." She smiled then led us to Prestin's office.

"I reached out to nearly every LGBT organization and our allies today about this matter," Prestin told us. "One of the online newspapers is set to publish a statement from you this afternoon. Afterward, the other media outlets will jump on it and reprint it as well. You should expect that most will reprint the picture, but will at least crop it or blur the explicit portion. Right now there's nothing we can do about people who may have saved a screen shot of the picture or retweeted it themselves, okay?"

Nisha and I nodded.

"Sugar, tomorrow morning you have both local radio and television appearances. Also, I have some contacts and I reached out to E's reps. They already caught wind of the picture and, as you know, for many celebs any kind of attention is good attention so they're cool as a fan about this. They don't care about your picture or who you're sleeping with, as long as that single keeps climbing the charts. Judging by some movement already, the picture is helping. There was even mention about you joining E on an interview or two."

"Oh, so now they want me in on the promotions?" We all chuckled.

"Now, Trendy. This is different for you. Mostly everyone just wants to know who the woman is in the picture. Some locals know you and Beau, but not the same as on Sugar's level. For both of you, people are going to want to know if you're a couple, especially after the song you performed. How do you want to address that?"

Nisha and I looked at one another. That was a piece of the aftermath we had never discussed: how we would define our relationship after the photos were published.

"I don't know," Nisha and I said at the same time.

"We'll figure that out. For now let's draft the statement you want to make, Sugar, and get it over to the media."

For the next hour the three of us wrote my statement to the press. When we were done, Prestin e-mailed it to her contact at a local magazine and we sat quietly, refreshing the magazine's online site every sixty seconds to see if the story hit. Once it was published, I would send a link to the statement via my Twitter account. After six minutes of wait time, the statement was public. Finally, I had my headline.

HOMETOWN DIVA RESPONDS TO ONLINE TWITTER
PICTURE CONTROVERSY

This morning, to the shock of both me and my fans, a photo was released by a Twitter account holder of me in the midst of an intimate moment. I understand that this photo has created disturbance among some, and I would like to address the matter at this time. The photo captured me and another woman, Trendy, a member of the Chicago-based band Beau, sharing what we thought was a private moment together. We regret that an unknown person chose to violate our privacy to capture and publish this photo. Should this person be in possession of additional photos, we ask that he or she respect our privacy and discard the photos. If any additional photos surface, we will take further action to determine the source of this leak.

To my fans, I understand there is confusion surrounding the fact that the photo is of me intimately engaged with another woman. As you know, over the past several years, I have spoken of having a man in my life and have not identified myself as anything other than a straight woman. Out of respect, I will not address my relationship with Franco. He has been an important part of my life and I will continue to honor him as a friend. At the same time, I would like to take this time to confirm that, yes, I am a lesbian and I have always known this fact about myself. This announcement is one I am proud to make and my only regret is that it was not stated sooner and revealed under a more positive circumstance. Please know that I make music for you and my music and singing will continue to serve you in the best way possible.

To my friends, family, my gems, and the community at large, I hope you can understand that I am an adult, and as an adult, sex is a normal part of my life as it is for most adults. I realize that as a celebrity I must take stronger precaution with this aspect of my life to ensure privacy for myself and those with whom I am involved. I apologize if anyone has taken offense to the photo.

I thank you all for your support and understanding during this time. I look forward to continuing to make music for you. Always, Sugar.

Okay, so we lied. We used the ironic twist of the situation to our advantage and it worked perfectly. Comments of support flooded the Web site and continued on the following sites that published the statements. Just as I had predicted, my fans didn't desert me. In fact, my fan base increased; when I checked my Twitter account that night, the number of followers had increased by several thousand. Before I closed my eyes that evening, comfortable in bed with Nisha resting at my side, I sent a good night tweet: Sugar @SugarChitown Lights, Camera, Action: the show will go on. ;) Thank you for your support my lovelies. Sweet dreams.

Chapter 14

Sugar Fly: Six Months Later

Momma once said that success was the sweetest revenge. She was right. After my breakup with Ace, I hadn't set out with intentions to get back at her for how she insulted my pride and injured my self-esteem. I didn't want to blast her name or bad-mouth her in any way, and I didn't. All I had wanted to do was to sever ties with her professionally and personally and move on. I also wanted to ensure that she knew the world would love me as a lesbian and as a full-figured woman. I was successful in accomplishing that goal.

The support I received from the gay and lesbian community was overwhelming. Some of the biggest names in the entertainment industry sent tweets and e-mails and praised my professionalism with how I responded to the matter. Many of them joked about their own public rendezvous and stated that it had only been good fortune and tight security that there were no photos of them caught having sex.

I was invited to call in to national syndicated radio shows and I made appearances on talk shows. All of the hosts wanted to know why I had hidden my sexuality for so long and to them I confessed only that I wanted my fans to recognize me for my talent first without focus on my personal life. "So how did you end up dating Franco?" they would ask. To that question I would simply say that what Franco and I shared was unique and special and because of the sensitivity behind our breakup, I chose not to elaborate further. Most hosts respected that request for privacy, citing that I hadn't been the first lesbian who ever entertained a man. Others, the more perceptive ones, argued that Franco must have been a cover. To that I would always say, "Come on, next question please."

E asked me to perform "Feel My Love" with him at several of his concerts and every week I packed my bag to travel to a different city. Fans went crazy whenever I appeared on stage and, ironically, they loved when E and I would hug up on one another as we sang about making love to one another. Oddly, they were turned on by our fake intimate interactions. We played into their horniness as far as our imaginations allowed, singing with E hugging me from behind, and still within FCC and Grammy rules and regulations as we performed our Grammy-nominated song on stage in front of our peers and fans seated in the balconies above.

When we won for Best R&B Performance by a Duo or Group, we received a standing ovation. Momma was my date for that night and she hugged me tightly before E and I went to the stage to accept our Grammys. Being the gentleman that he was, E allowed me to speak first. I first thanked God for His goodness. Next I thanked E for selecting me to partner with him on the song. I told him that I was honored and looked forward to collaborating with him again on my own album. As usual I thanked Momma for her support and my good friend, Trendy, who was in the audience somewhere that night with her band. I also thanked someone I referred to as "my baby" and spoke to her through the camera and said I couldn't wait to see her when I got back home. Finally, I said that I couldn't accept the award without deep gratitude to the person who had worked so hard and diligently at developing my career. I told her that

I appreciated her for reminding me that I deserved only the best in music and in love and that I wanted to assure that she knew that I did, indeed, have the best in both. Behind me E snickered, he being one of only a few people who understood the message behind my words. From what I had heard about Ace, she had begun to develop the career of a young singer named Cherish. Cherish was a short, average-sized girl, with a choppy blond haircut and fetish for wearing a variety of lace gloves; whether they were white, black, fingerless, or up to her elbows, it didn't matter, she was never seen without them. I couldn't help but speculate if she and Ace had started a relationship, as they had been seen together at various functions in the city and I was told that their interaction would suggest that Ace was more to her than just a manager. I guessed she had been honest that she felt more comfortable showing public displays of affection with a small girl.

When Momma learned the truth that Ace hadn't expressed her love for me because of my size, she wanted to confront Ace. If there was one thing Momma despised it was anybody who messed with her one and only baby Sugar. I had told her Ace wasn't worth the trouble and that's when she informed me that I'd have my vengeance through my career.

Franco was nowhere to be found for about three months after the controversy. We later learned that he had come out to his family and then sheltered himself in Derek's apartment in hiding. Last time someone told me that they saw him, he was dancing and partying topless in the club with all the gay boys.

After a night of partying with the most famous celebrities in the music industry, Momma, Nisha, Rock Sandy, and I flew back to Chicago the next afternoon. We had become sincere friends after the leaked photo incident, and had spent several nights heating up my sheets with one another. But we soon understood that even though we had the promise of a great sexual relationship, we preferred to be friends and collaborative music partners. We had performed together at many shows around Chicago and recorded "From Behind" as a single Beau would release on their own CD.

By the time I got home that night, the condo was quiet. I set my luggage in the living room, took off my shoes, and tiptoed softly to the bedroom. She was lying in bed asleep, and even though I tried to undress without much noise, she stirred and woke up.

"Ali, baby, go back to sleep," I whispered to her.

"I don't want to sleep now that you're here," she said. "No need to put on a nightgown. Come here."

I slid my naked body behind hers in bed. "I missed you," I told her and kissed the back of her neck.

"I missed you too."

Ali and I met through Prestin at an intimate gathering she and Jaye had at their house. Prestin and I had taken to one another after she assisted with the cover-up of the leaked photo. We had become friends, and I was soon invited to join their small circle of close friends, who turned out to be some of the finest lesbians I had ever met. Ali was a sweet, genuine woman, who humbled me with her generous and sensitive spirit. I was still Sugar and knew I was the shit, but in quiet, intimate moments like those lying next to her in bed, Ali had a way of reminding me that nothing was more important than being true to myself, my body, my music, and the love I had found with us. The message I tweeted just as the limo arrived to my condo said it all: Sugar @SugarChitown Still high off the best duo Grammy! Headed home to Ali, my best collabo of all. Ain't nothing like the real thing, y'all.

Queen Con

by

Ni'chelle Genovese

Prologue

A slight breeze played amid the tops of the nearby magnolia trees. Every now and again slivers of bright blue moonlight broke through the leaves, illuminating the otherwise dark ground. The low bustle from a dozen outdated washers and dryers in the apartment complex's little Laundromat hummed behind me. I couldn't believe tenants would actually drop their stuff off and just go back into their apartments. There was no way I'd ever leave my clothes unattended. Momma had told me a story about one of these kinds of places way back when. She said she'd left her things to dry and when she'd gone back to get them, someone had taken all of her stuff *including* her panties. Nope, if it were me, I'd be sitting right there with my laundry.

I sat quietly on the only raggedy wooden bench in the vacant playground behind the Laundromat, anxiously checking my watch. It was nine-thirty, way past my curfew, and he was late. The playground was no threat during the day, but at night every shadow looked ominous and every little sound made me jump. It seemed as if the news report every other day was about a girl being raped, beaten, or kidnapped, and I wasn't trying to become a statistic.

A soft breeze made the swings rock back and forth eerily, and I could almost hear ghostly childlike laughter as the chains creaked. At that exact moment my brain decided to remind me about Jankman. I'd never seen Jankman; only heard the stories everyone passed around the hallways at school. They were stories that my imagination now amplified and exaggerated. From what had been said he roamed around our neighborhood in a long filthy grey trench coat. Jankman started off just flashing little girls and running away, but after a while he upgraded to yanking girls up and disappearing without a trace. The fact that no one could ever identify him or find the missing girls left him as somewhat of an urban boogeyman. My best friend Brianna's four-year-old sister was playing alone in their front yard when he ran up on her two summers ago. He not only showed his twig and berries but he actually stood there and fondled himself before running away. The thought left me in a jittery panic and Carlos having me wait on him at night by myself was pissing me off.

The apartment security staff usually didn't start their rounds until after ten. This meant I needed to be gone since I lived in the houses across the street and not the apartments. Those stupid rent-a-cops never had anything better to do than harass kids on the property. I was pretty sure they'd have a field day if they caught me in the park; they'd probably say I was trying to vandalize something. Better yet, they'd probably say that I was trying to break into the Laundromat and steal clothes. I chuckled to myself at the ridiculousness of the thought.

A lonely black cricket skittered out in front of me and I kicked dirt at it in agitation. There was no way I'd ever break my curfew for this fool again. If my momma caught me sneaking back in she'd kill me, not to mention the hell I'd have to pay if she told my daddy. Trying to calm myself down I inhaled long, deep breaths of warm fabric softener–scented air tinged with a hint of magnolia flowers.

We always met at the same time and at the same place. Something had to be wrong because he would have told me if he wasn't going to make it. I'd decided to give him another five minutes when I heard what sounded like a group of guys approaching. My eyes scanned the darkened playground fretfully, but aside from some monkey bars, swings, a slide, and the merry-go-round, there was nowhere to hide, and no quick escape. Every lesson my daddy ever drilled into my head flooded me and here I was like a fool, alone, at night, and unarmed.

The guys were getting closer and I already knew there was no way I'd be able to outrun any of them. I could hear their crude and obnoxious jokes. A few sounded a little drunk and way older than me. Silently I crouched and made my way toward the Laundromat door, praying one of the tenants might have left it unlocked. It wasn't. What sense did it make putting a Laundromat and a playground behind an apartment complex without a single solitary light around it? Panicky I kept moving around the building, searching for any means of escape or camouflage. My hair snagged and I almost screamed, afraid that Jankman or worse yet, some kind of undiscovered human preying insect had snared me as my neat afro pony-puff came loose. It was a small wire rung that jutted out from the wood paneling of the darkened structure. There were more; they ran all the way up the back of the building toward the roof of the one story Laundroshack. I almost squealed and was suddenly happy that I'd kept it simple and worn my stonewashed capris and black Reebok Classics.

The roof couldn't have been more than six feet off the ground and after hefting my butt up there I was sweating, and out of breath, but it felt like I was on top of the world. I stretched out as flat as I possibly could and waited. The guys seemed to have all gotten hung up a few feet around a corner, lighting cigarettes and swigging out of a liquor bottle. Squinting, I could barely make them out among the shadows and bushes. Wiping the sweat from my eyes I fought to hold my breath as the group began to move forward.

"No lie, tenth-grade pre-calculus. I was dating Ms. Tuttle's daughter and she was out of town. She came home early and caught us sleeping on the couch. My dudes, on the life of my momma. Ms. Tuttle woke me up and I'm thinking she's about to go nuclear meltdown because I'm butt-ass naked on the couch with her daughter, but nah. She took me to her room and let me hit it," one of the guys said in a smooth voice.

His solid-looking frame towered over all the others. I didn't recognize him but he had to have graduated at least two or three years ago. I did however recognize Mrs. Tuttle's name, I had her fifth block and there was no way her prissy evil acting self could be doing all that. My mouth gaped open and I listened in utter stupefied shock. It was as if I were a real life fly on the wall, as their conversation floated up to my ears. They drifted through the playground and I kept my head pressed down into the rough, gritty shingles, praying they'd just keep walking through. The shingles were still warm from the sun beating down on them all day and the heat only made me sweat harder.

"Ha! Tyre, she still be on that after all these years. She got me when I was dating Shayla and she wouldn't put out one night. Got you too didn't she?" another guy responded, patting the taller one on the back before nudging a smaller guy wearing a baseball cap.

"Yeah. Just so happens . . ." the smaller guy had begun to respond.

Air whooshed out of my lungs and I lurched up onto my feet, completely forgetting the fact that I was even lying on a rooftop.

"Carlos!" His name flew out from in between my lips in an accusatory shriek.

The entire squad of seven guys all let out various sounds of surprise and alarm as they jumped in unison at the sound of my voice. I must have looked like a complete fright with the moon silhouetting me, and my hair sticking out of my ponytail in all directions. The fact that I just popped up on a damn rooftop probably didn't help either. The tall one they called Tyre yelped. Yes, he actually yelped, or maybe it was a squeal. I wasn't sure because it all happened in an instant. Before the sound was completely out of his mouth, his half-empty forty-ounce Olde English bottle was hurling towards my head. I tried dodging it, but I have a hard enough time getting out of the way of those bright as day red rubber beacons of embarrassment in gym class. On Friday's they make all of the classes play dodge ball, *at the same time*, in one group. It always winds up looking like a massacre and I'm always on the end of the playing field that believes the words "made in hell" has to be stamped somewhere on those balls. So, you can imagine my success dodging a glass bottle in the dark.

"Bae? What the hell are you doing up there?" Carlos called up to me.

His voice hit me at the exact moment that the bottle nipped my shoulder, and my foot went crashing through the shabby tilling on the roof.

"Shit. I was waiting for you remember?" I shouted down at him angrily, struggling to tug my foot free I winced at the pain in my shoulder.

"Aww damn, baby, I forgot. Do you need some help?"

Now that the surprise had worn off I could hear them all snickering and chuckling, "damn homie I ain't know you liked 'em thiiiick," Tyre whispered at Carlos which only made me angrier. Carlos had never mentioned Shayla in his list of exploits and he damn sure hadn't mentioned her mother. My foot jerked free and I almost fell off but quickly caught my balance. Shakily I made my way to the ground. He met me at the bottom. Shooing away his hands I turned and glared up at him.

"Baby, I have a meeting to go to at the library—" he began to explain.

Poking him in his chest with my finger, I cut him off. "You have a meeting? At the library, at this time of night, with all of your homeboys?" I tried to glare at him through the sweat that was stinging my eyes and failed miserably. He used the bottom of his T-shirt to wipe my forehead, taking some of my anger away along with the grime as he gently wiped my face.

"Look, go home and I'll meet you as soon as I'm done, I promise. I can't tell you anything more. You have to trust me on this." His voice was unsteady. He looked nervously over at his friends before giving me a weak smile. The smell of alcohol was faint in the air; he'd been drinking and he never drank. He was obviously nervous and lying about something.

I glared at him through narrowed eyes. "Yeah, all right. I'll see you later then."

Satisfied, he gave me a kiss that I didn't return, and jogged over to rejoin his friends. They all shot me huge grins and waved, saying, "Bye," in unison. I gave a huge fake grin that I didn't feel and waited until they were out of sight.

There was no need to follow closely behind them; the library was only a street over. If that's where they were all really headed I'd just wait a few minutes and tromp my little butt on over there. If he wasn't there I'd know for a fact that he was lying.

The library sat on the edge of our neighborhood, off a side street, surrounded by overgrown hedges. At first glance it appeared closed and my blood instantly boiled. Not only had I allowed myself to look like a complete idiot, believing such a stupid lie in front of all those guys, but I'd also come all the way over here in this heat for nothing. Angry at myself for not immediately following them, I blinked back a few tears that were threatening to spill onto my cheeks. It was then that I noticed lights in the windows of the library's basement.

Maybe he was telling the truth after all.

Glancing around quickly, I made sure there was no one around to see me before I scurried over and got down on the ground beside one of the windows. *Oh please, little critters and creepy crawlies, please don't come out. The last thing I need is for one of y'all to climb up in my shirt or some foolishness.* The shrubs did an excellent job at hiding me from any onlookers as I looked into the basement. I guessed I was expecting to see strippers or an illegal card game. What I saw looked boring to say the least. All of the guys, including Carlos, were seated at a rectangular table as if they were in class or something. The table and chairs were the only things in the dimly lit room, unless you want to count the dull cement floor. A lanky-looking older white guy stood in front of them, talking. The beat-up Van sneakers and oversized JNCO hoodie he wore gave me the impression that he was one of those skateboarder weedheads. There was a snake tattoo barely visible along the top of his calf-high black socks that appeared to runup his leg, disappearing just beneath the top of his knee-length shorts. That snake gave me a completely different, more menacing impression of him.

He handed something to Carlos but I couldn't make it out because he was sitting with his back was to me. Then the guy clapped his hands together and the guys all nodded and began to leave. I stayed absolutely still, afraid to get caught snooping twice in one night. After a few minutes of waiting I climbed out from the bushes and crossed the street to head home and wait for Carlos.

What was he doing for that guy? What in the world had I just seen?

Taking the long way home around the neighborhood I let my thoughts distract me from worrying about being in trouble for breaking curfew. I was so preoccupied I almost walked right up Carlos's back before I realized it was him.

"Girl, what the hell?" he asked, spinning around his eyes wide in surprise.

"Oh shoot hey boo, I didn't even see you." I replied nonchalantly.

"What are you doing over here? I thought I told you to go home and I'd meet you." His eyes narrowed as he began eyeing me suspiciously.

"Hell, you know how my mama is. I figured I'm already late," I shrugged dramatically and rolled my eyes to emphasize my point. "I might as well enjoy my freedom, so I'm taking the long way home."

He sighed and ran his hand across his forehead in frustration. "Bae, you can't be walking around out here by yourself. I, um, I need to get something out of my homeboy's car at the bowling alley and then we'll walk home together. Come on."

We walked in silence. The little neighborhood bowling alley was just across the four-lane highway that ran between the neighborhood and all the local businesses. Most of the teens hung out there on the weekends because it was within walking distance from home. That became the main reason any of the teens with a car hung out someplace else.

I watched from the side of the highway as Carlos ran over to a red Camry. He climbed into the driver's seat and all I could see at that point was his silhouette. It wasn't long before he was crossing back over and smiling at me.

"Ready to go home?" he asked me, sweat running profusely down his face.

"Yes, did you get what you were looking for?"

"That dumb ass must have forgotten to leave it. Nothing was in there."

"So do you have a key or he just leaves his car unlocked?"

"Girl, you are asking way too many questions. I have what's called a master-man key; it'll unlock you eventually. Let's go home, baby."

Chapter 1

Win Won, Lost One

They all wanted to know how I did it. How my sweet little quiet self ended up with the finest and most wanted senior as my boyfriend. He was Mr. Beautiful, baby face model fantastic and I was always referred to as "who?" because that's what they'd say when they'd see us together. No one could believe he was with "the average faced" nobody. Hoes had been trying to snag him since day one and he was hitting and quitting their thirsty butts left and right. All they did was make it easy as hell for me. Yes, so I kind of stole him from his last girlfriend but that was her own fault. Ladies, never let your man run off and vent to another female when y'all are having problems. All you're doing is allowing him to tell another woman what cards to play against the one's you're already holding. She'll use that information to be the bestest – yes bestest listener and friend he's ever had and then she'll use it to become his woman.

"Good morning, beautiful. I thought you were still 'sleep." Carlos raised himself up on one elbow and began tracing my eyebrows with his finger.

"No. I'm thinking about next year. What am I supposed do when you leave for college?"

"Who says I'm leaving? You know the boys want me to go into the business and I've really been considering it. Plus, I'd get to stay with you."

He nestled his head on my shoulder and my stomach filled with dreadful butterflies at his words. Was that what I'd seen last night, a meeting of some sort? Carlos was too smart and too kindhearted for that kind of life. Yet, the only real options open to get ahead in Norfolk, Virginia were to join the military, work at the shipyard, be a dope boy, or link up with the coterie.

They were a strictly male organization, more secretive than Masons, and in Virginia they wielded more power than the Illuminati. Carlos had no idea that I knew about their existence or his potential initiation.

The coterie, officially called themselves the Law of Talion, and just knowing that, by their standards, I knew too much. My grandfather was a seventh-tier imperial chief, the second highest title. When he got sick a few years back my daddy refused to take over, claiming their mission was no longer empowering people. He should have been killed, but instead he was cut off from the family, its power, and his inheritance. He'd told me enough about their symbols, their name, and their actions, making me promise to never deal with anyone affiliated.

"You know you're my God particle, baby; nothing could even exist in my world without you."

I couldn't help smiling at his choice of words; he always knew what to say to make me smile. His mouth was so close to my skin, I could feel each word as he spoke them. They struck me like miniature earthquakes that started at my ankles, fluttered up through my chest, and ended at the tip of my eyelashes, forcing my eyes to close. Even now with my eyes closed I could see his warm bamboo-hued skin and soft, toffee brown eyes.

I'd been waiting for the right moment. Most girls messed up by giving it up too soon, and his ex, Porsha's, biggest mistake was comparing him to everyone else. He used to tell me how he felt like he was always in competition to keep her. He couldn't stand feeling like he was constantly on some kind of game show. *"If this is really really real."* That's what we decided to call it when he first told me about Porsha and all her, *"If this is really really real, you'd punch that nigga for askin' for my number. If this is really really real, you betta' say something to that dude over there for looking at me while I'm holdin' your hand"*

Compared to all the other idiots in school my boo was a complete sweetheart and I was beyond in love with him. We were almost six months in and we still hadn't had sex yet. Oh, did he try though. At the moment I was a wild mixture of nervousness and excitement, the fear of us getting caught in my bedroom making me anxious. He teased me, sliding his body on top, nudging my legs open so he could nestle in between them, pressing his heat and hardness tight up against me. He sucked on my earlobe before kissing my neck. Sighing and biting my lower lip, I tensed as he dug his hips into me. For all I knew my panties and his boxers might as well have been gone. I gasped at the sparks of sensation that one motion caused.

"I'm still kinda mad at you for that shit you pulled at the park last night. Did you do all this with Mrs. Tuttle's old mean ass?"

"Damn girl, I didn't know you like that back then and yeah because I was failing the hell out of her class and they woulda kicked me off the track team. Every man needs a crash test dummy. We practice, crash and burn, run 'em into walls, "he began accenting each word with kisses, "just—to—be—able—to—do—this."

The heat from his lips seared my skin evaporating any further argument I may have had. He kissed and sucked his way toward my breast. My neck gave way, causing my head to fall back as I let out a whisper of a moan. Small pulses of pleasure radiated from his lips, into my skin.

They traveled like tiny ripples coursing around my calves and up my thighs, rolling like waves and crashing into the junction between my legs. Every brush of his lips painted a portrait on my skin that ended in bright bursts of orange and brilliant white sparkles behind my eyelids.

My hips wound in slow motion, dancing on their own accord to whatever song he was singing to my body. He slid himself down my body in a trail of kisses, sliding my panties off as he went with the ease of a magician. I needed him to sing that shit to the part of me that was now so alive with feverish energy it was almost unbearable. Pulling his head closer in between my thighs I shuddered, arching my back. The sensation was like hot water on frostbitten fingers as his tongue lashed out against my bare skin. Entangling my fingers into his thick hair, I draped my thighs over his shoulders, drawing the heat from his tongue deeper. I moaned out loud and then I literally told myself to shush.

My heart was doing some kind of crazy staccato rhythm in my chest as he made circles and swirls around my clit. He sucked it between his lips over and over, hard and fast. *Shit.* He'd never done that before. It was like I was running a race blindfolded. My body knew it wanted to get to a finish line somewhere out there, but just didn't know where or how.

"Okay, I'm ready. Please. Baby, I want you." I couldn't take it anymore. If he had a magical master-man keynis between his legs and it needed to guide me across the damn finish line, well then I needed him to whip that bad boy out pronto.

He pulled back and looked up at me shocked and concerned. "You sure? I can do this all day, sugar lips." He grinned, licking his lips for effect.

"Yes. I'm sure. Hurry up. Please tell me you got a condom."

He was gone and back so fast I didn't even have time to get cold. I undid my bra while he put the condom on, wondering if I was making the right decision. Hell, I was gonna marry this nigga, right? Any other doubts I might have had went out the window as he cupped my full double-D breasts. Oh yeah, that's another thing that pissed off all those Barbie heffas at school. My behind was not small by any means. I'd always been "stocky" as Momma put it. Yet, Carlos loved it. He said a woman was supposed to be soft, full, and curvy—that he couldn't stand a skinny, bony chick. He began massaging both my breasts in his large hands and alternated between licking and sucking my nipples.

That shit felt so good I didn't even mind the fact that his fingers smelled all the hell like latex from the condom. I could feel him slick, hot, and hard in between my legs and there was a moment of doubt, maybe even panic on my part. There was no way this would work.

The expression on his face was hard to read as he raised himself up over me. It was a cross between pain, pleasure, and extreme concentration.

"You okay, Carlos? What are you thinking about?"

He frowned even harder at me and my nerves frazzled. Maybe I was doing something wrong or there was something else I was supposed to be doing.

"I'm thinking about what every man thinks about, baseball and doughnuts. You're fine woman. Stop talking," he replied in a soft whisper.

We locked eyes briefly before he lowered his head and flicked his tongue across my nipple. My head rolled back into my pillow and then he bit down hard, pressing forward at the same time.

Flashes of pain hit me in two different places at the same time and I wasn't sure which one was worse. It was like having a serious burning, tearing cramp and getting my nipple pierced all over again. Tears burned my eyes and I tried bucking him off, and then I tried scooting away but he wouldn't budge.

"What the hell, Carlos?"

"I'm sorry, baby. I was trying to distract you. I saw it in a movie. Stop movin', girl. It's . . ." He sounded all out of breath, and I was just pissed, squirming, trying to get away and get him out of me, mad because all the feel good was gone.

"God. You've gotta stop moving. Oh shit. Oh shit."

His head fell onto the pillow beside mine and I was pinned under his weight as he wrapped his arm around me. I could feel him moving inside me faster and deeper. His breath pounded against my ear in short, hot bursts, like a bull just before it charges.

Squeezing my eyes shut, I began grinding my teeth, trying to block out the raw soreness between my legs. Realizing that I was starting to get a charley horse in my damn calf muscle, I flexed and tried straightening it out.

That slightest adjustment made a hellafied difference.

"Oooh," was about all I could manage to get out. Clutching at Carlos's back, I held on like my life depended on it and buried my face into his shoulder. I could feel him contracting inside me as his entire body tensed.

And then I felt warmth. There was a rush of heat inside me.

My eyes flew open as he stopped moving and completely collapsed on top of me. "Oh God," I whispered in agony. It was more to myself than to Carlos.

"Now you can talk? That wasn't God, baby, that was all me." He chuckled, like he'd done something spectacular.

"No, jackass, I think the fucking condom broke!"

"Oh the hell it did." He pulled out quickly, and sat back on his knees. I didn't even need to look. His expression said it all.

What the hell was this bullshit? This couldn't be what all the love songs and romance novels talked about. Somebody done lied to me! I closed my eyes and tried not to cry. I was now sexually frustrated and pissed off at this entire fiasco. I couldn't afford to get pregnant, and damn sure couldn't get an abortion. What the hell kind of cheap-ass condom did this fool have?

"You've got to be kidding me. *This* is what I come home to?"

My eyes flew open at the sound of my daddy's voice as it boomed loudly throughout our small two-bedroom house.

"Oh shit. Your pops is home? What time is it?" Carlos's voice was a frantic, rushed whisper.

I groaned, frustrated as hell. "It's way past time for us to get up out of here."

We both jumped up and I snuck out to the bathroom brought back a warm soapy washcloth for us to wipe ourselves down with before rushing to get dressed. I quickly tossed my yellow comforter over the small bloody spot on my matching sheets. That spot was all I had left of my virginity. I wasn't pure anymore, and I could only hope Carlos wasn't a mistake.

Peeking out my curtain-less window, the sky outside was just barely breaking into the light blue and grey streaks of morning. Cool white rays were creeping through the broken slats of my venetian blinds and I could hear a few birds breaking the morning's silence with their annoying chirping. I squinted at the battery-powered alarm clock sitting on the plastic bin I used as a nightstand and cursed. Damn, we was gonna be super late again. I was usually up and out the house before my dad got home from work.

"It's not that light outside, you can still go out through the window," I whispered. The arguing with my parents sounded like it was getting heated, which meant Carlos had a pretty good chance of hopping the gate in the backyard unseen.

This had become our routine. I probably hadn't slept alone for at least four of the six months we were together. Carlos would sneak in and out before Daddy got home or Momma woke up and we'd meet later at school.

"Next time will be better now that we got that out the way. Don't worry, no one gets knocked up the first time." He kissed my cheek.

I winced, thinking, *no one believes that urban myth bullshit.*

The side of my face was still sore from where the television remote had connected angrily with my cheek. I'd tried to prevent all the drama hours ago before I'd snuck Carlos in, quietly asking Momma to relocate herself from the couch to their bedroom. The remote was the closest thing to her so that was what she answered with, swinging it furiously toward my face. The lights had been shut off again because the bill hadn't been paid and I was scared to have any candles burning when she was like that. Otherwise, I might have had some kind of light to see the blow coming so I could've ducked in time. Gathering my things for school I fought a silent war on whether I should tell my daddy about *him.*

He'd brought her home drunk again. *He* was the main reason she'd been drunk by the time I got home from school almost every day this week, if she was home at all. When I asked her what she was doing with *him,* I was told to stay out of grown folk's business. But everyone in the neighborhood knew what kind of business *he* dealt with. It would hurt Daddy's feelings if I told him, and then he'd fly off and say something to Momma and Lord knows she'd take it out on me.

My mother's voice rose angrily, matching my Daddy's sharp tone. "Don't you dare come in here questioning me. *You* wanted this, remember? You wanted me; you wanted to be the family man. You made me choose and now all you do is stay at that job you love so much that you never come home!"

"Dammit, woman, it's called a double shift. This job is so we don't need nobody's handouts. You don't want to work, remember? You want to be Susie Homemaker or whatever it is you want to call this. I work enough hours to barely get us by; I'm paying rent on this piece-of-shit house while you sleep the day away dreamin' about a newer one!" Daddy roared back at her.

"We had a way out. I thought you were just righteous, but now I see it's because you wasn't man enough to take it. A real man would keep the lights on. Make enough money for us to use the air conditioner. I'm more of a damn man than your ass." She hurled her words at him with the same precision as the knife thrower I'd seen at the carnival. The little man could launch a razor-sharp blade and split an apple in half from nearly twenty feet away. Momma's words were the same, meant for cutting deep into Daddy's pride.

"I'm soft?" His question was barely audible. I had to press my ear against my bedroom door to hear him. "I ain't a real man? A lesser nigga would have put you out on the front lawn and changed the locks after whoopin' your ass. A soft nigga would have our daughter working to help out, instead of focusing on school."

"And a soft, scared nigga would do just like you," Momma snapped back. "You want to keep your hands clean yet you too stupid to realize you get 'em dirty every day, wiping the white man's ass for pennies."

Wow, did she really have to take it there?

Five, four, three . . . Counting the seconds down I listened sure as day at any moment they'd start swinging on each other.

"Nah, I'm solid. That easy money ain't worth the jail time for putting my hands on it. Neither are you."

I opened my bedroom door and it was as if the bell rang, signaling the end of a championship fight as the contenders retreated to their neutral corners. Daddy shuffled toward me down the hallway, yet something was different. This wasn't the look of a defending champion. It was the look of a fighter who'd seen too many fights, taken too many beatings, and at the end of the day finally realized that his bruised face and damaged pride wasn't worth the title.

"Mornin', Twinkles. What are you still doing home?" he greeted me.

I giggled at the pet name he'd called me for as long as I could remember. When I was little I'd asked him what it meant and he'd said it was because my eyes were as big and as pretty as the night sky.

"I'm late, Daddy. Have a good sleep. I love you."

He smiled tenderly before kissing me on the forehead. "I love you too. Have a good day."

It might have been my imagination but his smile seemed sadder than usual. It didn't quite reach his eyes, making them twinkle their usual bright brown or crease at the corners as they usually did. Damn, could he tell that I wasn't a virgin anymore? There was no way he could know I might be pregnant, was there? My conscience was already making me paranoid as hell.

Leaning over Momma on the couch, my nose wrinkled at the heavy dousing of White Diamonds she'd covered herself in. It was a sad attempt to compensate for the fact that she'd come home too drunk to stumble into the shower.

"Bye, Momma. Love you," I whispered softly.

She didn't so much as bat an eyelash.

Giving her cool cheek a small peck, I smelled the scent of White Diamonds, liquor, and something I'd noticed a hundred times before but could never place. The only reason I knew it now was because it faintly clung to my own body. It oozed out of my pores, danced behind my eyelids as memories, and lingered in my hair. Momma smelled like sex.

Chapter 2

Just Roll Over And Play Dad

I got home from school early. The record high was supposed to be close to a hundred degrees outside and with no AC it was almost inhumane to keep us in that brick oven they called a school. Besides, everyone got "the itis" after lunch anyway. When you combine that with those big-ass wind tunnel fans recycling hot air, even the teachers were either irritated or half asleep.

The house was insanely hot when I walked in. I was surprised to find the lights working and not surprised that Momma was nowhere to be found.

She could have at least cracked a damn window or two. Her absence was a good thing though; it meant I could watch my shows as long as I was quiet. Everyone at school had been debating over a new episode of *Oz* on HBO and I didn't want to miss it. Daddy usually rested in the afternoon before going to work if he wasn't already gone. The door to the bedroom was closed but I peeked in anyway just to make sure he wasn't home. No point in being all quiet if I didn't have to be.

There wasn't any money left on my lunch ticket and Momma had forgotten to put money up there so many times the lunch ladies were at their limit for giving me hookups. I didn't even think to get money from Carlos before school since we were on different lunch shifts. A few of my friends let me eat some of their fries and I played the "not hungry" role, opting to do my homework even though I was starving. Good thing it was a half day, because there was no way I'd have made it through a whole one.

Opening the door to the fridge, I stared inside as my stomach growled angrily. There was the ugly part left from a loaf of bread, mayonnaise but no lunch meat, no cheese. Shit, we didn't have shit! There wasn't anything in the cabinets except flour and an old box of biscuit mix. It was a damn shame I didn't have eggs or milk. Pissed, I opted for the heel of the bread. Smearing on a thick layer of mayonnaise and a sprinkle of black pepper for some flavor, I folded it in half and made do with my make-believe sandwich.

There were always a few minutes during each day when I'd sit on the couch after school and watch TV as if I were a grown-up in my own house living by my own rules. Crossing my legs I sat back and turned to see what talk shows I could find, but every local channel was showing an emergency broadcast. Something about the chief of police and a freak accident involving his air bag.

Every channel was airing footage of him in his uniform and his wife and family. He'd been the chief for over thirty years and his death was an unexpected shock. My sandwich may as well have been Styrofoam and sand. It lodged itself in my throat until I could work up enough moisture to swallow past the knot of disbelief. On the screen in front of me was a view of the chief's car. I prayed that for coincidence's sake he just so happened to drive a red Camry.

I decided to take a shower while the house cooled off. My make-believe half of a sandwich didn't do anything but irritate me, and just suspecting Carlos in something as big as the police chief's death didn't help matters. Confronting Carlos and then going to the police if he was involved was going to be insane. Besides, he'd said it last night, I even watched him go to Tyre's car. There were a thousand red Camrys in the area. I was probably just being dramatic. I squashed the thought for the moment as my stomach once again grumbled, only half content.

There was no telling when Momma would come stumbling back, and when she did she'd most likely be in no condition to prepare a meal. I wasn't allowed to even think about leaving the house unless someone knew where I was going. Hopefully she'd be hungry enough to leave her snide comments about my weight at the door. The last thing I wanted to hear was, "A missed meal or two ain't gonna hurt you none, girl. It's no wonder why we can't keep any food up in this house with your big behind suckin' it all down."

Momma loved to remind me that I was a little heavy. And, since I wasn't supposed to have a boyfriend, the most I could do was just think about how I'd like to shut her down. How I would love to one day get all in her face pointing and going off. It'd have to be on one of those days when she was so hung over it hurt to blink,that way she'd be a little slow with the slapping reflexes and I'd get a chance to say my piece.

Well, Momma, my boo ain't got no complaints. Matter of fact, he can't stand them Bones McGee–looking skinny broads. And he can't wait to slide all up in this big booty. So, poof, g'on somewhere. I'd be sure to pop my lips and roll my eyes for good measure when I was done. And after Momma's hand flew across my face and I got up off the floor I probably wouldn't remember my name or the last four digits of my social security number.

Giggling at the image, I just hoped she'd be hungry and possibly in a good mood whenever she finally came home. Maybe I could get enough money up out of her to walk to Brown's convenience store on the corner and get us some five cent potato logs or some wings.

My cell phone vibrated in my backpack on the counter scaring the living daylights out of me. It was a rinky-dink prepaid phone I'd gotten one day just so I could keep up with my friends. Momma looked at me like I was damn near out of my mind when I'd asked for a phone, and Daddy was all about money. The first words out of his mouth were "who's gonna pay for that?" when I'd asked. Fortunately some of the girls on the basketball team couldn't afford to go get their hair professionally braided. After two or three heads here and there, I managed to have enough to get my own phone. Flipping open the bulky little no-name thing I frowned at a text from my best friend, Brianna.

Text From Brianna 12:34: You busy?

Reply 12:34: no, bri bri, whatsup?

Text From Brianna 12:35: what happened with you and carlos?

Reply 12:35: Huh? Nothing happened. What do you mean?

Text From Brianna 12:36: Shit. I gotta tell u something. Please don't be mad.

Reply 12:36: What is it? Why would I be mad?

Text From Brianna 12:36: He asked me to meet him behind the stage in the auditorium after school but I told him no. He with you—that would be wrong. He said it was about you. But he wouldn't tell me until I met him.

Oh hell the fuck no, was the first thought that crossed my mind. Nobody ever went to the auditorium to just talk. Bri should have known that shit from all the stories we'd heard. I never knew her cousin's real name, just that she had a big old apple head, and that's what we all called her growing up; the name stuck to this very day. Hell,

Apple-head caught at least three STDs back to back up in there her freshman year, and if that wasn't enough the heffa still wound up getting pregnant.

Carlos was *my* damn boyfriend. Whatever she had to tell me was probably outside of her friend boundaries. Just the thought of him looking at her with his "come hither" eyes made my blood run molten hot. I wanted to wrap every strand of that straight black hair of his that he took so much pride in around my fist and just yank it right out of his scalp.

Carlos was in the twelfth grade and I was in the tenth, and I'd had a crush on him since I was in the third. That was when he'd first moved into my neighborhood and Brianna, "my best friend at first sight" as she put it, knew that. It was hard enough to get his attention, strategically placing myself in a position to become his closest female confidant. It took years to build that kind of friendship with him. Years of playing third wheel and watching him go on dates. Years of painfully helping him pick out flowers and gifts for other girls and talking him through breakups. It was even harder to finally make him do what I wanted all along and cross the friend line. All the hard work I'd put into getting him and now this?

Ugh! The fact that she even spoke to him without me around had me fighting the sudden urge to Hulk smash every piece of furniture in the house. I deliberately hadn't told her about this morning because I didn't want everyone knowing. Bri couldn't hold water sometimes and I hadn't made up my mind on exactly how much I wanted her to know.

Cringing at the thought of what she might have done with him, I could only shake my head. Why would he even go there, and with my best friend of all people? And Brianna's fake ass was just as wrong. I could just imagine her big-ass, *To Wong Foo Thanks for Everything, Julie*

Newmar Wesley Snipes in drag—looking man hands all over him! She always wore these bright-ass, made-up-ass exotic colors, like Pompeii Purple, Marry-me Mojito, or Passion Pink. All that bright polish and acrylic did was make you look at her hands and realize, *wow, that girl has some big-ass mannish hands*. The thought of her touching him and him letting her do it made me want to break his face and all of her fingers.

> Text From Brianna 12:43: You still there, girl?
> Reply 12:43: Yeah.
> Text From Brianna 12:44: He was all sweaty and nervous acting. So at first we just walked around and played with the props from all the old plays. Then he grabbed me and kissed me. I swear I was caught off-guard and when I tried to push him away he said that you weren't nothing like your flunky momma.

"My flunky momma?"

Grabbing my towel and a change of clothes I headed to the bathroom. I needed to calm down before I texted Carlos and cursed his ass slam-the-fuck out. The fact that he even knew about my momma and her escapades was mortifying. My phone vibrated but I didn't even bother looking at it. I didn't want to see the messages or feel the shame at whatever else they had to say about me, or Momma, or her activities.

Brianna was going to owe me so big whenever I finally decided to forgive her for her man-touchery. Juggling the phone and my underclothes I felt it vibrate three or four more times, before going silent. I was happy that I hadn't activated the voice call service. That girl was going to be texting me for the rest of the night because she knew she was wrong. I walked into the bathroom, flicking on the light, the words "flunky momma" whirring through my mind. They were bouncing between my ears, haunting me like the last song you hear after you turn off the radio after you get out of the car.

My "flunky momma." I was physically shaking my head at the exact thought when bright red flashes caught my attention. Gagging and gasping, I tripped over an invisible speed bump and went tumbling backwards into our small hallway. My things went spilling from my hands onto the once-tan, but now completely red-stained bathroom floor. Trembling, I just sat there momentarily petrified, staring as the few remaining stark white fibers of my bath towel slowly turned bright red. Buzzzz. Buzzzz. Buzzzz. Buzzzzz.

My heart lurched in my chest at the sound of my phone somewhere under my pile of my things. It was as if I were suddenly struck by lightning and jolted back to life at the scene of terrifying crime scene. This wasn't a dream; the tears burning down my face were real, the blood on the floor was real, and all the rumors about my mother were real. Standing on shaky legs, I steadied myself using the wooden door frame. "Please let me wake up, or let this be a mean joke," I repeated over and over, as I wrestled the dark feelings of desperation that were rising up to overtake me from the pit of my stomach.

Fighting the urge to vomit, sobbing and tiptoeing I forced myself forward to investigate. I was trying not to slip in the ice-cold slick puddle that used to be someone's life force on the floor. I edged my way into the bathroom carefully. No one should ever have to know what it feels like to walk barefoot through another human's blood; how it congeals, feels slimy, or how it slides in between your toes. I felt lightheaded and realized I'd been holding my breath; I inhaled and exhaled through my nose a few times, reminding myself to repeat the action every few seconds.

Reaching my hand out cautiously, tears clung to my lashes, momentarily blurring my vision, almost blinding me and I blinked them away furiously. I continued the slow process like when they took me to pet a pony for my fifth birthday and told me she was more afraid of me than I should have been of her.

The pony paid me no real mind as she chomped away at a stalk of grass, glancing at me every so often as I edged nearer, certain she'd take my head off at any moment. She peered at me eerily through enormous alien-like glossy black eyes that reflected my image to me. It was the only sign indicating her awareness of my intrusion into her space.

My parents were both there watching. Momma was eating my cotton candy I'd asked her to hold and Daddy was standing behind her, resting his chin on her shoulder, a mixture of pride and amusement on his face. He smiled and gave me a thumbs-up when I'd finally looked back at him shouting, "I did it, Daddy!"

My fingers met the cold, leathery flesh of his eyelids and I slid them down, gently closing them. I silently said good-bye to the reflection of me now mirrored in his lifeless eyes that were just this morning vivid and alive. I did my best not to look at the long, jagged gash that ran underneath Daddy's chin across his neck. His wedding band and chain, the only pieces of jewelry he ever wore, were gone.

Looking around I tried to see if maybe they'd fallen off. His Atum-Ra Egyptian medallion was important to him. It was a solid gold square with a carving on it of a man's body with a falcon's head; his arms were outstretched wings. A small snake hung from his beak, which I always thought was just nasty. His daddy had given it to him before he passed, and Daddy always had this saying about Egyptians being black. He believed we were all royalty:

kings, queens, princes, and princesses by inheritance. And now, the king of our little castle was slumped in an awkward position between the toilet and the side of the bathtub. Like a doll someone had gotten tired of playing the game of life with and just dropped. His wife beater and shorts were both the same nightmarish dark red as the pool beneath my feet. This wasn't an honorable death. This wasn't how my king should have died.

Buzzz. Buzzz. Buzzz. Buzzz.

Startled, I carefully traced my steps back to my things and knelt down to retrieve my phone. The worries I had moments ago seemed worlds apart from the worries I was facing now. There was nothing Bri could say at this point that could surprise me or piss me off after this. My little high school drama had immediately become irrelevant. What good was having a grain of sand once you realize you'd lost an entire beach? Flipping open the case I scrolled to her latest text.

Text From Brianna 12:44: He said he got caught up in the moment and was horny as hell since you won't give it up. He thinking about breaking up with you because you basically making him insecure, girl. When you gonna give that boy some ass?

I needed to donate my body to science. There was no way a human heart could possibly sink any lower than my heart had, but at the sight of her words, it surprisingly did. How could his lying, cheating ass do something so unbelievable? He got what he wanted and then just like that it was on to the next. *Wow.* It was time to pull myself together. I needed to go next door and get a neighbor to call the police. I'd started to close the phone when Bri's next words made my heart do one of those painful stutter thumps. That type of thump that sends a train wreck of thoughts to your brain in the form of an instant headache.

Text From Brianna 12:55: Are you there?
Text From Brianna 12:55: Girl, say something!
Text From Brianna 1:05: Are you that mad at me? You know I'm down for Korey right now. He's the star quarterback and he FINE. I'm not messing that up not for your little wanna-be playboy. Oh and, when we were leaving, Manny, rolled past with your momma and scooped him up.

Carlos got a ride with *him?* Was he in on this shit? If it was at that level was I next? I couldn't take any chances, especially not if *he* had anything to do with it. Whether my momma was with him willingly was still unclear. The police wouldn't be any help. They'd only get me detained until *he* got there because they worked for *him.* The only way I'd be safe was if I got out of here and as quickly as possible.

Chapter 3

Would You Bleed For Dead Presidents?

"What you mean you ran away? Girl, is you crazy?"

My cousin Charmaine was staring at me wild-eyed in the stuffy hallway of her six-story walk-up in Hell's Kitchen, New York. Her wet and wavy weave was braided into two frizzy plats that hung strait down both sides of her head. She'd come out into the hallway wearing nothing but a thin, almost see-through pink slip that barely reached mid-thigh, and one slouched white sock.

Where the hell is your other sock, woman?

An obsessive-compulsive war silently waged on in my head as I fought to refrain from asking her the question out loud. I kept glancing down at her bare foot, questioning over and over how someone could just walk around with one naked foot. One of my brain cells decided to raise the white flag of defeat, ending the battle. The need for fresh air outweighed the need for an answer. I was out of breath from walking up all the stairs to get to her door, and at the same time trying not to breathe in too much of the stale stank-ass air inside the hallway.

The entire corridor was filled with the faint odor of urine and dirty diapers mixed with the scent of someone cooking cabbage; either that, or the trash needed to go out. Car horns honked repeatedly, subway trains rumbled, and police sirens whirred in the distance outside. Inside babies wailed while televisions blared loudly behind each of the dark blue doors on every single floor, as if every single person was trying to drown out the sounds of the real world. Lord, I missed Virginia.

"Well, I'm waiting, girl," she said while impatiently tapping her ashy naked foot.

"I . . . I pawned some bangles Grandma gave me, and caught the China bus up here. You're the only one I could think of who was close by. Yo, why the hell don't y'all have an elevator?" The words tumbled from my mouth in a nervous jumbled cluster. Leaning forward I braced myself on my knees and stared up at her, sweat trickling in between my shoulder blades underneath my T-shirt.

She was a few years older than me from my daddy's side of the family. They had the same complexion and high, narrow nose. Swallowing past the lump in my throat I tried to find a steady voice to plead my case with her.

"I can't really talk about it; the less you know the better. I really just need some money and then I need to go. I'll pay you back, somehow, I promise. But they might come looking for me and if they do you ain't seen me. Life or death shit, Charmaine."

"You know I just had another baby. I really don't have any extra money right now, boo."

Tears filled my eyes at her excuses and I leaned into the wall. It sure as hell didn't look she'd had a damn baby. Jealousy tried to stick its long, ugly nose over my shoulder and look at the outline of her narrow waist that was so clearly visible through her slip. But, the shadow of dread that had been trailing me slowly clawed its way up my back. Its grisly shroud of misery erased all thoughts not related to my future, or the lack of a future if anyone caught up to me.

When I'd gone into my parents' room to get my bangles I'd found Charmaine's address on an envelope with a picture of the new baby inside, her phone number on the back. When the bus dropped me off in front of Penn Station I'd meant to call her first, instead of just showing up. I was just so determined to get away, and then shocked at actually seeing this "concrete jungle" I'd only seen on TV.

In Virginia, if you look up you'll see elm and oak trees, tiny finches, and robins as bright as stop signs. I'd seen so many different varieties of butterflies I could never name them all. Now my view was marred by endless stone and cold cement, pigeons, and squawking seagulls. It almost made me climb right back on the bus. Mouth hanging wide open, I honestly stood there, staring like a little country mouse.

Where were the gargoyles carved out of stone? How in the world did people have picnics or fly kites; hell, black people need a little bit of sun, that's how we get our vitamin D. I was trying to take in the scenery and people shoved past me. Elbows jabbed me and shoulders bumped me as they rushed to get their bags, and not one person said excuse me or I'm sorry.

My father always told me, "If you go somewhere you blend in; you don't stand out like a lost idiot. You walk with a damn purpose, and you get where you're going."

Fighting my way through the crowd I approached our bus driver, a little Indian man who spoke in very fast, choppy, incomplete sentences.

"Um. Excuse me, sir, how do I get here?" I asked him, handing him the sliver of paper I'd written Charmaine's address on.

He snatched the address out of my hand and frowned at the writing. All the while he was scratching at this suspicious "herpa syphylitis"–looking bump on the corner of his mouth. Uhhh! It was like one of the pictures they'd shown us in sex education class.

Please don't touch the paper, please don't touch the paper. Noooooooo! I screamed silently, cringing as he shook his head yes, and then jabbed the address repeatedly with his offensive contaminated finger.

"It is turty or turty-tree-minute walk. Or go one block dat way, take one train, is red number sign. Veddy cheap veddy quick. Ride train, take no time. Go last stop, get off, and walk uh, tree maybe fie block okay?" He shoved the paper back in my direction.

Speechless, I took my address back, trying to only touch the edges and simply nodded. *Paper-touching motherfucka, what the hell is a turty or a fie? A red what? Was all of that even English?* I walked away looking like a madwoman as I mumbled to myself—guessed I'd fit right in.

Charmaine sucked her teeth loudly, drawing me back to the present. "Come in, I might have a little something. Let me see what I can do."

Shuffling my backpack up onto my shoulder, I gave her a watery, sniffly thank-you and walked in, my eyes damn near bulging out of their sockets. What kind of *Coming to America* foolishness was this? This girl had a projection-screen TV on one side that took up the entire wall, exercise equipment, and those nice couches—the kind you see on display upstairs in the JC Penny's that they don't want you to sit on. I could even tell the carpet was plush and soft, and that was with my shoes on.

"So, my dear cousin, want to go with me to a dance tonight? You can probably make some money."

After looking at the layout of her place, I didn't need to think about it. Charmaine was obviously doing something right.

"Whatever it takes, girl," I all but shouted enthusiastically at her.

After taking Kendall and baby Shane across the hall to a neighbor we spent the entire day trying to find something for me to wear. There wasn't much to choose from since she was in like a size nothing and I sure as hell was not. I'd never had a reason to dress up before and looking at myself in the mirror was like looking at my evil twin.

"Is this really me?" I asked, as I twirled and preened in front of her full-length mirror.

"Yes, boo. I might need to get us a gun. Where you get all those hips and that booty from? I swear they putting something up in that milk y'all drinking. I ain't have all that when I was sixteen. I had to have babies to get what little ass and titties I got now." She then squeezed her boobs together for emphasis, making faces and laughing.

She'd managed to find a pink and black stretchy mini-skirt and a pink tank top with push-up cups made into the fabric so I didn't need a bra. The black button-up top she gave me to wear over the tank top was too small to actually button so I wore it open. Just having it on my arms made me feel less naked. We wore the same size shoes and I just tried on all of hers until I found a comfortable pair of low heels that I wouldn't fall out of.

"So the party is at this studio all the way across town in the Bronx, and these fools are talking about take the damn train. My homeboy is gonna come get us, because we'd have to take the one, then the C and I think B to D, and then the four train'll hit the six, which will put us at Westchester and Tremont; might be the longest way, too. Hell no."

She lost me when she switched from numbers to letters and then back. It sounded to me like New York just liked to make shit complicated. None of it really mattered though. I'd take a ride in a car full of strangers dressed as a hoochie over a train car filled with strangers any day.

The building felt like it was shaking. Charmaine's one window rattled worse than it did when the train passed, and the glasses in her wine rack clinked together. The duck-and-cover drill crossed my mind but what was I ducking and covering from?

A roach riot; is there a crackhead stampede down-stairs?

"C'mon, girl. Our ride is here."

My chariot for the evening was a dark green Jeep Cherokee with pitch black windows and chrome rims so big they were probably as high as my knees. Climbing in behind the driver seat I was surrounded by the spicy seductive scent of Black Ice air fresheners. Blue interior lighting ran along the floor and underneath the seats. Charmaine yelled over the music to introduce me to the driver, Tarique, and his friend, Chief. They barely acknowledged us, making me feel unwelcome, like an inconvenience or something.

"Rude asses. Well so much for Southern hospitality. Damn." Mumbling under my breath I got settled, content with just looking out the window.

"She introduced your little nobody ass and I nodded. Damn." Tarique sneered at me over his left shoulder.

Scrunching my face up at his ignorant self, I could feel my blood beginning to boil. "You calling me a nobody like you're a somebody," I spat back.

"Right now, I'm the somebody with the ride. You just a body. No car, no money. *Nobody*." He gave me a look in the rearview that could probably freeze water.

The music went all the way back up, cutting off any reply I would've made if I could have come up with one. The streets were a blur of taxi cabs, pedestrians, and city lights. It was all like a beautiful postcard in motion to my eyes. Jay-Z's "Feelin' It" vibrated through my back up to my jawbone through the gigantic subwoofer in the back. The album just came out and it was a helluva soundtrack to ride to through the streets of New York. Every street we turned on made me wonder if someone famous had walked down it or lived on it. We stopped underneath some eerie subway tracks that dripped down the front of the windshield. The greens and reds of the surrounding street lights reflected into the cabin of the Jeep, casting an unnerving glow.

"All right, y'all, we are here. We'll be up in a minute. Char, you got your shit?" Chief was the one who spoke. He was definitely the nicer of the two from what I could tell so far.

"Yeah, bae. I'm goodie like B.C. Powder white not birth control 'cause I got three. Mouths to feed. I do or die whatever ready," Charmaine half spoke and half rhymed in reply. Her eyes were practically closed. She was bobbing her head, rocking back and forth and snapping her fingers, even though there wasn't any music playing anymore.

Okay. Am I the only one who finds this . . . not normal?

Chief climbed out and opened Charmaine's door. "Good. Get in there then; call if you need us."

"Wait, you aren't coming with us?" I asked, while giving anxious glances in Char's direction. I expected her to speak up in our defense.

"You'll be fine. Charmaine got you," Chief replied and laughed, before lighting a blunt and waving me out of the car.

The studio was on the second floor of a brick three-story building that looked like it was wedged in between some other buildings as a last thought. The light buzzed overhead in the dimly lit stairway; it was so narrow we had to go one at a time. *Who in the world would put a studio in a spot like this?*

Charmaine knocked and a huge wall of a man opened the door with a scowl on his face that could probably curdle milk. He had very dark skin with dark brown eyes and a full beard that hid most of his face. Dude had to have been at least seven feet tall and was so wide he took up the entire doorway. At the sight of Char he pulled the door closed behind him and stepped out into the hallway. His face broke into a wide grin, revealing straight pearl white teeth.

"Mookie-Mook, you made it. I didn't think you were coming. But yay, you're here," he called out to her.

I immediately looked down to hide the wide grin on my face.

Did I see a tongue ring? Ooooh is his big butt gay?

"Hey, my Poo-Poo Percy. This my cuzzo. I told you about her on the phone," Charmaine replied in a slow sing-song voice.

He popped his tongue and swiveled his head, looking around the empty hallway suspiciously. He answered her, barely moving his face or his mouth, his voice coming out in a high-pitched squeaky whisper. "Bitch. I am working. You will call me P. Gunna unless we are in genteel company. Now, get y'all's behinds in here. You're late."

We followed him inside and it was like walking into a sea of people. The little dark room was packed wall to wall with folks everywhere. The music was playing so loud I couldn't make out the song. All eyes were on us as Perc, P. Gunna, led us farther into the place. We stopped just long enough to fix drinks at a table that was made into a makeshift bar. Char fixed mine since I'd never drunk before. If you could drink gasoline and not die, I was pretty sure whatever was in my cup was exactly what it would taste like.

"You gonna dance tonight, sweetheart?" someone screamed into my ear so loud and so close it made my eardrum hurt.

Yes. Thank you, another young person. I breathed a sigh of relief when I looked up at the young caramel-skinned girl with the nice smile standing beside me at the bar. She had on a Cleopatra wig that hung long down her back with bangs cropped just above her eyes. It gave her purple contact lenses a spellbinding look in contrast to the pitch black hair.

"Um yes. It's a party; of course I'm gonna dance." I leaned and yelled back into her ear just as loud as she'd yelled into mine.

"That's what I'm talking about," she replied, grinning like I'd answered the secret question before turning away from me to continue addressing the crowd. "Well then. Are y'all ready to get this party started or what?" Her voice boomed throughout the room.

Why is her voice amplified like that? When the hell did this heffa get a microphone?

But before I could figure out the answers to my questions my cup was snatched from my hand and I was hurled forward to follow her out into the mass of people she was parting like the sea. Five chairs were lined up across a wall and a blanket was spread across the middle of the floor. She spoke to the crowd like a queen commanding a court, and as she did so she slowly removed one item of clothing. The room went nuts and I looked around in sheer terror for my damn cousin.

"Okay, boys and ladies. Here, boo, hold my mic." She was addressing me like I was her own personal little butler or something.

Shocked, I took the mic from her as all of her clothes fell off. Literally, I don't know if this heffa had on a breakaway skirt and underwear set or what, but one minute she was clothed and the next she was completely buck-naked. *Oh, what the hell am I supposed to do now?*

Money flew through the air as she slowly oiled herself up, bending to do her ankles exposing her bare ass. Nervous, I could feel myself starting to sweat. When she sprayed something on her stomach and lit herself com-

pletely on fire I actually considered casually climbing
down the fire escape. There was no way I could follow this
up or do anything like this, and definitely not naked.

She finished and P. Gunna came out with a trash bag,
pointing at me to help him collect her money and take it
to the back. Charmaine walked past me on her way out to
the front. She was beside a chocolate brown girl who had
a curly black wig teetering on her head suspiciously, but
it was as if Char didn't even see me. The sound of the guys
hooting and cheering let me know she was dancing.

Little Cleopatra wiped off the baby oil and put on fresh
deodorant, getting ready for the lap dance set.

"Ma, you gonna go out there? The last set is just lap
dances. They sit down and all you have to do is take their
money." She addressed me, not missing a beat as she
oiled herself up again.

"I don't know," was all I could get out.

"Yo! You've got to come get your girl." Percy burst back
into the room looking between the two of us frantically.

"Get whose girl?" Cleopatra answered. She didn't even
stop what she was doing.

"Youuuuuuurs. Pleeeeeease. Mmmmmm." All the man
came up out of Percy and that's when I got worried. He
was doing what could have passed for "the potty dance."
Or, it might have looked more like that "oh, there's a spi-
der" dance you do when you see one run across the floor
and you try to sidestep it. His hands were in little fists
at his sides, and he was jumping frantically from side to
side. If I weren't scared I might have laughed at his big
behind prancing around like that.

"Go get your girl. Please, Lord, go help her," he squeaked
at me.

I rushed out into the front room and the lights were
up, the music was surprisingly low, and everyone was
standing by silently. Some people had looks of disgust,

and others were grabbing their things and leaving; their heads were low, not making eye contact.

"It's a fucking shame," someone in the crowd said.

Prepared for the worst I pushed past people ready to meet death face to face yet again. What had happened? Had she been raped or stabbed? Pressing through the last few bystanders I finally saw what they saw. Charmaine was writhing around on the blanket; her eyes were closed and her head was thrown back. I gave her a quick once-over and didn't see any cuts or bruises. My eyes darted back over the scene and that's when I saw it. Some of the bills were covered in splotches of blood, stained from the crimson river that was running from in between her legs.

"Charmaine, get your ass up, girl!" Yelling and ashamed at dragging a grown woman out of her own menstrual fluids I yanked her arm.

It was as if she wasn't even on the same planet with me. Her eyes opened and rolled in her head. She took my yanking as a cue to stand and dance. The entire room shouted "awww" in unison as blood droplets stained more of the money and the blanket. She stumbled and it dripped onto the carpeting.

"Yo. Nah. Nah. We paid good money up front, plus tips, and I want my shit back." Someone was arguing with Little Cleopatra in the back.

She stormed toward me, her face distorting into an ugly frown when she saw all the blood. Chief and Tarique appeared in the doorway and they both looked as if they wanted to run right back out of it at the sight of all the blood. Chief wrapped Charmaine in a towel, scooped her up, and carried her outside. Cleopatra turned, giving me a dirty look.

"When her ass stop rollin' tell her all her money paid me, because I had to pay the nigga back for cutting this short, plus everything her ass bled all over," she growled at me.

"So she doesn't get anything? It was an accident; she didn't do it on purpose."

She sneered before leaning down to pick up two bloody twenties, holding them like they were on fire before flinging them in my direction. I caught them. I'd walked through blood; the two splotches were nothing compared to that. Folding them with a heavy sigh, I turned and went to the Jeep waiting outside. Tarique opened my door and helped me inside.

"You okay, Char?" I asked her quietly.

She was leaning against the window looking half asleep. "Yeah, think I tore my stitches from the baby. That was some good ecstasy though; my ass ain't feel shit. But Chief's taking me to the hospital."

"You're more than welcome to chill with me so you aren't alone, ma. They might keep her a day or so. Real talk, you don't have to worry about anything." Tarique's voice was deep and raspy.

"Are you sure somebody won't feel some kind of way about helping a nobody?"

"Stop playing, girl. Char is my people. You need me I got you. You need me?"

There was something in the way he spoke that made me believe he was sincere and honest. *Should I go with him or go back to Char's place?* At least with him I wouldn't be a lonely sitting target. I also couldn't risk putting the little ones in danger if someone came after me.

With nowhere to go and no one else to call, I nodded okay to this new fork in the road of destiny, and I could have sworn I heard the devil laugh in the distance.

Chapter 4

Baby Wait. Baby W(e)ight?

My stomach had been in knots all morning. After finally getting sick of hearing Tarique's mouth for four months straight I couldn't take it anymore. None of the diets were working, I tried everything even not eating and I actually gained three pounds. Our friendship had skyrocketed into a non-stop flight to heaven if you'd let him tell it. Yet day by day I resisted the urge to ask him if he even knew where Heaven was, because we were always going through some kind of hell. He was angry all the time about every single thing and the fact that I was putting on weight didn't help. When I talked about enrolling in school he had a fit, if I talked about working he spazzed out. When and how he became this obsessive controlling dictator over my life I wasn't sure.

Balancing myself on the edge of the tub in our tiny bathroom I scrunched my nose in disgust. No matter how many times I scrubbed the floor it always smelled pissy in here. Like that boy just came in and aimed at the walls and ceiling or something. I stared at the little white test teetering on the sink ledge and prayed for a negative symbol in the little window. The only thing I was sure of was that I hadn't had a period in a while and couldn't remember how far back. Combine that with the fact that Tarique refused to wear condoms *and* he refused to pull out and we had ourselves a situation. I imagine chipper white women that be all in love, and love the thought of having babies made pregnancy tests. Because when that positive symbol popped up . . . I couldn't think of one positive reaction.

When Tarique got home I was a wreck from rehearsing what I'd say to him. He'd gotten mad on a couple of occasions and put his hands on me so I was hoping that the news would make him happy. Maybe just maybe, if we had a baby he'd treat me a little better, buy me some nice things. Maybe he'd think sometimes before he'd get so angry that he'd just let his fists speak for him. At least I knew that I wasn't some kind of physical anomaly and despite working out and watching what I ate this wasn't completely my fault.

"Why you standin' over there lookin' crazy as hell girl?" Tarique had walked in and sat down on the couch. I was so nervous I didn't realize I was motionless standing off to the side, out of striking distance.

"Oh, no reason. I um, was thinking about what we'd do for dinner I guess."

"I'm goin' out after I take a nap. You can do whatever." He flicked the TV on dismissing me and I fumed.

"Why don't I ever get to go anywhere, you leave me here day and night and I feel like I'm losing my mind. It's not fair Tarique." I all but cried as he just stared at the television ignoring me.

"I ain't got time for this, women would kill for someone to take care of they asses and you sit up here complainin'." He tossed down the remote in disgust stormed down the hallway.

A small mouse ran across my foot and I jumped as it scurried along the wall and seemed to disappear into a darkened corner. I crept over intent on catching it and knelt down examining the space. One minute it was there and in the next minute my forehead connected with the wall with so much force I'd have sworn my skull cracked.

"What the fuck is this? You pregnant! Really? Who's been up in here?" Tarique tossed the pregnancy test down onto the floor beside me. There was so much shock and pain still trying to register in my brain that I couldn't speak. Of all the things for him to think, when or how the hell would I have time to bring someone in his place, when he watched me like a hawk never letting me leave? The words were almost clear enough for me to say when I was yanked roughly to my feet.

"I don't believe this shit, I opened up my heart and my home to you and you do this?"

There was so much rage and hatred in his face it was a reaction I'd have never expected from him.

"Nobody's been in here. I swear on my life Tarique it's only been you, I've only been with you."

He wasn't hearing me through his anger and somewhere between the living room and the kitchen he decided to throw me out. *Literally.* There was a haze of yellow from the buzzing lights in the hallway as he opened the door letting in the crisp cold air. I remember seeing them briefly before every bone in my body was introduced to the concrete stairs one by one, and the world went black. I vaguely remember lying at the bottom of the steps in the apartment's cold moldy smelling corridor trying to figure out if I was already dead or dying.

My mouth was dry, I wanted water and it felt like the weight of a million sand bags were on top of my body. I tried opening my eyes and groaned as pain shot through my head.

"Don't move or you'll hurt yourself."

I froze inwardly cringing at the sound of Tarique's voice. I'd have given anything to slip back into whatever darkness I'd just drifted out of. At least I had some kind of peace while I was there. My eyes felt gritty and I blinked a few times trying to focus. He was lying on the bed beside me, a half empty bottle of Jack Daniels was in his lap.

"Can't do more damage than you already did." My voice was a dry croak through my parched lips.

"Doctor got you on some strong shit, he a friend of mine, stopped by to see you a few days ago. Said you might see and say crazy things," he hesitated clearing his throat nervously, "you know after losing the baby and all but you'll be fine." He picked up a cup from the side of the bed and put a straw to my lips before I could respond or react. Ice water never tasted so damn good, I almost choked as it felt like I hadn't had water in years.

"I can't make babies." Tarique said it so quietly, and in such a way that I actually did choke at that point. He sat the cup down and took a long swig from the bottle in his lap.

"My Pops was probably one of the biggest assholes in the world. He had this saying that there could only be one man in his house and that was him. I had to have been like sixteen and I'd been talkin' to this girl for a minute. One night I decided to bring her to the crib, I was tired of sneakin' around and Pop was on a drinking binge somewhere. Shit, the nigga came home caught me balls deep gettin' some ass under his roof and he went off. Beat me with a crowbar. Told me I wasn't a man and I ain't have his permission to use my dick." Tarique paused his eyes had a faraway look to them and I sat there in dumb founded numbed shock.

"He hit me so many times I had to have all these special surgeries an' shit. I been sterile ever since."

There aren't too many words you can say to someone that throws you down stairs because you're pregnant and they can't have kids. *I still want to kill you* crossed my mind. *We could have talked about this*, was another good one. Instead I ignored all of the pain that was flooding my heart and I blocked out the physical torture of the pain killers gradually wearing off.

"I was already pregnant Tarique, the day I ran away was the first time I'd ever done anything. I just didn't know it, we could have had a family." As hard as I tried to fight the tears I couldn't and I cried mourning the loss of so many things in such a small amount of time.

Chapter 5

When There's Nothing Left, Go Right (10 Years Later)

The sun climbed high overhead, driving it's unrelenting rays down directly into my forehead. Shielding my eyes with my hand I looked up and couldn't find a single cloud in the crystal blue sky. Placing my hat on I marched across the field, dead brown grass snapping beneath the heel of my stuffy, hot, black shoes. The scent of unbrushed teeth and too many cups of coffee filled my nostrils as I neared everyone else.

"Okay, Virginia Beach's finest. We have a hostage situation. Troughman, Taylor, and Cordello?" McKinley's coffee-tinged breath seemed to linger in the air.

"Sir," we called out in unison to Officer McKinley, the senior officer in charge of the situation. He'd gathered our team in a clearing a few yards from the one-story ranch-style brick house. The yard was a minefield of tires, car parts, and trash collected from various curbside heaps and refuse bins.

Pete Shaw, a middle-aged white male, came home and found his wife, Tabitha, and her lover, Abram Emerit, packing. She was leaving him and taking their four-year-old and two-month-old boys with her. Neighbors called the police when they heard multiple gunshots, saying he'd killed her lover. Pete had a history of psychological issues as well as anger management problems and upon our arrival he refused to let anyone in or out of the house.

"Mr. Shaw has agreed to have another phone call with me in ten minutes. Alicia, the side bathroom has a window we think you can fit through," McKinley ordered.

"Ha-ha. Not the way she's been putting away Oreos and Snickers," Lorenzo blurted out.

No one laughed at Lorenzo Cordello's joke. McKinley cut him an angry glance before going on. "I'll get him on the line and talking so we can get the window off. You get inside. Try to get a read on the situation and where the kids are. If you get the chance deadly force is highly permissible. Take. Him. Out." His voice was curt and stern. There was no breeze to relieve us, so I could physically feel the impact of his words.

"Yes, sir," I replied quickly, nodding my understanding.

My palms immediately began sweating. There were a million and one things that could go wrong and only one way that this could go right. Those were not good odds to bet with.

"All jokes aside, I got you covered, Al. Nothing will happen to you, I swear." Lorenzo's voice was a low murmur. I tried to smile, but couldn't as Lorenzo patted me on the shoulder, his hand lingering a second before handing me a heavy bulletproof vest. Its weight and my nerves only intensified the heat outside.

"Get in position. We're calling him now." McKinley's voice echoed in my earpiece and I was thankful he wasn't within breathing range.

Maneuvering through the dry soil of the yard was like walking through some sort of post-apocalyptic battlefield. A pale white doll head stared eerily up at me through its one remaining eye. *Two boys, why would they have dolls?*

Kicking it so it'd face another direction, I maneuvered around anything that might make a sound. I leaned against the side of the house and prayed silently while Lorenzo cut through the screen and pried the window up. We listened and could hear Pete inside on the phone. Lorenzo locked eyes with me and nodded before hoisting me up and into the window.

Sliding soundlessly onto the dirty green tile I quickly got to my feet, crouching and drawing my pistol. My breathing was so erratic I was afraid he'd hear it.

"Mommy. Mommy. I have to pee-pee," a child whined from in the living room.

Shit! Now, kid, really? Adrenaline was coursing through my veins so fast it's a wonder I didn't faint. *If she brings the boy to the bathroom, maybe I can get them out the window. Think, woman. Think. Seconds matter. Milliseconds matter.*

"Babe. Buddy has to go potty." Tabitha sounded frail and scared.

"You want him to grow a damn vagina, Tabby? He's a fucking boy. Be a fucking man and pinch it. I'll take you in a minute. I'm on the phone," Pete growled at them, obviously irritated. I couldn't place his exact location in the living room or how close he was to the kid.

"Can't pinch it no more, it hurts," Buddy responded in a tiny little voice.

There was some shuffling and I quickly climbed into the shower, making sure to leave the dark purple curtains as close to how they appeared before I got in, with a small slit for me to peek out of.

Relief almost oozed out of my body when I saw Tabitha walking toward the bathroom holding Buddy's hand. I waited until they were all the way inside. She was close enough for me to see bruises on her face and arms. The report said she was thirty-one but she looked so much older. Her mousy brown hair was pulled into a tight bun in the back of her head and her face was full of worry lines and creases.

"Tabitha, my name is Officer Taylor. I'm here to help you. Please stay quiet. My partner is outside the window; we can get you and Buddy out right now," I whispered through the curtain, glad she didn't scream at the sound of my voice.

"Mommy." Buddy pointed, his mouth geared up to spout out number three on the top ten questions kids ask. *Who's that lady?*

"Shhh. Go potty before Daddy comes in here with the spoon," Tabitha whispered before addressing me. "He has this damn wooden spoon he'll beat him with. What about my baby? He's in the living room, asleep in his playpen."

"I'll go get the baby. But I need you to go now."

She nodded hesitantly while helping Buddy with his pants.

"My partner is right outside the window, hurry. Get Buddy situated and out of here." As soon as I said the words I knew the window of opportunity had passed.

"You got a camel hump to empty that I don't know about? What's taking so long?" Pete called out curiously as his booted footsteps clunked in our direction.

He came into view at the end of the hall, limping toward the bathroom. He was holding a twenty-gauge hunting rifle, double barrel, the kind that sprays buck shots. Chief said take him out, and the timing would be perfect. I had the element of surprise on my side. Raising my .45 I felt like a poised cobra preparing to lash out at any second. Throwing the curtain back I aimed; he was dead-on in the crosshairs of my gun. Shock registered all over his face as I pulled the trigger. The bullet exploded from the chamber.

"No! Don't—" Tabitha's voice was cut off as the bullet meant for her husband lodged itself in her back. She'd jumped up, throwing herself in front of Pete. Buddy and Tommy wailed. Pete raised his shotgun to return fire as Lorenzo hoisted himself through the window and grabbed Buddy to pass him through it to another officer waiting outside. I fired again from the hip not aiming because in those seconds precision wasn't a factor, stopping him was. Pete flew backwards from the impact as he was hit square in the chest.

Kneeling down beside Tabitha I held her hand, waiting for an ambulance; and my heart was falling to pieces. Her lips were moving but I couldn't make out any words. I leaned in closer to hear what she was saying.

"You were wrong. He loves me so much, and he's good. Pete is so bad, the shack is bad," Tabitha stammered. Her hand was shaking in mine as if it were below zero in the house instead of almost ninety degrees.

She took her last breath as officers burst through the front door and a feeling of dread immediately spread through my chest.

"We got a live one in here," one of the officers called out.

I jumped to my feet and ran into the living room as they untied a middle-aged male from a chair. The right side of his head was bloody and his eye was swollen, but he seemed to otherwise be okay.

"I'm . . . I'm Peter Shaw. Where's my boy? Where's my son?" he stammered.

"Why don't you have a seat and fill us in on what happened first?" One of the officers asked and Pete shakily explained what happened. "The gunshot the neighbor heard was Tabitha, shooting that summa bitch Abram in the leg, wounding him. They been screwin' behind my back like jack rabbits for years. Where the hell is my son is he okay?" Pete was getting irritated.

Anxious for him to get on with his story I explained,"
Buddy's getting checked out by one of our EMT's they'll
bring him in when they're done."

Satisfied with my answer his piercing blue eyes seemed
to lose focus as he continued to relive and remember his
story.

"Abram had been pretending to be me on the line with
y'all this entire time. I heard them planning the ending of
me like I won't even here. Like, I hadn't given that woman
every single thing she owns." He stopped and cried quietly for a moment. I locked eyes with a few officers who
looked down and away out of respect as we waited for
him to pull himself together.

"He was going to lie on the floor and act unconscious
and she was supposed to untie, shoot, and kill me seconds
before yall barged in. My death was the only way she
could collect on the insurance and still live happily ever
after with him."

I quickly left the scene, suddenly saddened and dis-
gusted at trying to even comfort that woman in her last
moments.

Back in the squad car with the AC pointed directly at
my face, I laid my head back on the headrest and closed
my eyes to shut in the tears. Lorenzo climbed in and set a
cold bottle of water in my lap.

"You did an excellent job back there, Al. The chief gave
us the rest of the day off. Don't beat yourself up over this.
You can't help if she sacrificed herself or tried to set that
shit up."

"I could have delayed firing, or aimed lower, wounded
her instead of killing her in front of her son. Then maybe
we'd have at least one fucking person to take in, instead
of two bodies."

Grabbing my phone from the glove compartment I dialed my husband's number.

"Hello, my love," he cooed in my ear.

My eyes watered instantly at the soothing sound of his voice in my ear. "Hey, sweetheart, can you come home? I need you." My voice cracked. "I killed a woman in front of her son today."

"Oh my God. Are you okay, Alicia? You're not hurt are you?"

"No. I mean, yes, I'm okay. I'm not hurt just really, really upset right now."

"Ah. Baby, I've got a deposition to prepare for. We have a huge case coming up. I'm meeting Brandon in an hour at P.F. Chang's in Town Center. I'll be home right after that. Promise, okay?"

"I thought he was like your archenemy on cases or something. You know what? Never mind. Bye." I hung up without waiting for him to say good-bye back.

My marriage to Davin was nothing like I'd imagined at times. His job always seemed to come first if it wasn't life or death; my life or death to be more specific.

"Lo, Davin says he's meeting someone at P.F. Chang's to go over a deposition." I'd managed to ask the question in the back of my mind without actually asking it.

"You can't talk about something like that in public," Lo replied matter-of-factly, shaking his head and twisting his mouth up.

"That's what I thought."

"Is everything okay between you two? I mean shit, you just called your man about taking someone's life and literally got brushed off."

I took a deep breath and said, "Can you do me a favor? I can't use a squad car because he'd notice it and I can't use mine."

"Now, I'm used to women asking, you know, to get all up in the back seat of the Pimp Mobile and yada yada. But are you asking to use it for a stakeout?"

He was smiling at me mischievously, but that was exactly what I was asking. After what I'd been through today, Davin should have come up with a better excuse if he wanted to blow me off for an early dinner date.

After taking a quick cold shower in the station locker room and changing back into my civilian clothes it wasn't long before we were sitting across the street from P.F. Chang's.

I decided to make small talk to help pass the time. "Have you heard anything about where they're going to place the Sherman Case?"

Sherman & Waltman was a multimillion dollar investment company that had gotten robbed a few days earlier. Nothing was taken except several hard drives. One held a shitload of hot stock profiles and the others held every banking, checking, and credit card account for every one of their clients.

"Al, you did not hear this from me." Lorenzo looked around as if someone outside might hear us inside the car. "They were saying if we can get one or two more busts after the one like today it might be us."

"Yeah, right! Good joke. That would be like you actually getting ass in this car, Lo." I couldn't keep the laughter out of my voice.

"Woman, this is a 1987 Cutlass Supreme. My baby is a classic like Coca-Cola; that's why she's red."

I couldn't help laughing at him then. He was so damn serious, rubbing his hands all across the dashboard, making kissy faces.

"She's like you, *mi hermosa*. A classic." His voice was a low, sultry whisper.

"What's that supposed to mea . . ." The words caught in my throat and shock must have been written all over my face because Lorenzo turned in time to see Davin. He was walking toward the restaurant. But, with the way his arm was draped around the hips of the woman he was walking beside, I highly doubted that was Brandon. Before I could even think about what I was doing, I was out of the car and across the street.

"Who the fuck is this? This is Brandon? Is Brandon a Tranny? Why you got your arm around this bitch? This doesn't look like Brandon to me, Davin!" I slapped Davin on the back of his head. Tears were running down my face, streaking my eyeliner.

Davin jumped and spun around, throwing his hands up as if he were being robbed. People on the street stopped and stared; some of them pulled out their camera phones.

"Bitch? Who the hell are you calling a bitch?" She-man aka his date began to storm toward me. I reached into the back waistband of my pants and pulled out my personal .45. They always keep your service weapon at the station after it's been involved in a shooting. They gave me a pamphlet that mentioned something about, de-stressing and psychological kill switches. I didn't read it. I never leave home without a gun and a backup gun. Period.

"Davin, get her in check before I kill her."

"Alicia. What the hell are you doing here? This is my client. We are meeting Brandon. He's inside."

Lorenzo ran over and grabbed me around the waist. He picked me up, spun around, and was carrying me back toward the car before I could say or do anything.

"Now is not the time, Al. You have a career to consider. He ain't worth this shit."

***

Lorenzo dropped me off at my car and I drove the entire way home in silence. There was enough chatter in my head to keep me company on the ride. Davin hadn't been answering my calls all afternoon and here it was going on eight and he still wasn't home. Even though I was tired and drained there was no way I could lie in our bed not knowing what or who might have been in it. I was sitting on the couch when he walked in.

"I guess you had a good pre-deposition?" My voice was cold and dry.

He accidentally dropped his keys, quickly spinning around at the sound of my voice. "I didn't think you were home. Why are you sitting up in here in the dark?" Davin asked as he stared at me cautiously, waiting for his eyes to adjust to the dark.

"I don't know. Maybe it's because I had the honor of killing two people today. And it's shocking because I feel really bad even though my badge means I don't get in any trouble. I'm learning that killing people isn't hard. Maybe because right now I'm staring at my husband who hasn't been answering my calls all day . . . who I saw at P.F. Chang's with another woman and I'm thinking about killing again." I sat, unmoving, my eyes silently burning angry holes into every inch of his body.

His eyes finally adjusted and widened as they moved to my pistol sitting in front of me on the coffee table. A sheen of sweat broke out on his forehead. "Wh . . . what are you talking about? You were wrong for coming up there like that, Alicia. That was a very important daughter of a client I'm trying to persuade to take the witness stand. You almost scared her off and that could've cost me more than you'll ever know."

"You think real hard about that lie you're telling me." My voice was emotionless as stone and cold as the tile floor he was standing on.

He walked over cautiously and kneeled in front of me. "Alicia, you are my heart and soul. Baby, I need her as a witness. I also need the witness there in order to go over the questions that the defense is going to ask her. We spend enough time in our offices and courtrooms I thought it'd be a nice break. Brandon was already inside when we got there."

His forehead creased in a tight frown; then he asked, "Are you spying on me?" He spat the word "spying" out as if it tasted bad in his mouth.

"Just today, yes. Your story was suspicious. You know what I went through with my ex."

"Baby, I've told you over and over I'm not your ex, remember? Not everyone is bad." He kissed me softly before standing and pulling me up into his arms.

My guard dropped and I inhaled his warm, musky, masculine scent. "Mmm. You smell good. You started wearing your Armani again. I love it." Burying my face into his neck I kissed the letters "I'm sorry" into his warm, smooth skin.

He moaned quietly before stopping me. "Don't get me started, woman. You know I've got to be up early and you should be getting up to work out." He looked down at me seriously.

"Or my husband can work me out," I answered, giving him my best coy look while batting my lashes.

"I'm serious. You've been getting lax and your safety is contingent upon your reaction time and your fitness. Now, you know I love you more than anything." He waited, as was his custom.

Disappointed, I sighed and kissed his waiting lips. "I love you too, baby I'll weigh myself tomorrow."

Chapter 6

My Blood Brother

Long holiday weekends always bring out the freaks and the drama. Eleven p.m. on the Fourth of July weekend and I was stuck working the back end of a double shift on a Saturday night.

"Unit 440, we have a disturbance in Town Center at the Westin Hotel."

My police radio had been going off nonstop all damn day. It was that time of year when people drank way too much and between the illegal fireworks and barbecue fistfights my hands were full. I was sitting in front of a 7-Eleven while my partner refilled our coffee mugs inside.

"Ten-four. It's not like I have anything better to do. Shoot me the details."

My tone was overly sarcastic, but this late in the night I really didn't care how Liddy, the operator, took it. She'd been giving me attitude since the day she found out my husband was a criminal defense attorney. He was one of the most successful and well-respected men in Hampton Roads. Sexy, intelligent, and wealthy, yet none of that mattered at the precinct once people found out who he was and what he did.

The defense attorney's main purpose was to do the exact opposite of what we did as cops. They represented the criminally charged to try to get them a fair trial. Sometimes justice was served and sometimes you had very guilty and very dangerous people who walked away unpunished because of men like my husband.

"The hotel owner called in a fight on the eighteenth floor. We have a black male fighting loudly with two black females. Hotel security has them detained."

"Copy that, we're on our way."

Lorenzo got in the car just in time for me to put on the lights and siren. "Damn, another one?" He was irritated. We hadn't gotten a break all night.

"Now, my dear, dear man, you know I'm always Liddy's favorite. At least it's making the night go by."

I flashed him a smirk as I hit the gas, wheeling our older-model 2011 Impala out of the parking lot. Recent cutbacks had our squadron last on the list to get the newer Camaros everyone else was flying around the city in. I made it a point to drive our piece of shit like a stolen rental car every chance I got. Maybe if the wheels fell off or the transmission exploded, the commissioner would finally get up off of some money.

Town Center was the social hub of Virginia Beach. There were bars and chic restaurants all over the place. Restaurant patios were crowded with rowdy twenty- and thirty-something's enjoying the summer nightlife. We were making our way into the entrance of the hotel when something prompted me to look around. Nothing seemed out of place; couples were spaced out here and there enjoying the night. Armani For Him drifted toward me on a warm breeze and I immediately thought of my husband and smiled; it used to be one his favorite colognes. He was working late tonight too, stuck on an important case.

"Lo, can you go inside and handle this? I need to make a call real quick."

"Sure thing. They're all in the security office. Shouldn't be much to deal with." Even if it was a hostile situation I was pretty sure once they saw all 284 pounds of Lorenzo's six foot four inch Dominican frame coming, shit would die down.

I stood outside and dialed my husband's number. There were still trust issues on my side of the situation, and if he didn't answer in so many rings best believe we'd be swinging past his damn office. Leaning up against a pillar I tried to take some pressure off my feet. I'd only been out of the academy and in a squad car for a year and the shoes just seemed like they'd never feel right on my feet.

"Hello, my beautiful one." His voice was deep and quiet.

I could almost hear the smile in his tone. "Hello, handsome. I was just thinking about you. My night has been pure hell."

I glanced up, distracted as two young girls strolled past me holding hands. They were laughing, leaning into each other. I was secretly envious. Overhead locusts buzzed loudly in the few trees that lined the streets. Even from here I could smell the mouthwatering waffle cake batter and homemade chocolate sauce, indicating that the Häagen-Dazs parlor two blocks over was making fresh waffle cones. All the sounds and smells mingling with the salt-tinged ocean air were making me nostalgic to have my man with me.

"How are things at the office?" I tried to sound as nonchalant as I possibly could. There was no point in stressing him out. It was his salary that afforded us the house we lived in and the cars we drove. The little bit of money I made at the department sure as hell didn't cover half of the nice things we enjoyed. Not the ski trips to Aspen in the winter or our summer cruises to the Bahamas. My baby paid for all of that, not me.

"Oh, everything's fine. It's hell in here tonight too. I lost the Padilla murder trial today. They gave him life. It was some messy shit with honest and good police work. No one's gonna be happy about it, that's for sure."

"I'm sorry, baby. Want me to bring you something home to eat? I can stop by Boston Market or I can cook. You know I don't mind, even if it's late."

"Nah, we got a lot to hammer out at the office. Press conference tomorrow. I've got to make sure the partners are covered on this one. We're taking a pretty big hit."

A car sped past and instinctively my eyes followed it, calculating its speed. They should have gotten a ticket doing about forty in a twenty-five. It drew my eyes toward a couple making out in the shadows up against the side of the parking garage across the street. They were leaning into each other. One was kissing the other's neck as they leaned on the side of a building in the shadows. It was hard to make out any details, but I was on duty and this was Virginia Beach; an indecent exposure ticket would definitely help me fill my quota for the month.

"Well my shift ends at one and if Lorenzo doesn't issue any tickets or haul anyone in I should be home by one-thirty. You'll be home when I get there, right?"

A fire truck whizzed by on an adjacent street, sirens blaring, scaring the living crap out of me. As it moved farther down the street its echo rang loudly in the phone. *Impossible; it couldn't be.* I glanced around but there was no one else on the street. I squinted and waited for the blare of the horn to get out of hearing distance and my eyes zoned in on the two men still feeling each other up in the shadows. Heart racing, my mouth dried and my ears were on sonar and lie detector at the same time.

"Baby, I thought you were in the office. Why'd I just hear a siren?" I tried to sound as candid as possible. The last thing we needed was another suspicious wife argument.

"Huh? Siren? No, no sirens over here. Must have been a delay from the one I just heard on your end. You okay?"

"Yeah, I'm fine. It's been a long day. I love you. See you in a few."

"Love you more."

I put my phone back into the holster on my hip, my eyes never leaving the couple across the way. They'd started walking again toward a garage on the other side of the street. My police instincts kicked in, screaming for me to follow. I walked quickly, keeping to the shadows on the sidewalk. I was no more than ten feet behind them when my heart froze in my chest. Realization draped itself around my brain, and it was a dark, cold, and empty curtain of feeling. I recognized my husband's long, slow strides as they crossed the street to enter the garage. The entryway light illuminated them both and the sound of his laughter floating to my ears as he chuckled at something the other man said. I went through a mental Rolodex of faces I'd seen in his office, at his gym, friends from his golfing trips.

When it dawned on me, I knew he was walking arm in arm with Brandon, one of the newer attorneys I'd met at last year's Christmas party. The same one from P.F. Chang's. He was a gym rat they all suspected used steroids, but aside from that he was the second-best attorney at the firm. Walking next to Davin he looked like a thickly muscled caramel warrior in his fitted T-shirt and slacks. It was beyond ironic seeing them together, especially since Davin complained about him day and night. He claimed he'd steal his cases, slow down his research; even bad-mouth him to the other attorneys.

Momentarily dazed, I stood frozen in the middle of the street. I replayed the scene that I'd just witnessed in my mind, trying to convince myself that what I was seeing wasn't really happening. I lost sight of them as they walked into the garage and my feet felt like cement bricks as I made myself go forward.

He was drunk, and holding him up.

Who was drunk and who was holding who up?

And, he was holding him up against the side of a building kissing his neck?

And then arm and arm across the street?

There were a million conversations going on in my mind at one time, as if arguing with myself was going to clarify things. My hands were starting to shake and despite the heat of the night, I'd broken out into a cold sweat. I entered the garage not more than a few feet behind them and followed soundlessly as they walked toward Davin's silver Mercedes SLS coupe parked in a back corner. His "trophy" was what I called it. The only time he'd drive it to work was if someone big would be there to see him in it, or he'd be having lunch with a higher-ranking partner. It was also the one car he never let me drive or ride in because he said I couldn't handle it; it was a "man's" car. As if I could somehow depreciate its precious value.

I crept over and crouched slightly behind a blue cargo van with the words Sugar Shack etched on the side, and stared through the side window. My finger was clammy and sticky as I slid it along the butt of the pistol in my holster. *What are you thinking?* I silently asked myself, or maybe I asked Davin.

The question churned over and over inside my head, but there was no forthcoming answer.

I watched as they climbed inside the car. Brandon leaned across the center console and kissed my husband of two years full on the mouth. My reaction to the scene taking place before me was no less than that of gut-churning horror, disbelief, and disgust as my husband leaned into the kiss and returned it just as passionately.

They looked like two high school kids, sneaking to get it in before going home from a date.

I didn't know I was crying until the tears started to pool beneath my chin, making my collar wet and scratchy against my throat. My stomach was in a knot so tight it felt like I was going to break in half from the pain. Anger, hatred, disbelief, so many emotions were running through me all at once that my body physically shook.

There was no way that was my husband. That was not the man who stood in front of me at the altar with the loving gaze as he recited his own fucking vows before putting the ring on my hand. My head involuntarily shook back and forth as I stared in disbelief. There was no way that was the man who slept beside me every single night. The man I cooked for, cared for when he was sick, helped grieve when his parents passed.

Their hands were fumbling below the dash and I could only imagine what they were doing to each other as they continued to tongue each other down as if the world were coming to an end. Brandon was the first to break free; smiling seductively he said something and ran his fingers along my husband's lips before climbing out of the car. I could see the idiotic grin spread across Davin's face all the way from where I was standing as he popped the trunk and they both go out and walked toward the back of the car.

He was parked up against a back wall in the corner and it pretty much blocked anyone who drove or walked past from seeing them. But from where I was standing I could see it all. A movie played in my mind of me running over, screaming, and firing my weapon repeatedly, but I stood my ground. I needed to see exactly what would happen if they weren't interrupted so I couldn't be lied to or told something other than what I'd witnessed with my own eyes.

Brandon leaned into the trunk, bracing himself with one hand and the other holding his pants just below his waist. I closed my eyes as my husband freed himself from his boxers and shared with this man something that he vowed before God to only share with me. Their breathing was heavy, and I could hear them both making low moaning and grunting sounds. Someone's belt buckle rhythmically clanked against the bumper of the car accenting each thrust, grunt, and moan. Clank. Clank. Clank. Clank. Damn, why'd this particular experience have to be marked with the soundtrack from hell? Clank. Clank. Clank.

"Al? What in God's name . . . ?"

My eyes snapped open as Lorenzo's voice trailed off; instinctively I stepped out from the van toward him. His eyes moved from my distraught appearance to Davin and Brandon going at it behind the car. At the sound of his voice they'd both jumped, quickly trying to regain their composure and fix their clothes; but they hadn't jumped quickly enough. Lorenzo had seen enough to know what was going on. Everything after that happened in the blink of an eye.

"You motherfucka!" Lorenzo shouted, his voice echoing through the garage like a lion's roar. He launched past me across the garage and grabbed Davin by the neck, who was still fumbling, trying to get his pants up. Davin glanced briefly in my direction, his expression a mixture of surprise, fear, and pleading. His pants were hanging around his ankles as his manhood deflated and hung pitifully between his legs.

Well damn, at least his cheating ass wore a condom.

Lorenzo and Davin were about the same size; they were matched pretty evenly. Brandon rushed up behind Lorenzo and punched him in the back of the head, causing him to release my husband. Paralyzed, I watched my partner fight with this gladiator of a man who looked like he should be in somebody's arena, not working in an office.

In the midst of all this, Davin staggered back toward his car. Tears were streaming from his sad brown eyes as he pulled up his pants and tried to straighten up his clothes. He could barely make eye contact with me, and yet I couldn't take my eyes off of him. I watched his long, thick fingers as he fumbled with his belt and the clanking replayed in my head.

The fighting grabbed my attention as the two men slammed into the side of a rust orange Nissan 370Z so hard I was surprised it didn't tip over. Brandon landed a punch to Lo's jaw. Stunned, Lo fell backward and my husband, now suddenly full of anger and rage at being discovered and assaulted, seized this moment. Like a guided missile he launched himself toward Lorenzo as Brandon ran over to the Mercedes and reached into the trunk. Pulling out a .45 he turned and fired wildly without aiming.

I screamed. I screamed so loud that I didn't even hear the gun blast. My husband fell forward, his eyes widened in shock as he landed at Lorenzo's feet; he was dead before he hit the ground.

"Oh God, no. Davin! Davin!" Brandon's high-pitched wail resonated through the silent, empty garage as he dropped the pistol and rushed to kneel beside my husband. A place where I should have been, cradling my husband's head in my lap.

Before I could feel any more resentment, or hurt, loss, or even fury at this man on his knees crying over my man, Lorenzo drew his weapon, smashing Brandon across the back of the head. The blow knocked him unconscious and then Lorenzo fired one shot, killing him.

He kicked Davin's pistol closer toward Brandon's body and pulled his radio from its holder on his shoulder.

"Unit 440 calling in shots fired at the Town Center Garage. We were leaving an adjacent hotel. I overhead two males arguing. I saw one draw his weapon and fire. I returned fire when he refused to lower his weapon. Over."

"Ten-four, unit 440. Backup on the way."

Chapter 7

The Afterlife After Death, After Death

"No one's ever gonna find out about what happened here, Al. I already thought all the details through, sweetheart."

Shuffling the wool blanket tighter around my shoulders, I shivered despite the heat of the night. Scenes from what I'd just witnessed flashed before me. How could my husband have done those things with another man, and now?

"You just tell them you were in the car the entire time and ran to cover me when you heard the shots fired. Now, I already ran upstairs and deleted the surveillance footage so they can't prove anything more than what we tell them."

Lorenzo paced beside the squad car, his face drawn into a grisly frown as he quietly barked orders like some sort of insane commanding officer.

When the other units arrived I did exactly as Lo said. For appearance's sake it looked as though we were the first to arrive on the scene of a regular homicide. My part wasn't that hard to play. I was visibly distraught and upset when Lo explained what he'd witnessed to the other officers.

After all was said and done I was commended on how well I handled myself and given time off to recover. That was the longest and toughest six months of my life. I questioned everything, even my own life. I'd seen too much death and it was starting to break me down.

Most of my time was spent locked away in the house going over all the minor details, connecting the dots. Reporters, being the soulless jackals they were, didn't even give me time to mourn or recover. They were everywhere, even at his funeral.

The third most devastating day of my life had to be when I found out the only things I'd get out of his death were the house and two cars. Technically our marriage wasn't legal because he was already married. His attorneys wouldn't and couldn't tell me anything more; they were apparently under some kind of legal gag order. The fool actually had a living will where he had the audacity to list me only as his "live-in mate," and I waited for the woman's name but she was only mentioned as the "intended late wife and distributee." If he weren't already dead I would have killed him then and there.

I'd gotten questioned relentlessly about some Sherman & Waltman financial holdings he'd miraculously liquidated right before their hard drives were stolen and his murder. I all but laughed in the investigator's face, telling him I did not have my husband murdered for the money. If I was clueless to the fact that my husband had a secret gay lover and another wife, I sure as hell wouldn't know if he was planning to defraud and rob a multimillion dollar company.

Lorenzo did all he could to keep me from killing myself, or eating myself to death. It's a shame but I probably survived on ice-cold beers and chocolate chip cookies; there's probably no better combination in this world. Baking and drinking were the only things that kept me from going insane. It wasn't the healthiest strategy, but it kept me sane.

"Woman, you can't survive on cookies and beer forever; you have to rejoin the world eventually."

Lorenzo always stopped by to check on me after work and bring groceries that I never touched. He was busy putting Lord knows what into my fridge and I was just praying he'd remembered my Coronas.

"I'll be fine, Lo. Did you try to pull the files from the last case he who I wish not to name was working on?"

It was a sunny afternoon but you wouldn't know it from the tightly drawn curtains in the entire house. I hit one of the dimmer switches and set the lights to low so I could peek through the paper bags. My heart sank.

"No files. You've been gone for a minute, woman. The chief wants the department to be the new guinea pig for this new system call PATTI."

"PATTI? What the hell is that?" I'd never heard of the system before my leave started.

Lo stopped what he was doing and gave me an empathetic half smile. "Paperless Accounting Tracking Transcribing Information System. Needless to say, a team went in and uploaded our case files." He paused and took a breath. "Um, they shredded the originals. We went live and, uh, they're still working out all the kinks."

"Kinks? What the hell do you mean kinks? And you can't justify getting rid of hard-copy case files, Lo. What kind of shit is that?"

He crossed the kitchen and pulled me into a tight hug. I struggled against him and he fought just as hard to hold me. So many things were working against me that I just wanted to bend under all of it, break down, and never get back up again.

He cooed and clucked like I was some kind of scared puppy. "Calm down, *bella,* sweetheart; everything will be fine. Lorenzo will take care of it. Let me take care of it." He kissed the top of my head softly and anger, frustration, hurt, all these emotions welled up within me.

I wasn't his to take care of. I didn't need taking care of by anyone. Someone always seemed to be taking care of me.

Breaking free of his hold I glowered at him. "I don't need this. Not right now. Take care of me so what? So you can be having 'guy only' meetings at the gym or, what, a side ho? Get mad and want to put your hands on someone or kill someone? We've seen how you take care of things, Lorenzo!" I yelled and tears fell down my face.

Lorenzo bit at his upper lip and nodded in understanding. "I'll see myself out. You need time and I was way out of line. Your Coronas are on the bottom shelf. You know where I'll be."

He let himself out and I collapsed on the couch, content with staring forlornly at the same Hello Kitty pattern on my house pants that I'd been wearing all week.

I couldn't help wondering how many nights he spent with his real wife, and how long they were actually married. Where did she live and why did he marry me? Did they have a bad divorce, maybe, and she refused to sign paperwork or faked signing paperwork? Was she a real woman or was she transgendered? Maybe that's why he married her. Did he try to keep her in the gym or have a fit if her weight changed?

I tried to squelch the thoughts of my ex-boyfriend but they wouldn't stay at bay. Davin was no better than Tarique. They both distorted my self-image. But, thanks to my husband I was down to 18 percent body fat, walking around looking like a skinny, well-muscled boy, and for what? Because Davin actually preferred well-muscled dudes over women.

Anger still seared through me at the thought of how he'd pushed me to work out when we'd first met. Telling me how good I'd look if I'd just drop a few more pounds.

I'd worked so hard to recover from the mental damage Tarique subjected me to after my father's murder.

He basically molded me into the woman I'd become. And maybe he was scared that I'd leave him because his mother had abandoned him when he was little. Maybe that's why he felt he needed to break me both physically and mentally in order to keep me. I'd never know. For five years, I was a firefly in a mason jar. My refuge was also my purgatory.

There were so many nights when I'd do nothing but lie in my bed, physically bruised and mentally drained, crying, wanting nothing more than to go home, and I couldn't. Tarique would find me and kill me for leaving; he'd told me in more ways than one and with so much passion burning in his eyes that I believed him.

That seemed like a lifetime ago now. A foggy picture in a fuzzy frame, from a grey, dreary, and rainy day that was so old it'd started fading. Sometimes I'd try, but I could never remember exactly which direction the rain fell from, how cold or hard it felt as it hit my face in the form of fists or Timberlands. In a few years this mess with Davin would feel like that too. I'd considered quitting the police force but decided to stay on. The main reason I'd joined was to bring some kind of peace to women who suffered as I had.

The second reason I joined was to find my father's murderer; it was still an unsolved cold case file. I scoffed. PATTI better not have lost that file or I'd go ballistic when I got back. My mother was somewhere in the area but I'd never bothered looking her up, just like she'd never bothered looking for me. Lorenzo was like my blood brother now—my one and only true friend.

"Hey. Don't you dare run from this fucking ass whooping," a voice shouted from inside.

I was standing on the stoop outside of a run-down Section 8 home off of Little Creek Road. Lorenzo was a few feet behind me with his hand on the holster of his weapon. He nodded. I always got anxious when we answered domestic disturbance calls.

My thoughts turned briefly to Tarique and our one-bedroom tenement in New York. It was crammed between a twenty-four-hour Chinese spot and a building that served as a studio, pool hall, and a barbershop. Our kitchen was twelve ashen grey tiles long. I'd lain there enough times to count them. Even now, the scent of Chinese food drifted over from the China King on the corner. The pungent odor of stir fried garlic and General Tao chicken was making my stomach churn. Funny how his tough love still affected me. The only way he knew how to show love was with his damn fists. It seemed like such a long time ago, almost ten years to be exact. Long before I'd joined the police force and many years before I'd learned my value as a woman.

A woman's high-pitched cry from inside the apartment drew me back to the situation at hand. I knocked solidly and loudly on the wooden door, red paint flaking off with the thud of my fist.

"Police. Open up," I called out, deepening my voice to sound more authoritative.

The crisp November wind shuffled brightly colored leaves and Doritos bags across the yard, cooling my face and neck. It had an almost calming effect on my nerves and my queasy stomach. A tall, light-skinned female with shoulder-length dreads opened the front door. She was dressed as a male in a black button-down shirt and khakis, a "stud" I assumed. That's what they're known as throughout the gay community. A community I'd taken a strong disliking to after Davin's little incident, but I couldn't let my disdain for someone's sexual preference show in my treatment of them. I could clearly smell marijuana reeking from her clothing and from within the home.

"Someone called in about a domestic disturbance at this address. Do you mind if we come inside and check things out?" I asked, looking up at the tall, boyish, somewhat attractive woman.

She cocked her head back, rubbing her lips together while she frowned down on my heavy, five foot four inch frame through glassy, high eyes. She was calculating. I looked small, hard to wrestle but easy to outrun if she could get past me. She glanced just beyond my shoulder at Lorenzo, my partner in crime prevention, and I could see the thoughts of fleeing or fighting me leave her mind almost immediately.

"I don't know what the hell they call you for. Ain't nothing going on in here for nobody to need the police," she replied angrily.

"Either you're going to let us in, or I'm gonna take you down right now and make my way in. The option's yours. My way's gonna involve some pain and maybe a night in a holding cell, so I'd suggest you just step aside." Lorenzo moved forward to stand beside me, his hand still on his pistol in the holster.

"Well fuck it then. *Mi casa es su casa,* shit."

Lorenzo walked in ahead of me and I motioned for the female to move back inside. I followed closely behind her to make sure she didn't try to bolt through the door. It took a minute for my eyes to adjust to the dim interior and I took everything in at a glance as we were taught in the academy. The apartment was scarcely furnished and it was a complete mess. Evidence of a fight or a struggle was apparent. There was a coffee table turned over onto its side and one of the legs was broken off. Clothing was scattered along hardwood flooring that probably needed a broom, a Swiffer Wet Jet, hell maybe even a sandblaster taken to it to help remove some of the dirt. My shoes felt like they had suction cups attached to the bottoms. They stuck to the floor with each step I took, fighting not to openly cringe at the obvious filthiness of the place.

I turned to address the female. "Where is she?" I knew she was scared. She was probably in the bathroom trying to fix herself up to look like nothing happened. That's exactly what I would have done; well, what I used to do.

The stud walked over and sat on a black leather love seat that was so tattered and torn it must have been a scratching post for someone's kitten in its former life. Dropping her head into her hands she started to pour her heart out to us.

"She was cheating on me, dude. Flat out fucking somebody else and lying to me. I pay all the bills up in here, every single one. I don't make her pay for shit, and she return the favor by giving my cookie away." Tears streamed down her cheeks, through her hands. "How the fuck you gonna do me like this, Tia?" She jumped up in an angry outburst and began pacing.

My hand flew to my holster on my hip and Lo stepped forward, ready to take her down if needed. Lorenzo looked in my direction, his eyebrows raised in confusion.

"What's your name?" I asked sternly.

"Everybody call me Vee."

Lorenzo stepped forward, "Okay, Vee? Let me get this right, you got us called out here over some cookies? Is that code for something or, or some kind of slang term for marijuana? I smell it all up in here." Lorenzo's question was so far off the mark I wanted to slap him in the forehead for the poor girl.

"Naw, dude, she was giving my pussy away. Cookie—pussy. It just don't sound so crude man. Damn. Where you from? What do it matter though? Either way she a cheating-ass ho!"

"Okay, Vee. I'ma need you to just calm down and take a seat while I go check on Tia okay?" I stared at her, waiting for confirmation.

She nodded and I nodded to Lorenzo to watch her while I made my way farther into the home to look for this Tia woman. The place was small so she had to be close by. To the left of the living room was a tiny kitchen, if you could even call it that; it was more like four linoleum tiles with a refrigerator and a long counter. I glanced past the counter just to make sure no one was there. A darkened hallway was to the right that led to the bedrooms and bathroom behind the couch where Vee sat. I made my way in that direction, my eyes roving back and forth, searching for movement.

"Hello, ma'am. I'm an armed police officer and I'm here to help you. I need you to come out or answer me if you can't."

I could hear muffled crying from behind a closed door at the end of the hall. There were two other doors on either side and I opened them and did a quick sweep just to make sure there was no one else in the home. Satisfied, I walked back to the closed door that I assumed to be the bathroom. I checked the knob; it was unlocked. I took a deep breath and turned the knob slowly.

Tears instantly sprang to my eyes, mentally shaking myself. It was pep talk time. *Turn off your "care switch," Alicia; let the cop take over. You need to be the cop now; you are not a person.* She was lying on her side on the floor, facing the bathtub, wearing nothing but a green cotton bath towel. I took in all the details that I could just from looking at her. *Female, early to mid-twenties, twenty-four at the oldest. Height four foot nine inches or five feet even. Ethnicity, biracial possibly. Drug user? Possible. Injuries, not life threatening but should seek medical attention.*

"H . . . hello, Tia? I'm Officer Taylor. Are you okay, sweetie?"

She was curled into herself, hugging her knees to her chest. She shook her head no but she wouldn't turn to face me.

"Taylor? You good back there or what?" Lorenzo sounded like he was getting impatient.

"Yeah, we're good. Give me a minute," I called back before crouching down a few feet away from the girl. "Sweetie, I need to make sure you're okay. I can't leave unless you tell me everything is fine. I need you to turn around and talk to me."

She sat up slowly and turned to face me. My heart instantly went out to her. She was beautiful. Not your average kind of everyday beauty, I mean beautiful like supermodel or TV-star beautiful. There was a small cut on the corner of her mouth but I could visibly see no other marks on her heart-shaped face. She looked up at me through slanted, cat-shaped brown eyes with golden flecks, and I paused. I quietly took in a few deep breaths but couldn't figure out why she seemed somewhat familiar.

"I'm good, Officer. We just had an argument. We argue all the time and this one was the worst but really, ma'am, I'm fine." Her words gave me time to recover.

"You sure about that? This looks like more than an argument to me, sweetheart. Shouldn't nobody ever put their hands on you. Can you tell me exactly what happened?"

She hugged the thin cotton towel closer to her body and looked away as tears rolled down her cheeks. "I left my laptop signed on and she checked my Facebook page. Niggas flirt with me all the time and I flirt back but I don't do anything. . . ." Her voice caught in her throat.

"Do you wanna press charges? We can take Vee in until she cools down but you'll have to press charges against her. I also suggest you get to a hospital and get yourself checked out."

She tried to talk between crying hiccups. "No. She doesn't mean it. I'm good. She'll be fine once she calms down."

I moved closer and knelt down beside her, compassion written all over my face. My heart always went out to women who allowed themselves to stay in these types of situations, gay or not.

"Sweetie, love isn't supposed to be like this. Love isn't supposed to beat you up no matter how hurt or mad love gets. Here, take my card." I handed her one of the business cards I'd had made with the precinct's phone number and my cell phone number. Her fingers were ice cold as they brushed slightly against mine.

"I said don't fucking move." Lorenzo's voice bellowed through the walls.

Commotion from the living room and Lorenzo's tone made my blood run cold. I rushed to my feet and ran back toward the front of the house. Vee was lying on the floor, blood trickling from her nose.

"What happened?" Wide-eyed I stared at Lo, waiting for an answer.

Tia dashed past me and dropped to her knees beside Vee. "Really? What did you do to her? What the hell did you do?"

Lorenzo's eyes widened angrily for a split second at the towel-covered girl, before sneering down at them and cutting his eyes angrily in my direction. "That's it. We're taking her in. She made a move like she was going for something, I told her ass stay still and she didn't. I ain't takin' any chances out here."

I quickly regained my composure. This wasn't the time or the place to second-guess him; I needed to back my partner up. We would go over the details later, but in front of civilians we needed to be on the same page.

Letting out a loud sigh I looked down at Vee and said, "Stand up and turn your back to me please."

She was moving slowly, still hazy from the blow to the face and still heavily under the influence from whatever she'd smoked or drunk before we arrived. Tia was staring up at us, anger, maybe hatred, and something else mirrored in those ghostly familiar eyes of hers.

"Do you have anything on you, in your pockets that I need to know about? Any drugs or syringes? I need to pat you down and I'm not one for any surprises right now," I asked her in a dry tone.

She shook her head no and I gave her a quick pat down, taking her ID and handing it to Lo before pulling my cuffs out and handcuffing her hands behind her back. We led her out of the house; neighbors were standing on their porches, loitering around nearby in the street. I looked back at Tia standing in the doorway still wearing nothing but her bath towel, tears streaming down her cheeks, her wavy hair falling wildly around her face. I couldn't help feeling sorry for her, but I damn sure couldn't show it. Compassion, caring, and all that other BS are the main reasons women on the force are given such a hard time. I climbed into the driver's side of the patrol car and focused my thoughts toward all the damn paperwork we were about to fill out, and how the hell we were going to explain Vee's busted nose.

"Eh, momma, look like you got yourself a few warrants in Norfolk and Hampton. I guess you're going to be staying up in our house for a little while huh?" Chuckling, Lo continued looking over the rest of Vee's file on the car's computer.

I wasn't laughing though. All this meant was that poor girl back at the house was going to catch even more hell behind this domestic disturbance when this girl finally got out.

My head was throbbing and the lines on the road looked like they were running together. Maybe I'd rushed things and come back too early. I probably should have taken a little more time off. My blood pressure was up, and I hadn't been working out or doing anything to prepare myself for this type of stress.

"Lo, you handle the paperwork on this one when we get back. I need a break."

"What's the deal, Al? First you come back all extra thickalicious and, what, now you got a hot date you trying to skip off to?"

My grip tightened on the steering wheel. I'd had to hear all kinds of bullshit about my weight since coming back. Granted I'd gone from a size nothing back to my "normal" weight, but damn. The guys were all shell-shocked and I was shell-sick of hearing it. It wasn't Lo's fault, I couldn't blame him; he didn't know how self-conscious I was about my weight gain.

"No, Lorenzo, my mind just needs a moment to wind down after stuff like this. It's been awhile, you know that." I gave him a weak yet reassuring smile and he nodded in return.

Chapter 8

Define The Word "Con"
(Tia's Definition)

"No, Hemingway, I swear this really ain't my fault."

"Anyone ever tell you that 'ain't' is not a proper word? It offends my ears. Refrain from using it in your conversations with me. Anyway, explain to me, whose fault is it then, Tia? Rumors about my money spread faster than a ho in a houseful of diamond phalluses, sweetheart. And rumor has it, no one dropped off those hard drives from the Sherman job. So, did you really just call me asking if I could help bail your mannish woman friend out of jail?" Hemingway's voice was sickening sweet and unnervingly soft in my ear.

My hands and my voice were both shaking. "Hemingway, that's why I need her. We had to—"

"Oh, Tia, still the needy one are we? Well, I am going do you a favor, sweetheart. I am giving you a crash course in empowerment. It's seven days long and all it costs is your life."

I stared at my Samsung Galaxy 3 in disgust as the line went silent. It cost too damn much to throw, and even though I didn't buy it, it was a gift from my ex, but I was so mad I definitely considered launching the thing across the room. I swore whenever things with Vee were going good that girl would find a way to go and mess them up.

This mess was getting old and fast. The last thing I wanted to do was leave her locked up but I damn sure wasn't looking forward to the rest of the ass whooping that I knew was coming when she got out either. I could only see one way out of this situation and it wasn't going to be promising if I didn't get those hard drives for Hemingway. Vee said she'd had something set up but that was before I'd pissed her off so who knew where she'd stashed them or if she'd even tell me now. After this foolishness there was no way I could call my cousin or family for any favors to help out. Nobody liked Vee, and once my family found out she'd actually put her hands on me they'd all be up in arms ready to fight.

Leaving my Facebook open was by far one of the dumbest mistakes I'd ever made. Vee wasn't lying when she told that cop she took care of everything. She did, but she also treated me like an inmate in the process. I had to cut off all my closest friends, all my side hoes, side dick, too—especially my side dick. Hell, I was cool working my three to eleven p.m. shift up at the call center. It was Vee who cancelled that out.

She was all like, "Bae, you ain't gotta work, and I takes care of my woman from all perspectives. You just live here, look beautiful, and let me bless you with the best I have to offer."

Based on my lifestyle some people might call me a gold digger or a con artist, it's whatever. I'd personally like to consider myself nothing more than an opportunist. My last boyfriend, Capone, was a medical tech in the Navy. Each and every one of his friends was nothing more than a straight-up ho. They were constantly getting caught up for picking up underage girls at the high schools, mostly because they were young and foolish enough to fall for their wack-ass game. Capone was known for hooking his homeboys up for what he liked to call his "J Fund." Since he had easy access to the clinic's pharmacy, when they would get hit with chlamydia or trich he'd sell a few treatments on the side and use the money for new Jordans and jump-offs.

I had to correct that once I learned that a jump-off was his definition for chicks he dated just to get on, in, and then leave, aka "jump off." I made myself useful, suggested we partner up and start selling Plan B emergency contraceptive pills during lunch and study halls over at the high schools to any of the girls who needed it, not just the random ones his homeboys smashed and didn't want to get that support call from nine months later. I got myself a fake ID and everything just so I could blend in with the students.

It was golden until that fool got lazy and realized he could make more money if he substituted sugar pills in place of some of the actual Plan B pills. I couldn't lie; some of those high school chicks looked like grown women. I had to move three times just because one of them recognized me in my neighborhood after her Plan B failed. She didn't go for that whole "you probably waited longer than twenty-four to seventy-two hours" routine either. There's absolutely nothing funny about almost getting beat down by a three-months-pregnant seventeen-year-old Amazon.

Sincere was a dude I'd met while Capone was out to sea on deployment. He worked at the pharmacy at a twenty-four-hour Walgreens where I'd go to get hookups because they were just too lazy to ID on the boxes of Sudafed with ephedrine in it. At the time, you could buy a ton of those and sell them to the good old boys out Ocean View for triple what they cost because they'd use them to make meth. This was before they'd just scan your ID into the system. They couldn't buy them because they'd gotten busted so many times the police would camp out and watch for them, but I'd never been arrested so I had no problem.

You know how they say a woman knows if she'll want to sleep with a man within the first five minutes of meeting him? Well, let's just say that I knew within the first thirty-five seconds of laying eyes on Sincere's gorgeous ass that I was definitely going to cheat on Capone.

I'd take his dog tags that I'd been wearing on full display around my neck and stick them in my back pocket, purse, glove compartment; anywhere but in plain sight. Sincere was always working the late shift when I'd come through and that night was no different.

It was late summer, one of those kinds of nights where it's so hot you want to walk around naked. The damn AC in my little beat-up Honda was out so I hated life at the moment, and was riding around with all the windows down. Usher's "Follow Me" was playing on the radio as I pulled up to the pharmacy drive-through. That Negro was behind that glass, looking like a made-for-me version of Reggie Bush. His biceps made his crisp white lab coat fit a little too snugly in the arms. Something about his looks and that lab coat just didn't mesh. It was like he was meant to be moonlighting as a stripper for a bachelorette party, except that wasn't a damn costume. And all I wanted to know was what in the world was underneath all of that stiff professional material?

"So, umm, what are you doing later besides buying up all the Sudafed in Hampton Roads?"

I did my best to hide the ridiculous Kool-Aid grin that was fighting to spread across my face. As many times as I'd come up here, he'd never said more than, "Have a nice day." Guessed his man senses were on point and he could smell Capone's scent all over me every other time.

"I'm not sure yet; got a couple of invites to some parties but it's up in the air. What about you? What you getting into?"

Biting my lower lip I waited, as Usher sang in the background, "You came just in time with what I needed."

"Mmm, I was hoping you . . . I mean, damn. I meant to say, I was hoping you and I . . . I mean we could maybe . . . ah . . ."

I laughed so hard. He was fine as hell, smart as hell, and unbelievably awkward when it came to dealing with women.

"It's okay, sweetheart. You can do all the above. 757-303-0306. Call me when you get off."

We met for drinks at Martini Blue and it took him about a half of a bottle of Cuervo to lighten up. I tried to be good but I couldn't do it anymore. Capone had already been gone for two months, plus I'd been hearing all of these rumors about a girl out Newport News he'd gotten pregnant. On top of all that I needed my vitamin D, aka my daily dose of dick, something fierce.

Sincere was slurring, going on and on about some boring chemistry lectures. The only way I could think to shut him up was by kissing those sexy, thick, pink-pillow lips I couldn't seem to keep my eyes off of all night.

That was all it took. My body instantly felt like one of those fires that burn so hot and fast they consume all the oxygen in a closed room. With all the air suddenly gone the surfaces look cool and calm and the flames vanish, as if they've been magically extinguished. When in all actuality it's more like a bomb, and all the room needs is air.

I slid my hand out, creeping it up his leg to do "the test." It was like a door was flung open or a window was broken and the quiet flames all over my body were fed fresh oxygen as I damn near exploded in my seat. I hadn't even made it halfway up his thigh before my fingers struck gold and oooh wee this Negro was hard and huge.

The farthest we made it was to his Navigator parked out back. I guess the tequila made him bolder than he'd normally be as he pushed me up against the passenger-side door. He kissed me with those lips and simultaneously slid his thigh in between mine, wedging my legs apart. Instinctively my hips did their own thing and I ground into his strong, muscular leg. We both moaned, and I bit his lower lip just enough to let him know I wanted more.

He growled, and the sound made the hairs on the back of my neck stand up. Pausing for just a second he opened the door and spun me around into the car. I was leaning into the passenger seat as he stood behind me, lowering my panties from underneath my sun dress. Caught off guard I squealed in surprise when his hand roughly pressed down on my lower back, pushing my face farther down into the truck. That quickly turned into me trying to bite the stuffing out of this fool's peanut butter and dark brown leather seats.

His nails raked across my bare skin before he parted the seas and went straight deep sea diver on my ass from behind. Flicking his tongue softly across my clit one moment before stiffening it and thrusting so deep I had to look back and make sure it was still his tongue. On my life, I tried to pull away because the last thing I wanted was his nose all up in the crack of my sweaty ass. But he just wrapped his hands around my thighs, roughly pulling me back into his oral assault. The rhythmic lapping of his tongue suspending me in between a state where I didn't know if I wanted to cry or pass out. Shit, I was just happy I'd shaved that morning; he'd have been upset if he'd dropped them panties and found Chewbacca looking back at him.

My fingers had gone numb from gripping the seats so hard, and I was flexing them when I felt that first quiver. You know, that tremor that usually starts the avalanche. Letting out a deep, throaty moan that almost scared myself, I threw my ass so far back in his face I was surprised

I didn't knock him over. And then he stopped. I heard the condom wrapper tear open and I screamed and almost laughed, cried, and died at the same time.

It hadn't actually occurred to me how big of a big he was until I felt myself actually stretching around him. Size matters, girth matters, length matters. Dammit, it all matters. I swore he had to have been about as thick as a damn soda can. Every damn second was agonizing. It hurt so damn bad and so damn good at the same damn time. My entire damn body instantly went limp; it was absolute and complete damn sensory overload.

"Damn, damn, damn, damn," I whispered in between each stroke, my legs shaking like a drunken game of Jenga. "Damn? That's all you got for me, love?"

Yes, that's all I got, was the shouted-back reply in my head. I was downright stuck on some kind of "damn"-driven autopilot. And everyone knows you done ran up on some good dick if he got it so you can't even talk. Or if you can talk, I don't care if you got a doctorate degree in linguistics and can speak four languages fluently, if all you can say is one word because he's gone and knocked every other word you've ever known in your entire life completely up out of your vocabulary except that one, you done ran up on some good dick.

He actually laughed at me before going so deep I damn near screamed, "Damn," a couple of damn times. Leaning forward he started biting the back of my neck, sucking on my shoulders, giving me little back-gasms that took my breath away. Then to top all that off, this fool could make his dick pulse on command and he liked to get right there, so deep we probably looked conjoined. He pressed hard right up against my G-spot, and wrapped those big tree trunk arms tight around my waist, and started sucking on the side of my neck, and then thump. Thump. Thump. It felt so good, I started begging for him to stroke it, tap it, hit it, or kill it. I didn't care what he did as long as he did something. I was about to start pulling on my own hair, and he'd get a kick out of teasing me right up to that point of desperation. You know something, I never even thought about Capone's ass after that.

Well one day me and "Thumper" were lying around after one of our love sessions. When I finally regained my ability to hear, I noticed he was complaining about a system glitch that dispensed an extra two to four unregistered pills on certain prescriptions. All he saw was a headache, and I immediately saw dollar signs. I suggested we go into business. If he could find a way to get them out of the building, I would sell those vitamin V's or Viagras, Vicodins, Percocet, and whatever else to the dudes down at the shipyard on paydays.

Frankie Senior, or Sugar Daddy as I called him, was actually my first customer. He was my best friend Rica's support system; anything she needed she'd call on Sugar Daddy. I once asked her if they were, ahem, "having relations" and of course she said no. He couldn't function anymore. That was the way she'd explained it to me. She said they'd tried once and he sat there and tugged and pulled on old faithful, damn near gave himself an Indian burn and a heart attack trying to get himself hard. Well, one day I had a tree rat or something in the wall behind the cabinet in my kitchen and she sent his old crotchety self over to my apartment to investigate. That particular month the system was kicking out Viagras left and right so I had all these blue pills I'd stored up from Sincere and no real idea how to really get rid of them, and I also had no cash to offer Sugar Daddy after he'd caught the rat. So, I offered him the next best thing.

Needless to say Rica called me later that night because Sugar Daddy was standing in her living room and was refusing to leave. He'd dropped his pants and showed her his flag was flying at full mast. He was ready for her to pay homage to his die-hard wrinkly dinkley. I laughed so hard I almost peed a little. I didn't even have the heart to tell her it was mostly my fault. But thankfully he was one of the shift leaders at the shipyard and he let all the old timers know exactly what was up after that. Fifty dollars a pill and he and I were in business.

Shonique messed it up for both of them though. Capone came back and wanted to battle it out with Sincere. Sincere couldn't believe I'd played him and he was the side dude, while I tried to tell him that he wasn't. I'd grown to love him and started thinking about a future with him and then everything pretty much fell to pieces. I was holding my world in both my hands and it was still slipping through my fingers. And then there was Shonique. Not only did she show me how the world and the game turned; she taught me how to run them both.

Chapter 9

The World Is Yours—Only If You Take It

Shoni had me backstage with the who's who of the celebrity world at concerts. That same night we'd be up in their luxury penthouse suites at the after–after parties, and a month or two later we'd be up at Hillcrest, stealing abortion clinic sonograms and threatening to FedEx them to that dude's wife, the press, whoever, but for five to ten thousand it would all disappear. Those rappers and singers did so much dirt all it took was a picture or a text to remind them of what went down after that show. It was easy money for sex that I would have had with a regular man for free. It was risky because sometimes they'd say, "I don't care. Have the baby. For all I know you were already knocked up." But there were those times that they wouldn't that made it worth the try.

I first met Shoni when we were both working the register at the BP gas station out Five Points in Norfolk. At the time, I couldn't figure out how this nineteen-year-old was on her own, working part time, pushing a Lexus, and still killing it. She'd come in every day with the insane Gucci purses, the real ones, and they'd be the newest, just-released current line. Not the ones everyone got from the flea market over on Little Creek before it burned down, with the faded straps and the bubble letters poking out of the pleather. Everything Shoni had—I mean everything— was in style, and there was no way she was getting it off of eight dollars an hour.

She was thick like Monique, intelligent, beautiful, and had an ass you could make into a coffee table, nightstand, and probably even hide under when it was raining. If she was feeling nice enough to let you, she was obsessive-compulsive as hell about people being close to her and what not. Niggas used to love her, and she'd let them think she loved them too, but on the low Shoni loved women.

I'd never been with a woman, but I'd thought about it once or twice here and there. Honestly, after dealing with Sincere, also known as Thumper, I just couldn't figure out what a girl would actually do with another girl aside from be bored. One day Shoni and I were having that very same conversation and I guessed I hit a nerve.

"So do you think when you kiss a woman it's anything like kissing a man?" she asked me, her Sister Souljah voice turned up on ten, hands thrust on hips. I was not going to win this battle no matter what I said.

"It's a woman so it's not supposed to be like kissing a man right?" I asked her.

"That's not what the hell I meant and you know it, woman. Come here." Her snippy reply meant I was going to get some sort of lesson.

Reluctantly I walked over. It was like I was seven again, being called up to the teacher's desk at the front of the classroom. We were at her place, or the Sugar Shack as I liked to call it. Her decorating sense was always a little sensual met modern if I had to describe it. Strands of black or dark chocolate–colored Japanese thread curtains called *Wooshie* hung over the doorway to each room. They were more like the modernized version of those seventies beads everyone else was used to seeing in their momma and them's houses.

"I know it ain't what you meant. You got any tree, Shoni?" I asked her, glancing around, not really paying attention. Her house was just so . . . interesting.

Every wall in there had at least one piece of WAK art that was in existence at the time. I sat beside her on the couch beneath the gaze of the mahogany brown woman with braids, pregnant, with an image of the earth. Pink Sugar invaded my senses. She always smelled good; that was her signature scent as she liked to call it. The smell reminded me of warm, melted cotton candy and vanilla, but if you let her tell you she'd say it reminded any- and everyone of Shoni's yoni: the Sanskrit word for vagina, because she couldn't bear to hear or use the word "pussy."

Indigo Blues candles were lit all over, their woodsy, earthy, masculine scent clashing pleasantly with her feminine one. Both fragrances blended nicely with the Kush aromatics, even though one of the blends she had was so new I just called it Christmas Tree because the buds all stank so good they smelled like raw pine needles to me.

"You know I always got that good-good. Here." Handing me a blunt, she turned, focusing her radiant deep brown eyes directly on me, the attention suddenly making me nervous. She focused in on me through the smoke, pointing a sharp red painted nail at me before continuing.

"Women were actually made to be the lovers of each other. Only a woman can truly appreciate another woman's emotional complexity and vulnerability. Because any hole that a man finds in a woman's countenance, he'd just assume it was meant for his dick to fill before he tries to do any emotional patchwork."

Now, I didn't know what she meant by that, but we were high as hell and it seemed to make sense, right up until she kissed me and I tasted cotton candy and a soft, sweet sadness that tasted like nothing no man on this earth deserved. And when she moaned into my lips, I felt something give way in my chest that I never even knew was there, and I realized that was the emotional hole she was talking about.

The one that every man tries to fill by "fucking" it away, when all a woman really needs is for someone to call and say "I love you" or send her flowers for no reason. That hole that goes away when you tell her that she's beautiful first thing in the morning before she's brushed her teeth even if she looks like hell. It's a weird thing that hole is; it makes you watch someone when they're asleep, lightly tracing the shape of their nose with your finger, whispering quiet promises to their ears. I learned about all of that with Shoni.

It was Shonique who also taught me how to grab credit card numbers. We'd go shopping off other people's accounts and then quit whatever job we were working at before loss prevention could even figure out what happened. When we both worked at Sprint, we'd set up fake accounts and have our homeboys in tech support issue equipment refunds against them. Send out new cell phones to phony PO boxes and then we'd go sell the phones at the mall on military paydays. This was before all the high-tech security checks they put in place, so back then we could make anywhere from two to three thousand a week like it was nothing.

She opened my eyes to a world of white-collar scams, where the money was bigger, easier, and my hands stayed cleaner. We had so many different scams and schemes going on at one time that I couldn't keep up with half of them. As soon as one became obsolete we'd just sit, brainstorm, smoke a little, and then, bam, we'd have a new one. This was all a part of my development, learning how to fly and be out on my own.

Now, granted, compared to all that, the best Vee had to offer me was a two-bedroom Section 8 home in her sister's name, but what the hell would I look like turning down a chance to not have to work for once? But no man or woman has ever told me that before. If I'd known she was only doing it out of her fear and paranoia about my bisexuality I might not have been so damn eager to say okay.

I'd told Vee from the get-go I don't mind a little lesbo action here and there, but I love . . . Wait, let me rephrase that. I needs me a good, solid-testosterone, sweat-pouring, make-it-hurt dick down and, no, not that fake plastic piece of crap strap-on. Vee, like all studs, thought she could change my mind and my heart, and worst of all Mrs. Smuckers. You know what they say, "It has to be good." Yes, my punani is good, as I'd been told so on numerous occasions, but there would be no changing her mind; she definitely appreciated the D.

Sometimes the sex with Vee was so insatiable. She'd be staring at herself in our bedroom mirror doing the Dougie behind me, making kissy faces. I was pretty sure I could have propped up a couple of pillows and as long as she could slide in and out without losing momentum, the change would have gone unnoticed. I blame my Facebook slip-up on my ass being in heat. I was not of sound mind or sound pussy, and now I needed to find myself a new mark or at least a temporary live-in fuck buddy.

I had one number saved in my phone under DNA: do not answer. City Boi or C.B. was one of the grimiest industry niggas in the area. There were all kinds of horror stories about girls who would go in business with him and wind up strung out, missing, or pregnant by some anonymous dude. But, truth was he could make things happen if he wanted to. I'd tried to work with him once on a video shoot when a bunch of rappers were in town.

These dudes were as legit as they came. I'd never seen so many bottles of champagne and diamond chains, but to be the legitimate moneymakers they were you'd think they'd never heard of a bank. Not one of them was without a book bag, fanny pack, or some kind of duffle bag full of money. C.B. had me going for a minute until he hit all the girls with this "hang around after hours and entertain the squad 'Ho Chi Minh Ho' style." That's when I got pissed off and carried my ass. I was not about that life.

My mistake back then was running with too many females who were known for that type of foolishness. I didn't separate from myself from the pack and I was mistaken for one of the sheep.

"Yo, this City, who this?" His raspy voice gave me instant chills of both foreboding and expectation.

"Um, hey, you. Thi . . . this is Tia." I waited.

"Who the hell is Tia?"

"You know Tia . . . Tia. From out Oakmont Tia. I used to chill with your girl Rica and, uh, Shonique."

Rica used to be my best friend. She was one of the only girls I knew of who actually made it from her connection with C.B. She got picked up to do a couple of *King* and *XXL* magazines, moved to Atlanta, and then she got brand new, erasing all of us and Virginia from her vocabulary all together.

"Oh yeah, li'l mixed breed with the pretty eyes. Long time no hear. I'ma be up in Venue 112 tonight, got a couple of tables, we popping bottles. You should come through."

That was all the work I needed to do. Once he saw me the rest would take care of itself. Everyone always said with my features that I should or could model. It didn't make any sense to just keep letting this face and this body go to waste. I was twenty-four with no kids, no real family ties, and I didn't do the college thing for real because I hated school. The only reason I'd tried to go was to get a refund check, but you can't do a damn deferment or forbearance on those loans forever so school was out. This was my first and last chance to make a good impression on this dude to let him know that I meant business this time.

It didn't take me long to get dressed. Despite the temperature only being in the low fifties I still wore as little clothing as possible. I put on a pair of super-tight leggings I'd gotten from Olive Ole and a long-sleeve see-through black Dolce Vita pheasant-print shirt that tied up in the front. Spinning around several times, I made sure no tags or panty lines were showing through my tights. Shoni always said that as long as your top spoke high fashion and your shoes were on point you could always get away with a decent pair of jeans or tights if the pockets or the label weren't showing. My hair always hung in black wavy curls down my back because I was too lazy to spend the four hours it took to straighten it out or style it any other way. I sprayed some Dolce & Gabbana Light Blue behind my ears and in my hair, and I was ready to go.

The club was packed, just as I'd expected, and the line to get in was around the building. I called C.B. to let him know I was outside. A couple of security guys came to the front door and let me in, no ID check, no cover charge, nothing. I liked this shit already.

"Damn you look better than I remember." He stood up and gave me a tight hug. "Smell good, too."

I returned his embrace and tried my best not to look nervous or uncomfortable. His entourage was small tonight, just another guy I didn't recognize and his girlfriend, I guessed. City was a short, muscular, light-skinned dude with a full beard and his edge up was always razor sharp, like his barber used a ruler to make the lines. He reminded me of one of the husbands from *The Real Housewives of Atlanta*. I couldn't remember the guy's name. Vee let the cable get cut off before I could ever really get into the show. He was stupid sexy; yes, he could definitely get the goodies.

"You smell damn good yourself, sir."

I gave him a shy smile and took the seat next to his. I was immediately happy I'd worn leggings instead of a skirt, as his hand instantly slid up in between my legs.

"So you want me to make you a star, love?"

I thought about Vee and our run-down house, the fact that I didn't have a job or even a damn checking account. I lived off of her and my first cousin, who dropped me some money every now and again. Closing my eyes as if the darkness would make the shame of my situation go away, I silently nodded my head yes to his question.

"Good!" City replied eagerly. "First we celebrate because a star you already are; I can look at you and tell. Later we'll go to my place and relax."

I had a momentary break as he ordered two more bottles of champagne. When the server brought him his change he handed me a one hundred dollar bill out of it. My heart pounded in excitement and I quickly squirreled the money away into my clutch next to my phone before he changed his mind.

"So, Tia, you see all these men up in here looking at you?"

Glancing around I noted a few stank stares from some hoodish-looking girls nearby, and some men sitting at a table next to us were looking me up and down like wolves. The attention made me uncomfortable and I quickly averted my eyes. People often stared or looked at me but men did that naturally; it was in their nature.

"I've never really paid much attention to men." I took a sip of my champagne to cover up my obvious unease at the change in topic.

He didn't notice, and continued without missing a beat. "Those are what I call money glances. Imagine if we put you on a magazine or in a video. They would all willingly pay for the same glances they're sneaking at you right now for free, love."

He put his arm around my shoulder as we laughed and toasted to "money glances." Two bottles later I was feeling extra nice, and I didn't know how it came up or when I'd even told him that I liked women or was bisexual or any of that shit, but I wish I never had.

"So you be out there pulling chicks? Really? Have you ever been with a man? How long ago was it? You strap up or you get strapped? Could you pull a chick right now?"

He had a barrage of questions. Before I could answer one he hit me with another one. He pulled out a band of fifty dollar bills. "This is two thousand. I'm a gambling man. I bet you can't get a girl to come chill with us at the house later."

His homeboy chuckled and I looked at him like he'd grown a second and a third head. His emphasis on the word "chill" made it all too clear he wasn't trying to sip Moscato and watch TV. Now, I wasn't saying that my ass was the player type or conceited or anything like that, but hell, all women in my mind were inherently lesbian. The most I'd ever had to do was give a woman a few drinks, smile real sly while saying that I like women, and they were usually nothing but spaghetti girls: straight until you get them wet. I smirked. Something was suspect about his little bet and I wanted to know exactly what it was.

"You gonna give me two thousand dollars for something you can have any given day of the week? What's the catch, C?"

"Any given day of the week it hasn't been with you, and the catch is I get to pick the girl. And she just walked through the door."

Following his gaze my mouth dropped open slightly, and it was as if a million butterflies had been released in my chest all at once. Her back was turned to us, but I'd have known Shoni anywhere in this life or the next one over. We hadn't spoken in over a year, not after I fell in love with her only to find out she'd been married the entire time. Her reasoning was that it was only for the money but that didn't matter to me. I was devastated nonetheless.

She stood at the bar now, the explicit center of all the money glances. Even now I admired the full thickness of her hips. There was something about that woman's body that made her look exactly like that—a woman. Gold pumps laced up around her ankles; a deep brown and gold dress that belted loosely around the waist further accenting her big old booty. She turned to walk toward the bar and my breath caught. I almost fainted, fell out my chair, and pointed like the village idiot mouth hanging open and all. No, not because she was gorgeous; she was beyond that. Her skin was a golden brown hue; her high cheekbones were a bright rosy pink from the cold air outside. Even from this distance I could see the deep dimples in them as she politely excused herself past people, smiling at the quick compliments the men were throwing her way as she passed. There was no way I could go through with this.

I just began shaking my head back and forth. "Anyone but her."

"Ha, she thiiiiiiick. Gorgeous isn't she? Makes you nervous just looking at her. Well, we don't have a bet then."

He started to tuck the money back in his pocket and mentally I cursed myself out. $2,000 could go a long way. I could get a place to stay for a few days, pay my cell phone bill up for a couple of months. Not have to ask for anyone's help. I needed that money. Me and my damn luck. Figure the odds, out of all the places to go and all the people in the world to choose from. That definitely was not Shoni. This fool would just so happen to casually scan a crowd and pick out the same damn cop who only hours ago had just arrested my girlfriend.

Chapter 10

All's Well If Al Is Well

The few close friends I had in my life were either married or socially awkward. Besides, I already knew how they were about a last minute girls' night out. Somebody wouldn't be able to find a babysitter, somebody's boo wouldn't like it, and somebody's money wouldn't be right. The social no-goers were always like "Club? Why do you wanna go to a boring-ass club? Let's stay in the house and order takeout." Or they'd say, "Let's go out to eat." Lord knows I didn't need anything else to eat right now. But, it happened every single time without fail. This night was going to be me all by myself, and I was okay with that. Besides, Davin and I had stopped having sex long before he was murdered and now that I knew why we'd stopped, it was time for me to find myself an extracurricular plaything.

I needed to get out the house and away from jail and the other cops and laws. Most people didn't recognize me out of my uniform anyway, especially with the weight I'd put back on. Add that to the fact that I'd worn makeup and let my natural shoulder-length twists hang loose, the odds of anyone recognizing me were slim to none. I slid the valet ticket into my back pocket and reminded myself to get cash to tip the guy on my way out. Davin was probably rolling over in his grave at the sight of me driving his car, let alone clubbing in it. That car was one of the few things I had. I made sure I drove it everywhere completely out of spite.

"So, um, are you allowed to come and party with us common folk?" someone said from behind me.

I was standing facing the bar when a small body pressed up against my back, sliding a champagne flute onto the bar in front of me.

"My friend wants you to come have drinks with us, and I owe you a thank-you as well."

I looked down at the glass, wondering who exactly was thanking me. Contemplating the situation I leaned my head to the side, casually sliding a test strip from the department's lab from my bracelet and dipping it into the glass without anyone seeing. Yeah, being a cop makes you stupid paranoid about stuff like roofies. *Five, four, three . . .* I counted silently, and without turning around I addressed my visitor over my shoulder. "Hmm, free champagne and invitations. Might this be my lucky night?"

The strip didn't change color indicating any GHB, Rohypnol, or ketamine; it was clean. I lifted it to my lips and took a sip, turning to face whoever she was. I immediately choked and sputtered on the bittersweet bubbles as they slid down my throat.

"T . . . Tia? Right?" I stammered at her in complete shock.

"Yes, um, Offi—"

"Alicia, just call me Alicia. I guess you're okay? I'm, um, sorry about your friend."

"Oh, it's fine. That situation was over with anyway. Besides I have new friends and they'd love to meet you. I'm modeling now. This is kind of a little celebration thing."

She smiled and waved toward a table in the VIP section, I bit my lower lip at the light-complected bit of goodness who waved and smiled back. All I needed was for him to say he could pick up or bench press 190 to 200 and we'd be best friends.

"Okay, Tia, but just don't say anything about what I do for a living and we are fine."

She winked a silent promise and I winked back before following her past the "no-fly zone." That's where all the hating-ass chicks who ain't fly enough to get in stood and hated on everybody else in the VIP area.

This was against all of the precinct's rules. I should have turned and left as soon as she recognized me, but to hell with caution. I needed an adventure. I needed to live again. Life was so boring, especially after only dealing with Davin and all his stuffy friends and our married friends. Martinis at Ruby Tuesday was definitely not my idea of getting out of the house or living. After his death, this was the closest I'd been to human interaction outside of the station.

At the table Tia introduced me to City Boi, aka my future "Thunder Buddy." There was another guy who reminded me of the version of Shaggy from *Scooby-Doo;* his name was Nova and his girlfriend was Portia. I took a seat in between Tia and City Boi and finished my glass of champagne. My phone buzzed in my back pocket and I quickly ignored a text from Lo asking if I was okay or needed anything. What I needed was sitting right here beside me smelling like Yves Saint Laurent For Him and looking even better.

"Sweetie? Um, City Sir? I'm not calling a grown man anything like that. What did your mother name you?" I smiled politely but I was dead-ass serious. I would not be yelling out, "Ooh, Ci . . ." I couldn't even think it without smiling to myself.

"I don't usually do this. But since you asked so seductively, you can call me Chason. Kind of like, don't be chasing me after I finish tasting you." He winked.

The only reason I didn't put him on blast for that corn-ball line was because he was fine as hell. I flashed him a pretty smile and replied, "I asked like I was inquiring, and I don't chase, nor do I give out tastes. This is a meal fit for a king, not boys." I winked back and took a sip of my champagne. The table broke out into laughter.

"Oh. I think I just fell in love and lust!"

We exchanged small talk. Chason owned a successful model management company. He'd placed girls in several major magazines and videos. I honestly couldn't care less. I listened just to be polite but my mind was doing all sorts of impolite things to this man's body. Tia seemed to be a ball of fidgety nervous energy beside me, double-dutching in and out of our conversation.

It wasn't until I leaned back to laugh at something Mr. Sexy Everything said that I noticed her sitting a little too close to me. The warmth from her breath brushed against my ear. It was when I noticed that I could damn near count each of her lashes if I wanted to that I needed to address the personal space issue.

"Um, Tia? You okay, sweetie?" I asked her peculiarly.

"Mmmm hmmm. Are you okay?" Her reply implied so much more as she swooped her eyes seductively up and down my body from head to toe.

Shockwaves swept over me. It was like yin and yang. Chason's thick, warm, masculine hand encircled the back of my neck and he gently massaged my shoulders as Tia's long, slender, warm fingers . . . .

Oh the hell no, she was not. Had I been in uniform I'd have twisted her wrist and taken her to the ground without a second thought. I inhaled sharply to cover my mental gasp of shock at the fact that this woman's hand was slowly gliding somewhere it definitely did not need to be going.

"Let's excuse ourselves to the ladies' room right quick." My tone was sharp as I cut my eyes at her, daring her to tell me no.

I grabbed her by the hand I'd just considered breaking before she could respond and marched toward the restroom. The line was ridiculous, as it always was, with women lined up chatting, doing the potty dance; and some were too drunk to even stand on their own. A male came out of the men's room and I jumped in, pulling Tia with me.

"Girl, are you that drunk? I know I didn't imagine—"

"Ugh. You didn't imagine it. I'm sorry; please don't get mad. City bet me two grand that I couldn't get a girl back to his place for a threesome. I said okay; he picked you randomly out of the crowd. I really need the money. I'm leaving Vee because we did something insane and stupid, like took these har—" Someone banged loudly on the door.

"Occupied," we both shouted in unison.

We were both standing in a pissy men's room, trying to diffuse a situation that actually felt like the most fun I'd had in forever. The giggling started out of nowhere and I couldn't help it. The entire situation was hilarious when I thought about it. Tia just stared at me like I was crazy.

"Look, Tia. I don't get down with that gay mess. Up until I met you, I didn't even know if I liked gay people. But, you are lucky because I want that boy out there something bad. Maybe we can fake it?" I shrugged.

The smile that spread across her face was a good enough answer for me.

Chapter 11

Two Birds—I'm Stoned

Leaving the club, Chason was smiling so hard he looked like the cat that swallowed the canary. I was just thankful his condo wasn't too far away.

"Welcome to Palace de. I don't speak that mess so just fill in the blank with a sexy French word of your liking. Please feel free to get comfortable," he said as we walked in.

Surveying the place, I had to admit he had damn good taste. The walls were painted in a soothing slate grey with large framed black and grey movie posters in foreign languages. Some of them were from plays; others were scenes or names of movies from around the world. A floating fireplace hung on another wall. The flames appeared otherworldly as they danced seductively from a crystal bed that made them turn mesmerizing shades of purples, blues, and greens. I'd have bet money he had those little MidSummer's Night Yankee Candles hidden somewhere. They were my favorite and the smell was everywhere.

Propped neatly next to the wall on the farthest side of the room was an actual all-black BMW motorcycle. Had this fool never heard of a garage? The place was extremely spacious and in the center of the living room he'd opted for an oversized round black and grey microfiber couch with matching throw pillows. I took a seat, running my fingers back and forth over the fabric, admiring its softness. He disappeared down a long hallway just as the recess lighting dimmed. I looked at Tia and smiled and nodded. She smiled and nodded in return, taking a seat on the other side.

And then I nearly jumped out of my skin. If I'd had my service weapon I might've actually fired on him a couple of times. I swore this fool had to be half ninja. He'd somehow silently manifested directly beside me in a cloud of blunt smoke, wearing nothing but a black silk robe and white gym socks. I hid my surprise and the temptation I was fighting at wanting to reach out and run my fingers through the thin sprinkling of straight black hair on his chest. Slowly my eyes followed the trail that ran down the center of his one, two, three, four, five, six, whew. There wasn't an ounce of fat on the man and he was thiiiick. He had to be addicted to working out.

"Ladies, I think you are both entirely overdressed for this occasion."

"And I didn't know I was coming to a pajama party. Um, do you have on underwear, sir?" I teased him, playfully tugging at the belt of his robe, trying to sneak a peek underneath.

He took a drag off his blunt before offering it to Tia, who accepted.

"I can give y'all some T-shirts and sweats if you want to get comfy. Just let me know."

I hadn't thought about taking my clothes off, and I honestly doubted with his little tapered V-shaped waist he had any pants that I could fit my hips into. I could feel myself getting nervous, and hot, and anxious just thinking about what would happen if this were to go any further. I hadn't been with a man in so long and, now, with my new body and Tia with her perfect little skinny self. *Ugh.*

Tia caught my gaze and looked at me strangely for a split second before shakily extending the blunt in my direction. *Oh, to hell with it,* I thought, suddenly irritated and frustrated with the entire situation. I snatched it quickly from her fingers. She'd obviously expected me to turn it down as she'd glanced sideways and made a soundless "okay" motion with her mouth. I narrowed my eyes at her as I raised the nasty-smelling thing to my lips thinking, *humph. Girl, please don't try to predict me.*

Taking a larger pull than I probably should have, I did the exact opposite of what we were trained to do in the force: I inhaled. My throat burned, my chest burned, even my lungs rebelled against the smoke's intrusion into my body.

"Relax, ma. That's that good-good. I guess I should have warned you."

He chuckled and slid closer to me, rubbing my back. His body heat seared through the fabric of my dress, making me even more aware of how long it had been since I'd been touched by a man, and I coughed all the harder. Tia was reclining calmly on the other side like a little Persian kitten, just watching me with a smug expression through lazy, kittenish eyes. And then. . .

"You good, ma?" Chason asked, eyeing me with concern.

"I . . . I . . ." Pausing, I had to think about it, because I honestly didn't feel like I could make complete sentences for a second. "I don't remember what happened before shit happened," I muttered with the most confused look on my face, I was sure.

They both burst out laughing and I sat there, confounded. I couldn't for the life of me remember what club we'd just left, the type of champagne we'd drunk, not even the name of the condos we were in.

Oh hell. I was a police officer and I was stoned, high, turned all the way the hell up, whatever you wanted to call it, and it felt awesome. There was something about being in that state of mind that made me not care about anything. It was suddenly very clear why people risked getting arrested just to chase that kind of relaxation. My phone vibrated and I clumsily silenced another text from Lorenzo before completely shutting my phone off.

Chason was saying something to me but I couldn't make my ears line up with the sounds coming out of his mouth. His beautiful man-nipples were poking out from his man-chest. They kept drawing my eyes downward every time I'd try to focus. It was as if my fingers weren't my fingers anymore. I watched in amazement as another woman's hand reached out and a single index finger pointed and then moved forward in slow motion. It was like E.T. trying to phone home or something, before it homed in and slowly began tracing one soft, erect nipple and then the other.

"Can you feel that?" My voice was a slow, deep foreign sound to my ears.

"Yes, baby, I can feel it. It feels nice, too."

"Who would've ever thunk it? E.T. likes nipples and shit." I giggled at myself.

"Woman, how in the hell you get up there with E.T. already? You ain't even get to ride my rocket ship yet."

Leaning toward me, he began running his hand up my thigh and in my high state it felt like he had ten hands going in ten different directions. Standing wobbly, I steadied myself as the room shifted slightly and I stood, placing myself in between his legs. There was a gleam of appreciation in his eye that gave me the confidence I needed to undo my belt, and slowly lower my dress to the ground. Thank the Lord I'd actually worn a sexy bright blue satin bra and panty set with pink stitching that I'd picked up on sale at Lane Bryant. He drank all of me in with thirsty eyes before pulling me down impatiently onto his lap.

Straddling him, I could feel him hard and ready, straining against the fabric of his robe. He was pressing tight up against me and the pressure, the heat from him, sent a shockwave from my core to all the way down to my toes still enclosed in my heels. I closed my eyes and moaned as his oversized hands tangled in my hair. He flexed his fingers, massaging my scalp, and I was pretty sure I all but purred. He was grinding up against me while simultaneously pulling me down into a rough kiss, and that sent shockwaves from my head to my fingertips.

It was getting so damn hot up in there. Leaning my head back to give his roving lips better access to my neck I almost peed on the man. There was no way he could be standing over me and kissing my neck at the same but he was.

"How are you, sweetness? I'm Big Country. You get tired of the City, you rest assured that you can always cum on over to the Country." He gave me a devilish smile while biting his lower lip and my head almost fell slam the hell off my shoulders.

Big Country and Sweet Baby Jesus in a manger, twins, really?

Mad she wasn't getting any attention, Tia snatched him up before I could even think about getting greedy. It was like watching a live-action porno in slow motion. Tia stood, stripped, and put her arms around his neck, pulling herself up onto his body. They kissed like they'd been lovers for a lifetime as she wrapped her legs around his waist. Mark my words, this girl had some skills. I watched in amazement as she used her legs and feet to slide his boxers down with flawless execution. The man was standing at full attention and I prayed they were perfect carbon copies from head to, um, head.

When she lowered herself onto him, she squealed and he grunted in satisfaction. Chason grabbed the back of my neck, roughly turning me around to face him and it was on. Or so I thought as he came in for what I believed to be a kiss. The fool turned his head and bit my cheek, yes, my cheek on my face. That shit hurt so damn bad, shocked, I grabbed his dick through the hole in his boxer and yanked it out through the slit. Sliding my panties to the side I forced myself down onto him, biting his cheek back just as hard if not harder, getting a mouthful of beard and everything. He growled, and pulled my hair so hard my eyes watered while he drove himself into me over and over, sucking and licking at my exposed neck.

"You gonna come for me?" he growled at me, not missing a single stroke. Shit, I was trying to answer him but all I could do was hold on and moan.

"You hear me? You gonna . . . come for . . . me or what?" he growled, pumping harder than he did the first time. "Answer me."

My ass was trying to concentrate and this nigga was talking too damn much. I figured if I kept quiet then maybe Papa Pump would pump harder, and then, hell, maybe I'd get there faster so I just bit my lip and moaned. He dug in and I just kept riding him, getting closer, and closer, until slap! I stopped moving and my eyes flew open. I looked around trying to figure out what the fuck hit me.

"Don't get mad, girl. Smack me back. C'mon!"

Now this fool done lost his ever-lovin' mind. I smacked him back as hard as I could and crossed my arms, glaring at him. Tia and Country were still going at it on the floor somewhere behind me, from the sounds of it.

"Damn, baby, you mad. You was liking that rough shit earlier."

"You actually hit me."

"All right. I'm sorry. Let me make it up to you."

He leaned me back onto the couch and stood to remove his robe. My eyes followed the thick build of his shoulders down through the full span of his chest. Taking in an angry breath I let my eyes once again rove down his well-sculpted body. He had on black Versace silk boxers that clung to every inch of him, and I blamed the weed, and the alcohol. I blamed my inability to control myself when I was sober magnified times hundred when I was intoxicated. I clutched my sides, tears began rolling down my cheeks. I couldn't breathe because I was laughing so hard.

This Negro had the skinniest, ashiest little toothpick legs, like he'd spent every hour of his life in the gym working on his upper body and he'd completely forgotten all about his legs. Oh yeah, he was strong all right—upper body strong. If anybody ever wanted to rob him, all they'd have to do was kick him in one of those little weak-ass legs and run.

"What the hell is wrong with you, woman?" Chason was standing over me, getting angrier by the second.

"Licia? You all right, girl?" Tia stood beside him, holding a pillow over her chest.

They were all standing there confused and concerned with my sudden descent into madness, and my grown ass rolled off the couch and on the floor, laughing at this fool so hard my sides hurt. A sudden knock at the door made everyone jump and we scattered in various directions, trying to get dressed.

Chason went outside for a few moments before coming back inside and glancing at his brother anxiously.

"Uh, Country, your man is outside about the part for your bike." He spoke slowly, emphasizing part and bike.

I'd been in the game long enough to know a setup or a sale when I saw one. I locked eyes with Tia and cleared my throat, nodding toward the door.

"Well, boys, I guess we will be getting ourselves up out of here since you two seem to have guy stuff to tend to."

Stepping toward the door Chason blocked my path. "Now, now, you ain't got to leave just yet. I think you might want to meet our friend. He makes movies."

I rolled my eyes at him. He wasn't about to let one of his friends film me or run a train on me or any other kind of foolishness. My mouth had just tooted itself up to say as much when the door opened and a man backed in with a young girl flung over his shoulder. She was obviously unconscious and couldn't have been older than thirteen or fourteen. He was making his way over to the couch to lay her down and I used that moment to break for the open door. I glanced just long enough to see if Tia was following and caught a brief glimpse of the face of the man I'd helped save with the two boys. I almost tripped over my own damn feet in disbelief. What the hell kind of business did Peter Shaw have with these two and that unconscious girl?

Chapter 12

It Is What It Is Until It Isn't—Or Is It?

Sitting at my desk, my elbows were resting on a report I was supposed to be looking over. My hands propped my face over my cup of coffee so close it fogged up my Michael Kors shades.

"Good to see your fingers aren't broken. You know, since you can't return texts or anything."

Lorenzo's voice echoed behind my eyelids, and I moaned. Leaning back, I cringed at a wave of nausea. The last time I'd been hung over . . .

"So what's up? You so high profile now you can't even speak when promoted? And don't tell me you're pulling the paparazzi thing with the shades."

"What the hell are you talking about?" Speaking was tiring, not to mention the number my own voice was doing on my headache.

"Damn, Al, it's right there under your coffee. We're on Special Division Investigations now. Turns out that Vee girl we picked up is willing to gnaw her way out of here and bite the hand that pays her in the process. She's willing to help bring down Hemingway. And *we* are the ones who brought her in, and everyone's in a good mood since Pete Shaw from that case with the two kids got brought in last night turns out he's"—he did an imaginary drum roll—"this legendary Jankman."

He danced in place doing some sort of salsa two-step before flashing his new badge in my face. *The motions, so many motions. Why, Lord, can't this man keep still?* I blinked several times before squinting at the bright gold shield that now replaced his old silver one.

Glancing down, frowning, I focused on what I thought was just another report on my desk. Wow, it sure was a reassignment, promotional detail. All I had to do was sign. We would work hand in hand with the FBI on special cases. The salary was almost double what I made now.

"Wow, he's Jankman." I was all but in shock.

The man who terrorized our neighborhood for all those years was alive and in a cell. All because I'd had a drunken fling.

"Yep, someone spotted him carrying a girl into a condo last night and called it in. They searched his place, he had another missing girl in the shack behind his house. They've been sending in DNA all morning from these SUGAR SHACK vans he had planted all over the city. He broke down and admitted everything, said his dead wife has been coming to see him every night tellin' him to stop. Forensics been at his place all night, so far five bodies have been pulled up out of the ground in the yard."

I was floored by news. That's what his wife meant when she whispered the words about the shack being bad. That's why there was a doll's head in the yard that day. A smug grin spread across my face and I was thankful he didn't see me last night; yet, I couldn't help feeling so sad for his sons.

"Well, Lo, as soon as I can focus and find myself a pen I am in. No more damn patrol car for me. And, they're going to let me on, even with Davin's situation?" I frowned, confused about that small piece of this large pie.

"Chief wants to see you. I've got to go make another victory round." Lorenzo sauntered off to share the news with the rest of the division.

It was a proud moment and sadly I didn't have any family or friends to share it with. A small smile spread across my face as I remembered fleeting moments from the night before.

Tia dialed 911 from her cell and reported what we saw. I couldn't be connected since I had drugs in my system but when the unit showed up the guys were thankfully still upstairs.

We giggled all the way to the house, all the way up the stairs, and it was close to four a.m. when we climbed into my bed. Tia was still wide awake and full of so much chatter.

"Alicia, where's your man? I mean why don't you have one? Or do you?"

"I did, I don't now. He's gone. He died. Why do you date abusive women? Somebody do something to you?"

"No. I was with a good woman, I loved the hell out of her for a long time, but she was married. I didn't know until he got shot by his boyfriend or something in a parking garage one night. Some kind of high-profile lawyer or whatever fighting with his lover. She slipped up and told me. You remind me of her, the way you look and carry yourself. But I'll love whoever will love and take care of me. Male or female. It's that simple."

The chances of that kind of coincidence were one in a million. I couldn't help asking, "Her husband got shot? How long ago was that?"

"I don't know, not long before we broke up and I met Vee."

"What was her name?"

"Shonique Padilla. Why?"

The first name didn't sound familiar but the last name, the last name made my palms clammy. Davin's last case, the one that he lost, was the Padilla murder trial. I raked my brain trying to remember if he'd told me any details about it but he never discussed his cases with me. This Shonique woman, whoever she was, was somehow related to the man Davin was representing, and she inherited all of his money when he died. She not only left me penniless, but she also was the reason my marriage was fake as fuck.

Yawning and glancing at the watch still on my wrist I could only shake my head as I stuck my arm out almost smacking her in the face.

"I was just curious. Why the hell does my watch say ooy? Aww damn. I think I broke it."

She burst out laughing while taking my watch off and trying to answer in between gasps for air. "Girl, it don't say nothing about ooy; it says four o'clock."

Her fingers lingered on my wrist a second too long and I snatched my watch from her hand. Frowning, I grabbed one of the umpteen pillows from behind me and stuffed it in between us, making myself a pillow barricade.

"Don't you be trying to touch, taste, look at, or sample these cookies. I don't care who I look like or remind you of. Don't . . . get . . . it . . . confused. I'll shoot a bitch." Giggling probably took some of the severity out of my tone, because even though I was serious it was the craziest threat I'd ever had to issue to anyone, let alone to a woman half my size.

I might have been dreaming, might not, but I could have sworn as I closed my eyes I heard her whisper, "Don't worry, I ain't got to take it. You'll be begging me to taste it by the time I'm done."

Staring down at my promotion on my desk, the only person I could think to text was the person I woke up next to this morning.

Text To Tia 8:49 a.m.: Good morning, woman! Make my bed whenever you get out of it. Oh and I got a promotion. Yaaay!

"Partner, you ready to get to work or what?"

"Yeah, guess I don't have a choice since you so damn gung-ho today."

Pulling a pen from my desk I quickly scanned all the pages and signed my name across each of the documents. The first order of business after I admired my new badge was to get this private meeting with the chief out of the way. It was probably to discuss my weight. Chief Reid was a gruff, no-nonsense asshole from what I could tell. He had all these dents in his cheeks and I didn't know if they were from some sort of skin condition or a birth defect.

Entering his office on the fourth floor was like walking into an executive suite. He was seated behind a large mahogany desk and stood to greet me.

"Taylor, welcome to my dungeon," he called out, chuckling at his own joke. I smiled politely and waited for him to continue. "I called you in here to discuss the Sherman & Waltman case file. Although you come highly recommended, the manner in which the drives were taken indicates an inside job. We have an informant, an unreliable informant, who says you might be connected."

"That's insane. I already said I didn't know anything about Davin's business, sir," I burst out in outrage.

"Like I said it's an unreliable informant. Hence, I'm not withholding your promotion. I think you are an excellent officer. Look, a great writer once said 'we are all apprentices in a craft where no one ever becomes a master,' and

you are by far one of my best apprentices. I just can't let
you work the case. Second . . ."

From that point forward I heard nothing else he said.
This was ridiculous, and I could probably sue someone
for slander. He was talking about my weight and their
standards and I couldn't care less. I was happy with my
weight, loved it, matter of fact. My husband tried to control it, my ex. I damn sure wasn't going to let anyone else
do it and especially not an overweight white man with a
"foopah." You know, that bit of belly fat that usually only
women tend to get below their belly button over their
abdomen. Well his ass had one, and it was weird as hell
to see a man with a flat stomach up top and this big ass
"foopah" at the bottom.

He had a habit of crossing and uncrossing his legs like
a woman, and I fought the urge to scream, "You are a
man; why the hell do you have to keep doing that?" How
did he buy pants, or underwear? He was married; how
did his wife feel? Did she "lift" his "foopah" to give him
head if she even still gave him head? And how dare he
talk to me about my weight when he looked like he might
be seven months pregnant!

And then I saw it. Faded and smudged, blotchy and
somewhat unrecognizable yet there all the same. It was
just above his blue dress sock among the varicose veins
poking out of his calf. My mouth dried and my brain emp-
tied as he uncrossed his legs and his pants leg fell down,
covering the hideous snake tattoo that I'd forgotten all
about from all those years ago. He was the guy I'd seen
meet Carlos in the library that night. He had to have been
the reason the old chief had that accident.

We tersely shook hands. I then nodded as if I'd heard
and agreed with every word he'd said and took my leave.
My mind was a cluster bomb of angry musings. Why was
I facing so much backlash behind a man who never even
loved me, and if Chief Reid was dirty, how dirty was he?

My next order of business was looking up this Shonique woman's information so I could pay her a visit. She wasn't hard to locate in the computer system and was actually not far from where I lived, which kind of pissed me off. I jotted down her information, hell bent on getting answers out of someone, and marched off for number three on my list: speak with Vee before she was transferred to a secluded holding cell away from the other detainees, and out of my reach. I silently escorted her to an empty interrogation room.

She glanced around skittishly and asked, "What's this about?"

I leaned onto the desk across from her and answered, "This is about me needing a favor. Vee, what I can or can't do depends on what you do. Did the name Davin Taylor or Alicia Taylor ever come up?"

"Nah. Not that I can remember. Look can you just get word to Tia? Tell her to get somewhere safe? Can't you put her in that witness protection shit until this blows over?" Vee stared at me pitifully.

Tia's safety had honestly never crossed my mind. I stood in the doorway of the interrogation room while I tugged on my right ear lobe in thought.

"Uh-oh. I see *mami* tugging. What's the problem?" Lorenzo walked out of a room across the hall, a recorder and clipboard in hand.

I nodded in Vee's direction. "She wants witness protection for her girlfriend."

"We don't have a huge budget, Vee. We don't even know if what you say will bring anyone in." Lorenzo's tone was snide and overly condescending, as if he were addressing a young, spoiled, rotten child asking for a toy at the store.

"What! Soon as I start saying what I have to say, they gonna know who's saying it. I can give you everything.

She doesn't get any kind of protection, then I'm not talking and you can kiss that upgraded gold piece of shit on your chest good-bye," Vee retorted. She stared up at the ceiling, defiantly chewing the inside of her lip.

I grabbed Lorenzo's arm and dragged him into the corridor, closing the door to the interrogation room so Vee wouldn't hear out conversation.

He snapped at me as soon as the door latched in place, waving the clipboard to accent his point. "We don't have to give her witness protection, Al; that's wasting money from our budget that we can direct toward other things." His jaw was crooked to the side; he wasn't going to budge on this, I could already tell.

"Lo, the girl can stay with me. I'm just as good as witness protection. Think about it. I'm not on the case."

"You're what?" he yelled in my face, the vein throbbing out the side of his neck.

"Chief Reid told me just now. I'm too attached. Think about it: no one knows where I live, I can keep an eye on her. And, we won't have to spend a dime."

"You sure? You don't have to, you know."

My phone vibrated and I looked Lorenzo in his eye, answering him, "Yes, I'm sure. It is what it is right? This will be for the greater good of the case. We just tell Vee whatever she needs to hear, and I'll smooth everything over with her girl. The chief cannot get wind of this shit though. I just got this badge; I'm not trying to lose it."

Lorenzo lifted his head in agreement before going back into the interrogation room across the hall. I walked back in and nodded at Vee, giving her the okay.

Relief swept across her face before she leaned forward and whispered, "Don't tell anyone, not even your partner. We talking billion dollar files, not millions. Go to the house; they taped to the top of the ceiling fan blades. I condensed 'emto terabyte flash drives no bigger than lipstick tubes. You'll find five." She leaned back and acted as if she said nothing.

Lo came in to escort her out. I looked away to read the texts from Tia to hide my shock at actually knowing where they were and their worth.

> Reply From Tia 10:16: Ahh! Congrats! We gonna celebrate! I made the bed Lol!
>
> Text To Tia 10:16: I have a guest room. You should just stay with me for a while.
>
> Text To Tia 10:16: Look, You need to. For your safety. I'll explain later.
>
> Reply From Tia 10:17: wow and um ok? I guess I need to go get a few of my things from the apartment. I can take a cab. I'll Brb.

Sighing, I went to put in a leave chit for the rest of the day. I had some things I needed to get in order if my home was going to be a damn safe house.

Chapter 13

Trouble With Two T's

The drive to Shonique's only took thirty minutes and I was relieved to see a black Audi sitting in the double driveway. *Humph. Most likely purchased with Davin's money.* My heart sounded like an army of ants marching in my ears as I approached the three-story brick house. There was a wide balcony that ran along the second and third floor and the yard was lined with evergreens trimmed into triangles. As I climbed the steps I rehearsed what I'd say, how I'd smile and shake her hand. Maybe offer my condolences even though it would feel strange.

The door flung open just as I was about to ring the doorbell. She screamed at the sight of me; she was obviously on her way out and wasn't expecting anyone to be on her front porch. I screamed, because I recognized her immediately. She was a little shorter than me and we were about the same build. Jealousy was my first reaction because up close and personal she was actually beautiful, with an oval-shaped face and large doe-like eyes.

"You're Shonique Padilla?" It was as if I were accusing her of being herself. Shock was registered on my face.

"Yes. Why are you on my front porch, Officer? Can I help you?" She didn't recognize me at first, but her eyes widened when they landed on the name Taylor on my uniform. The department still hadn't changed my tags due to funding issues.

"You were at P.F. Chang's with Davin that day. I don't want any trouble. Please I just really need to understand what happened. Why he married me if he was already married to you."

She looked warily at the gun perched on my hip and I raised my hands to show I meant no harm.

"Okay. Come inside."

I followed her inside and was in awe at the massive amount of art on all of the walls. We sat in what I'd call a formal living room and she began to explain.

"Davin was my father's attorney. He was paid to keep him out of prison. There aren't too many people who know who my father is or that he even has a daughter. I stay to myself. Father didn't trust him so he had him marry me as insurance. In the event Davin didn't hold up his end of the deal and father went to prison. Davin's assets were willed to me. That's all there is to it."

Her story made sense and yet it still made absolutely no sense, it didn't explain why Davin would marry me. "And you're sure your marriage was legal and binding?"

"We went to the justice of the peace and everything."

"Do you have any idea then why he would marry me and not tell me about you or let me believe my marriage was real? Do you know anything about his Sherman & Waltman accounts?"

"Maybe he thought he'd win, and he'd be able to annul our marriage? I can't answer for a dead man and I don't know about his accounts. All I know is he cost me more than anything his money could ever buy me." Her eyes took on a sad, faraway look.

"If you mean Tia, I think she misses you."

"Ha. Tia is still a confused little girl looking for a dick long enough to reach her heart. That's the only way she'd call it love. What's done is done. I have things to do. I am sorry for your loss."

She stood, and dismissed me. I left with more questions than when I went over there. But, I felt somewhat at ease that Davin wasn't living a complete quadruple life. Their marriage was more for paperwork and that was still crazy but I could wrap my brain around that.

After running around getting groceries, extra towels, and things for the house I was beat. Vee's place was last on my list of stops to make and I prayed no one would pay too much attention to me as I went into the rental office and requested a key.

"You're the second cop to come around here today," the young girl said from behind the counter between pops of chewing gum. I froze with the key suspended in mid-air and stared into her blue-green contact lenses.

"Who was the other cop?" I asked her suspiciously. No one else should have known about the drives; there was no other reason for a cop to go in there.

"I didn't even think to ask him. Just gave up the key like I'm doing right now."

Something told me it was Lorenzo; there was an unmistakable intuition I couldn't shake as I walked out and made my way to the apartment. The power was off and the faint scent of stale marijuana and aftershave lingered in the air. Placing on a pair of my latex gloves, I climbed up on the couch and ran my hand across the top of the fan blade. Clumps of dust fell around all around me, and just as I suspected there was nothing there. Tired and pissed at someone getting the jump on me I cursed and returned the key. I'd have to figure something else out, but for now it was time to take my ass home.

The last thing I expected when I pulled up to my house, ready to open a bottle of wine and relax, was to not be able to get into my own damn driveway. Somebody's Escalade had my driveway completely blocked, forcing me to park on the side of the house on the street. Immediately pissed, I texted Tia, telling her to move her shit or her friends or whatever. A good five minutes passed before I started to get nervous. She hadn't replied and I was supposed to be her "witness protection." *Shit.* What if whoever was after Vee had followed her back from picking up her things?

No windows faced the street in this direction so I couldn't peek in. I'd have to actually go take a look. Creeping quietly out of my car I made my way up toward the house. I couldn't pull my weapon in broad daylight; my neighbors were too damn nosey. All it would take was for one of them to see something going on and we could have a hostage standoff before I could even get a look at the situation. The house was quiet as I made my way toward the door on the side of the garage. I never locked it, and once inside I'd be in the laundry room on the opposite side of the kitchen.

I made it all the way through the garage without making a sound. The house was quiet except for what sounded like the TV, and I cursed silently as I tripped over a stack of newspapers by the laundry room door.

"Hey? Hey? Y'all hear something?" The muffled sound of a man's voice floated toward me. I strained to hear more without having to open the door.

"Nah, you scared Hubby the Unfriendly Ghost gonna float up in here? Get back over here; we got business to handle," another male replied.

I could now clearly make out two distinct male voices.

"No. No. Please, I said stop. Stop!" Tia sounded frantic and scared.

My instincts kicked in. I had the advantage. I knew the layout of my house better than a blind man trapped in a cactus patch. The element of surprise was on my side and they were breaking and entering, assaulting, and I could only imagine what else. Shooting to kill would be in my favor if I had to.

"Grab—" One of the men had started to say something.

Before I could lose my nerve I flung open the laundry room door and bolted forward toward the direction of their voices, my .45 leading the way, aimed and ready.

"Don't nobody grab a damn thing. Police, on the ground or I'll shoot."

A guy in a gold sweatshirt dropped to the ground so damn fast you'd have thought he fell through a trap door, but the other was still standing beside Tia. His eyes locked defiantly with mine; his hand was raised or raising. Grazing the trigger ever so softly, narrowing my right eye, I took aim. He wasn't dropping, and I specifically said, "Drop." The blood rushing in my ears was like a foreign object, an alien spaceship was landing in my brain and the bathroom floor was covered with blood.

"Tajah?" It was just a whisper. It could've been my subconscious but it broke through my mental haze as if it were a scream. My hand shook as the .45 suddenly seemed to double in weight. I'd gone and officially fallen off the deep end. Was my daddy talking to me now?

They were both still staring back at me, as my vision focused and everything became clear.

Tia was the first one brave enough to speak. "Everything's okay I swear. I was just telling him to please not pour anymore in my shot glass, Licia." She was wide-eyed, talking extra loud, and extra slow, like I was psychotic, deaf, and dumb.

My eyes never left the guy beside her. Frowning, I tried to figure out what it was about him, and why was he watching me strangely? When he tilted his head to the side I realized it wasn't defiance creasing his eyebrows and clouding his eyes, it was recognition. And, if I'd taken in more of the scene I'd have probably noticed the shot glass in his left hand.

"Licia? Umm, I feel extra safe and everything but can you please stop aiming the gun at my cousin?" Tia asked before taking a timid step toward me.

Slowly I lowered the pistol, confused at being called a name I hadn't heard out loud since I'd changed it.

"Well damn, Tia. Let me find out you done moved in with Darkie Morgan. Dexter Morgan's other sister, the one they don't talk about on the show." Goldie was talking a lot of shit from on the ground. Especially considering the fact he was the only one to hit the deck, and he hit it quick at that. He stood slowly, brushing invisible dirt off his blinding gold sweatshirt.

Holstering my pistol, I straightened my uniform and smiled as they all laughed at his attempt to lighten the situation. It was awkwardly funny.

Tia did the introductions. "Licia, that's Jin in the gold and this is my cousin—"

"I think we already know each other. Don't we, Alicia?" the one she'd called cousin interrupted.

"We do?" I asked sarcastically.

There was something I couldn't quite place about him. My first instinct was to worry that I'd arrested him or one of his relatives for something and he'd looked up my background. People did that sometimes; they'd take their anger out on the arresting officer for their loved one's bad decisions.

He ignored my attitude. "We need to all take a shot while you think about it. Hell I'm going to make mine a double after the entrance you just made."

It wasn't until he turned to grab the tequila from the other counter that I noticed the long jet black ponytail hanging down his back and I could feel the fogginess slowly burn away from memories I'd long ago locked up. The texts from Brianna, the way I'd found my father.

"Why are you here, Carlos?" My tone was immediately demanding and emotionless.

"Got-damn! Quick Draw McGraw over here gonna give me a condition. Man, I shouldn't have smoked that shit. I told y'all I don't like to smoke in places I don't know. Tia, get ya girl. Get ya girl." Jin jumped when he was once again confronted with Destiny. Yes, I'd named my service weapon.

My pistol was cocked and aimed back on Carlos before any of them had a chance to even tip back their shots.

"Tajah . . ."

"Call me that again and Jah is exactly who you'll be talking to next."

"It's not what you think, Alicia." Carlos's hands went up in surrender. "I didn't know you were going to be here. Tia really is my cousin. She said come celebrate and have some drinks with her. I said okay. I'm just as shocked to see you as you are to see me. I thought you were dead."

"If it were up to you I probably would be," I retorted. Everything in me wanted to believe he was lying. But there was something in those eyes of his that took me all the way back to high school.

"Taj . . . Alicia, I was being watched because I found out what was going to happen to your pops and I was the only one against it. I asked Brianna to meet me after school to warn you without getting myself caught up. They were following me and listening so I had to act like I ain't give a damn about you to try to warn you."

I glanced cautiously at Tia and Jin. "Should they even be hearing this?" I nodded in their direction.

Jin grabbed Tia's arm and began dragging her from the room, shouting, "Huh? What? I ain't heard anything. Look, ma'am, I don't have kids but I want to live to have kids hopefully with Tia one day if she'd just stop acting so damn saddi—"

"J, chill," Carlos shouted at him before turning back to me. He went from night to day, anger to sincerity in the blink of an eye. "Alicia. They good, they've been with me through much worse and Tia is blood. Manny picked me up after school so I couldn't interfere, that was it."

I just felt so tired from so many years of carrying a burden on my shoulders that no one could lift or carry for me. Lowering my gun, I walked over to my kitchen table, grabbing a shot off the counter, and sat down. Without thinking I slammed the shot back and fought not to choke as the tequila burned its way down my throat, warming my stomach.

"Who murdered my father, Carlos?" My voice cracked from the tequila, from the emotional drain of finally having a conversation that I'd not had with a single living person in over ten years.

He covered the space of my huge kitchen in three long strides. Kneeling in front of me he stared up at me with regret and compassion. "You know I can't betray them by naming them specifically. I'm bound by blood. But I'll die helping you find them. I owe you that much for not being able to stop it. I've been in hiding for some time. They tried to recruit my little brother . . ." His voice caught and he stopped talking.

"They didn't." I vaguely remembered his little brother. He was at least seven years younger than me.

"Yeah, I refused to let him join. He had a scholarship to play football and . . ."

"You found him with his throat slit? Because no one refuses the coterie. What made you think you could protect him, Carlos?"

He didn't respond right away and lowered his head. I offered him some comfort by rubbing his back. Tears were streaming down my own face at all the resurrected memories.

"And that red Camry? The old police chief?" I asked warily.

"I was being initiated. I only followed orders. I was in before I'd realized what I'd even done. Maybe I tried to protect my brother because of the things I've done but it was sincerely because I couldn't help you. You were my God particle, my heart, remember that? When you disappeared, I blamed myself. This is some kind of re-union huh?" He tossed back a shot that was sitting on the kitchen table.

"Yup. Sounds like a real party," I joked back. I must have looked bipolar as hell. Tears were streaming down my cheeks and I wiped them away angrily while smiling at Carlos.

Jin who had apparently been eavesdropping poked his head around the corner, "Aww, Carlos. You are the clos-est, man; move her gun away and I'll call everybody in for a group hug. She looks like she needs a hug."

That one made even me laugh. He was such a charac-ter.

"Fuck a drink. I need to smoke after all this murder, death, kill talk." Tia always wanted or needed to smoke something.

"Alicia, you gonna smoke this one with me?" She looked at me expectantly.

"To hell with it; it's definitely been one of those days. Why not?"

We all relocated into the living room and once again I let the relaxing calmness overtake me and my eyes kept wandering over Carlos's face. He looked older and yet still seemed to have remained exactly the same. He'd removed his leather jacket and I could see that his shoul-ders and chest seemed wider and broader. They stretched the fabric of his plaid button down and it tapered at his narrow waist. He was sitting beside me on the couch when he turned and caught me staring.

"You're going to give me a complex if you keep doing that," he said quietly before chuckling.

"Sorry, it's just that you bring back so many memories. Good, mostly bad."

"Well I have something for you. I kept it." He pulled his wallet out of his back pocket and unzipped a side compartment.

Time felt as if it had stopped and I sat there motionless with a million and one emotions running through me, as I stared at my daddy's necklace hanging from his fingers.

"They always take a trophy. I stole it and Tony's class ring as retribution. It was the least I could do."

The gold medallion was cold against my skin and yet it felt so alive and so vibrant with Daddy's energy that I could almost hear his voice.

"I want you to know," Carlos began saying, "Atum-Rah was believed to be the first Egyptian god. When we take the oath of the coterie we are branded with a falcon holding a snake. Talion is the Latin word for retaliation."

I'd started to get up and hug Carlos when the doorbell rang. We all looked at each other questioningly and I reached for my pistol, confused at it not being in its holster until I remembered I'd left it in the kitchen. No one ever came to my house unannounced.

Signaling for everyone to go upstairs, I retrieved Destiny and sprayed Febreze as I made my way to the front door. Relief swept through me when I saw it was only Lorenzo.

"Hey, Lo, what are you doing here?"

"I called and sent you texts, didn't get an answer. Came to make sure y'all were okay." He marched inside without an invitation, which immediately annoyed me.

"We're fine. I went to the grocery store and Tia was upstairs asleep."

"Whose truck is that out front?"

"It's mine. And how are you, cousin?" Tia came downstairs in one of my bathrobes.

"Big truck for a small woman. Do I smell marijuana? Al, may I see you in the other room please?" He marched toward the kitchen before I could answer and I followed, but not before giving Tia a wide-eyed stare that clearly stated, "Cousin? What the fuck?"

Who *wasn't* this girl related to in my circle of people.

He didn't say anything at first, just stood there. I noticed Carlos's jacket hanging over the back of one of the chairs and moved to the opposite side of the kitchen.

"Alicia. You're high, and don't tell me otherwise. We do this shit for a living. If Chief found out—"

"No, if Chief found out Tia's your family that you didn't even want to pay to get witness protection for that might be interesting. Or that shit at the house with Vee. What were you really doing, letting off some steam because she put her hands on your baby cousin? The case that got us our break could go to shit if that girl says two words. 'Police brutality.' Don't come in my house threatening me about what Chief finds out."

"Al. *Mi hermosa.* No. No. That's not even why I came over here." He walked toward me, speaking that Spanish shit that I didn't understand.

"*Mami,* you know we've had this connection ever since you found out that *punta* husband of yours wasn't shit. I took care of that for you, remember. I got you out of that. Think, *mujer.* I want you. I can take care of you now. You don't have to do this cop shit anymore; it's beneath you. I've always wanted you to be mine."

Lord, I was too damn high for all of this foolishness right now, and not with all the information Carlos had just thrown into the equation.

"No, Lorenzo. You are my partner. We can't mix. That was all circumstantial; it just happened that we were there. Speaking of you being somewhere, since Tia is family and all, tell me about your little visit to her place earlier today."

He scowled before turning and walking angrily away from me toward the kitchen table. He'd started to sit down but stopped when he saw Carlos's jacket.

"Oh, I get it now." His back was to me. He gently touched the sleeve before turning to face me. Staring at me silently, I could literally see his expression grow distant. It became stormy, resentful, and colder than the temperature outside.

"Business huh? So you gonna pay me for handling business then? Your husband wasn't no Boy Scout. He was taking money to make innocent men guilty and guilty men innocent. The Padillas paid him crazy money and they were content with the favor I did them since Señor Padilla is behind bars. I even did you a favor and told them you didn't know about the money."

Wide-eyed, I stared at Lorenzo. Did everyone know what the fuck Davin was doing except for me? "That wasn't a favor for me or anyone. You saw exactly what happened that night. What I saw." My mind was reeling, trying to replay every step of the night in the garage.

Lorenzo walked up to me, his overbearing cologne reminiscent of Heinz 57 Sauce. *Did he have to douse himself in that mess? Good Lord.* He was so close I could see the light brown stubble underneath his chin and smell the slight scent of gin on his breath. He trailed his rough finger down my cheek.

"You fuck whoever you have upstairs and then you send them on their way for good. Go ahead and get it out of your system. Or, you come up with the 1.3 million dollars your husband squandered for Señor Padilla's life. If not, I talk to Chief and then I talk to the Padillas. A drug test will prove my word over yours at the station, *mi hermosa.*"

Jerking my chin away I ground my teeth together, my eyes glaring.

Lorenzo saw himself out, as Tia darted into the kitchen, looking at me questioningly. My high was causing all of this information to form in crystalline perfect images in my head.

My husband was a dirty lawyer being bought by the highest bidder and when he'd failed to win a case, Lorenzo was bought to kill him. The garage just worked in Lo's favor. I didn't get any money when Davin died because my marriage was fake. Shoni got all of his money. I only got to keep the house and the cars. And Lorenzo was now trying to blackmail me into his bed or out of more money!

Grabbing the tequila bottle off the counter I took an angry swig before launching it across the kitchen. It was time for Tajah Cardin to come back from the dead.

Chapter 14

Deter-Money-Tion

"Is everything okay?" They were all in the kitchen in a manner of seconds after the glass shattered. All I could do was nod. It was Carlos who asked the question.

"I need a shower. I do my best thinking in the shower."

My room felt farther away than normal, and the climb up the stairs seemed to take longer than usual. So much had happened within the last couple of hours from Carlos to my daddy's necklace to Lorenzo's craziness that it left my head spinning.

I lathered myself in a peach vanilla body wash; the water was cold and the bottle was empty by the time I was done. All of this just seemed too surreal for me to process at one time. My mind was someplace else as I put on my bathrobe and walked out into my bedroom. I jumped when I saw him reclining on my bed.

"What the hell are you doing in here, nigga?"

"I thought you might need some help lotioning up or something. I love me a big girl." Jin had his shoes off and dirty white socks all up on my white down comforter.

"Carlos! I'm gonna shoot your boy if you don't come get him." I stormed back into the bathroom, and I could hear Carlos burst in as Jin ran out.

"I'm sorry. You know we've been drinking all evening and Tia been acting kind of off since some chick called her a little while ago." He was towering in the doorway. He'd definitely gotten taller since high school.

"It's fine. I wouldn't have killed him, just wounded him." Not thinking, I placed one leg on the chest at the foot of my bed and began to lotion my ankles and feet.

"You know I really did miss you. Thought about you all the time." He'd come up behind me and I continued as if I didn't hear him, but I was soaking in every single word.

"I tried searching for you, did a ton of those Internet searches. You changed your damn name on me." My hair had fallen out of its bun from the steam in the shower and it was hanging in damp twists over one shoulder. He touched my hair so softly I almost thought I imagined it.

Turning to tell him exactly what I thought of his bullshit half-ass Internet search, my words were cut off as he leaned down and pressed his full lips into mine. My lips parted and my knees almost gave out as his tongue met mine. Damn, the man tasted just like I remembered except this time there was the faintest hint of tequila.

Smiling into his lips, I couldn't help thinking that this was what the fuck a kiss was supposed to feel like. Pulling back, I traced his lower lip with my tongue and it was like walking down a favorite path or revisiting a favorite place. All the firsts that we'd had together, well all the firsts that I'd had with him, made me feel so open and confident. My robe fell open and I pressed my body up against his.

Grabbing his hand I guided it down in between my legs, I wanted him to feel how wet I was. My grown ass must have forgotten who I was dealing with. He slid his hand back and forth, appreciating the sound of my ocean sloshing against his fingers. Before knew it, he parted the sea and buried two middle fingers so deep I almost cried. He kissed me hard to keep me quiet because the door was still open, but ask me if I gave a damn. I used what little sense I had left to unbutton his pants so I could give him his own torture.

He was hard and ready; my hand closed in as tight of a fist as I could make around him and I started stroking him upward. The harder I stroked him was just reason for him to show me how much harder and deeper he'd could go with his fingers. Stopping just for a second I used my free hand to undo his zipper and pull his pants and boxers to the floor. Davin, Tr . . . Ta . . . Who? I couldn't even remember the other nigga's name. But they ain't neva do what the hell Carlos did.

This fool put one of my legs up on his forearm and in one fluid motion he was so deep inside me all I could do was wrap my arms around his neck and try to remember how to breathe. I hadn't worked out or stretched and every muscle in my body was screaming but I was dealing with it because he was stretching the hell out of the important one right that second. It got to the point I was up on my damn tippy toes, and I tapped him pointing towards the bed. Ladies and gentlemen, I am a creamer. He pulled out and there was Tajah sauce all over him.

"Now you know how women feel when y'all cum all over us," I said while laughing.

"Ha ha, except I love this." He smiled at me while pulling off his shirt, before closing the door. Then he wiped my juices off of himself and licked his fingers like icing off a Krispy Kreme doughnut. My mouth fell open and stayed there, until he fell on the bed in between my legs to get whatever he didn't get off of himself.

If Tia and whoever he was, whose name I suddenly couldn't remember, downstairs didn't know what we were doing, they knew now. My fingers clawed at the sheets, because this mothafucka had learned some tricks over the damn years. His tongue was telling a story to my clit and he'd slid those thick-ass fingers back inside me, doing come here's and go there's and dosey do's. I didn't fuckin' know. I damn near stopped breathing when his free hand slid upward to tease my nipples. That was all it took to have me scared I was gonna break his fingers. My muscles started convulsing, and I could feel the first twitch, the first hint of the damn finish line. That's when this fool decided to hop up like a fucking surfer and ride the big wave in.

I screamed. I've never screamed during sex in my entire life. My nails clawed up his back and Carlos moaned, taking that as fuel to dig even deeper. He pinned my arms above my head to keep my nails out of him and I resorted to biting his neck and shoulders. There was only so much I could take as wave after wave washed over me. Just when I thought I was done, he released my arms and reached underneath me. I gaspedat what had to have been a pinky easing ever so slowly into the only other unoccupied hole down there, and it all started again. Flashes, sparks, explosions, and all kinds of foolishness were going off inside of my head until I was just lying there breathless and unable to move.

"I bet you feel real calm now, don't you?" He had this smug smile on his face that I'd have loved to wipe off with a smart ass comment if I could.

"Mmm hmm," was all I had the strength to say. Minutes passed before I had the energy to actually hold a conversation. "Carlos. I lost the baby."

His hand, which had been making lazy circles on my shoulder, stopped at my words. "What baby, Tajah? You mean—"

"Yes, I got pregnant. It happened that first time."

He pulled me into his chest and held me. The slow, steady beat of his heart bumped against my ear, comforting me, and I finally let go. All the years of pent-up hurt, anger, and frustration came out in a rush of tears. My body shook from gut-wrenching sobs and I soaked his chest. All the while Carlos just rubbed my back, telling me everything would be fine.

"Can you tell me what happened?" he asked quietly against my hair once I'd finally calmed down. I nodded, taking a deep shaky breath, and I started at the moment I left Charmaine.

Carlos sniffed quietly and I knew he was crying over a child he'd never get to see or hold. I'd already done the same on many occasions myself.

"Well after Tarique calmed down enough for me to explain, I healed and things slowly got back to normal, but I never forgave him. He couldn't have children and yet he stole mine from me. One night he came home irritated at something and he took his anger out on me for the last time. I fixed him a drink with a couple of crushed sleeping pills to make him drowsy. Drew him a steamy, hot bath and waited until he was in the tub, as was our custom. I laid a hot washcloth over his eyes and a copperhead on his chest. Then I locked him in the bathroom, took his cell and all the cash out of his wallet, and I waited until the splashing stopped."

"Where in God's name did you find a copperhead in New York, woman? You actually handled a venomous snake." He shook his head in disbelief.

"I did. One night when I was lying on the floor in pain I thought I was hallucinating. There were these eyes staring at me, yellow demon eyes from hell. It took me a couple of beatings to remember I'd seen them. Each time I would have the same vision. I remember regaining consciousness one morning and having my heart stop. She was drawn to my body heat and was coiled in a ball in between my breasts. The snake was a baby when I found her, or you can say she found me. Tarique didn't let me have any friends or see my cousin, and I was desperate for something to love. There were plenty of mice to feed her and you know we have plenty of 'em 'round here. I knew she was venomous but I didn't care if I lived or died so I picked her up and kept her hidden in a shoebox when he was home. Left her out when he was gone."

"So, the name change, this Alicia person you became, was because of him?"

"I still didn't know who was looking for me so I felt it would be safe to just reinvent myself. Start all over."

"Well since we're baring our souls right now I think there's something else you should now, Tajah. Even though I'm out of the coterie, there are a few guys in there who keep me up on non-confidential stuff. I threw your partner's name around. I think he's trying to buy his way in."

Well I'd be damned. That would explain why the hell Lorenzo wanted all that damn money all of a sudden. You had to either be born in or recruited; otherwise, I guessed it cost, hell, $1.3 million to get in?

"I'm so glad you found me, Carlos. I think I might need your help."

"You know I'm here for whatever you need."

Chapter 15

The Devil In You
Brings Out The Snake In Me

Slipping into the station bright and early wasn't a problem. The only way I could come up with over a million dollars overnight was by taking it from the evidence vault. There were a couple of massive pallets of money inside from various robberies and drug busts. I hadn't set up a code yet but Lorenzo's was easy enough to figure out. He used the same numbers for everything, 38-36-42: his dream woman's measurements. Once inside I grabbed enough cash, a micro-transmitting device, and a detector.

Carlos and Jin were waiting at the house for me. Tia had left to meet up with Shoni sometime during the night and sent me texts swearing she'd be fine. I couldn't force her to stay in "witness protection" and since Lorenzo was her cousin, she was more his responsibility than mine. Back at the house I began prepping the briefcase and the money for my exchange with Lorenzo.

"Damn! Lemme hold a stack. No? Okay, lemme hold a twenty?" Jin was sitting across the kitchen table from me, damn near salivating. Carlos was at the stove making breakfast. He had the whole house smelling like steak and eggs. I was too nervous and too focused to eat.

"Tajah? What if your police people notice the money is gone?" Carlos seemed extremely frazzled by that piece of the equation.

"They won't notice. No one inventories the evidence locker until the end of the year, and they only pull evidence for specific cases. I pulled this from old case files and I used Lo's access code. I don't even have a code set up. They'll think he took it. I just need him to take the cash and leave me alone long enough for me to get what I need."

Carlos nodded at my answer before returning his attention to his steaks. My attention went to cleaning my personal weapon. If anything happened later today I didn't plan on using my service-issued pistol. Destiny would not be choosing anyone's fate this time.

Time seemed to take forever to go by and at I texted Lorenzo promptly at three p.m. to meet me at my place in an hour. *Okay, gentlemen, let the games begin.*

I'd dressed in jeans and one of my favorite oversized hooded sweatshirts so I could wear my over the shoulder holster underneath. Carlos had moved his truck two streets over and he and Jin were in the laundry room just in case Lorenzo decided to act foolish. He showed up at four o'clock on the dot as expected.

"You've got something for me?" He was out of uniform as well, dressed in dark blue jeans, a white Ralph Lauren sweater, and Kenneth Cole shoes and jacket. *Nice clothes for a cop,* I thought.

"Yup. Here." I stuck the briefcase out in his direction and he walked inside and laid it on the coffee table, opening it and thumbing through a few stacks of bills before snapping it shut.

"Nice doing business with you. Glad we could see eye to eye on things." He winked before smiling wide and striding out of the front door. I let out the breath I'd been holding. Carlos and Jin rejoined me. They both looked ready to go to war.

"Okay. What do we do now?" Carlos was looking at me intently.

Pulling out the tracking device, I turned it on and it immediately began picking up the signal for the transmitter I'd planted on the briefcase.

"Now we see where he takes the money. Whoever he's paying probably has something to do with everything that has happened to me and Davin. Lo isn't smart enough to do all this on his own."

We climbed into the truck and followed the signal. It was almost an hour's drive before we stopped in a neighborhood of Pleasure House Road out Ocean View. He was obviously making sure he wasn't being followed with all the extra hoops and hurdles, and he didn't do a good enough job. He parked in a cul-de-sac that accessed the beach. We pulled up beside him as he was getting out, and Carlos walked up and casually stood in front of him, placing his pistol tightly against his chest.

"You signal or call whoever it is as you would normally do or I'll be more than happy to blow your damn head off." Lorenzo looked around, realized he was outnumbered, and scowled.

"I call and then I walk up to the house two doors down." He nodded at an enormous white sandstone house with a three-car garage.

"Well then make the call. You so much as stutter and it'll be the last sound you make. Jin, come assist our friend here." Jin walked over and reached into Lo's coat. He found his service weapon and handed it to me. He then grabbed Lo's cell and handed it to him.

"I'm outside. I've got it." He hung up and stared Carlos down angrily.

"Now, I go into the house." Jin handed him the briefcase and he started walking as we followed.

The house didn't look like the type of place for this type of transaction to occur. Then again, that's probably what made it the perfect location. The front porch had one of those large family-style swings on it that swayed with the breeze. The streets were pretty much deserted this time of year but I was sure they were buzzing with people in late spring and summer. The front door was unlocked and my senses were on high alert as we followed him inside. Spanish mariachi music was playing throughout the dimly lit house. Lo led us through the main foyer, past a large, fancy dining room with china place settings.

"Braullo, is that you?" My heart sank and Lorenzo, or Braullo as he was just called, burst out in anger.

"Tia, what the hell are you doing here?" Lorenzo shouted.

We walked down five steps into a large sitting room. Winding staircases ran along the top floors on both sides overlooking the open area. There was a large fireplace sunken in the floor in the center. It was regal almost, elegant looking, decorated with red and gold carpet and Versace furnishings. Sitting around the fireplace staring back at us were three faces I never in a billion years though I'd see in the same room together. My pistol with its custom silencer was out and in my hand before anyone could say anything to me.

"Tajah. Is that anyway to greet your mother after all these years?" Gone was the doped-up alcoholic degenerate I remembered. In her place was this statuesque queen-like matriarch with rubies in her ears and rocks on her fingers so large they looked unreal. I blinked several times just to see if she'd disappear, but she was still there, with Tia and Shoni on either side of her like they were having some kind of fucking tea party.

"Momma, Braullo has been playing both sides. He somehow managed to set up the man you'd found to marry Shoni and protect the Padillas' assets with Tajah. Then he killed him and he's trying to blackmail Tajah."

Had Tia just called my hoeing-ass momma "Momma"? I felt lightheaded. Now I knew why Tia had looked familiar the first time I'd seen her. Next to my mother, I could see how much she resembled her. It was like looking at a portrait from years ago and an age-progression image side by side. There were hundreds of questions but I couldn't get a single one of them to come out of my mouth.

"Braullo? What do you have to say for all of this? I trusted you." My Mother's voice was quiet and sweet; it didn't even go up an octave as she addressed him.

Lorenzo just stood there with his head lowered; his shoulders were heaving in anger. I knew him well enough to know he was thinking of how he could fight his way out of this situation.

Then it happened so fast if I hadn't been standing there I would have never believed it. One minute he was standing and in the next he was on the ground in pain, blood seeping from a small knife sticking out of his leg. Startled and shocked I looked at Carlos, who was just as stupefied as I was. Even Jin was quiet.

"He was a fag and careless about it. When Al . . . I mean Tajah joined the force she wouldn't give me the time of day." Lorenzo groaned before continuing. "I just told him to marry her and I'd keep quiet about it. All he had to do was keep her at arm's length, make her miserable, and then I'd make her see her worth and take her off his hands. It was selfish, I know. He fucked up and lost that case and I got the orders to take him out."

"Tsk. Tsk. Tsk. You disappoint me so much. Lorenzo Braullo Cordello, give Davin my love." My mother spoke the words so carelessly you'd have thought we were discussing the color of the carpet. Her hand raised and she was poised, ready to fling another small blade with deadly precision in Lo's direction.

"Now, now, sweetheart, there's no need in killing the boy." Before she could flick her wrist, Chief Reid walked up behind her and kissed her softly on the cheek.

For the second time in a day, I was absolutely speechless.

Tia stood up from her seat, clutching her chest theatrically. "Hold the fuck up, I know that voice. Hemingway?"

I'd have laughed at her expression if I weren't in just as much shock as she was.

"No, no. Please sit back down. Alicia, thank you for all your hard work in getting us the files. We owe you more than you'll ever know." He smiled down into my mother's face and they kissed. I silently gagged. They were like sinister evil commandos as they smiled at us after letting each other's lips go.

"You two. Go wait on the porch please." My mother addressed Carlos and Jin. They gave me worried glances and I nodded, letting them know it was okay. She waited until they were outside. Silver whirred through the air.

It was when Lorenzo grabbed his neck, letting out an eerie gurgle that I'd realized what happened. Momma got some of that bite back into her tone that I remembered so well. "Men don't tell me what to do anymore, dear. Braullo disrespected my daughters and my rules, which means he in turn has disrespected the queen. No one gets away with that. Do you still have a problem?"

Chief Reid shook his head back and forth quickly as he backed down to take his place quietly behind her chair.

"So, my oldest has finally decided to find her way home?" She focused her calculating, devious snake eyes on me.

Hard as I tried I couldn't find an ounce of love in my body for the woman. Not after she'd gotten my father killed and especially not after all I'd been through. "Not really. I was just following Lorenzo and here is where he led me. Um, Tia called you 'mother.' So are we half sisters or something?"

"No, you're as sisterly as sisters get; she just took after my side and you took after your real father. Taj, or Manny as you knew him, was both your and Tia's daddy. Me and him hit a rough patch when I was pregnant with you. I dated and married the man you called Daddy honestly, because he was the last male in his family. He was supposed to run the Lot; we were supposed to be damn near royalty. Your play-daddy had no backbone. He didn't like what the Law of Talion stood for anymore. He even named you after another man. He was so poetic, always trying to turn a negative into a positive."

She was laughing maniacally, like a crazy woman, and all I wanted to do was break down and cry. Everything I'd ever known was a lie, a story, manipulated by this monster in front of me.

"So that means Carlos is my cousin, too?" I had to know; there was no way we could continue if we were truly blood.

"I don't know him to be kinfolk; who told you that?"

"Momma, he's not a real cousin. Just someone I'm real cool with." Tia smiled nervously at me, and for once I was thankful to have a cool sister, even though the circumstances hurt me to the core of my soul.

"And I didn't find out you were my sister until Shoni called me. Trust me, I was all like ewwww. I looked at my sister's ass! Then I was like well my sister hot though, thick as fuck, too. Good genes up in here. Thanks, Momma."

"Tajah, are you ready to take your rightful place where you belong? I've made history. No woman has ever even been allowed as a member of the brotherhood, the coterie. Look at your momma now. I've managed to turn this shit into the sisterhood. We have damn near every cop, lawyer, judge, drug dealer, and congressmen under our pretty little painted thumbs."

"What happened to Manny?"

"Manny happened to Manny. Too busy running his mouth, and showing off how big his balls were all over town. While I was doing all the thinking behind the scenes for his dumb ass, Momma got jealous." She pouted before continuing. "Momma wanted some big balls to show off too. So Momma cut off Manny's balls, they're there in formal living room on display in the curio cabinet with my crystal. I had them preserved of course. Now Momma has the biggest fucking balls in town."

This shit was like a Quentin Tarantino movie gone wrong and my momma had somehow become the psychotic unstoppable bad guy. She'd offered me a position in the coterie and turning her down meant death. You were born in, recruited, or you bought your way in, but once you were chosen you did not turn down an offer.

Now everything made perfect sense. The reason why she let me become a cop, because she could have shut that shit down at any given time, was so I'd have the inside hand with the police. She probably even worked everything out so Tia could learn a street hustle outside of the drug game. She'd managed to con her way into my daddy's life even though she was pregnant with another man's child. She'd then conned Manny and somehow found a way to get off her back and lying up underneath him, to being on top. She was a queen con woman.

"Tajah?" Her voice was shrill and high. I jerked at the sound of it and looked up, my expression puzzled and dark. "What took you so long to handle Tarique?"

A chill ran up my spine and something began to come alive inside me that I'd locked away the same night I'd locked him in the bathroom with my copperhead.

"Obviously I left your bangles and that damn address. I also wanted to teach your little ass a lesson about running away. He was cheap labor. You never questioned why he had such a nice truck and such a rundown apartment? He obviously worked for us."

Every beating I'd ever endured, every single busted lip, bruised or cracked rib, all the black eyes and the verbal abuse, even losing my baby was all because this bitch just said she was trying to teach me a lesson.

"Lessons involve climbing trees and learning not to climb on weak limbs. A lesson is when you learn not to reach across a hot iron or fry bacon naked. You knew where I was and what I was going through, and you didn't bother to do anything. He damn near tortured me daily. Almost killed me, and on more than one occasion. I nearly starved to death."

She raised a finely arched eyebrow before asking, "Where do you think the snake came from, my love?"

She laughed and clapped like she'd just watched the ending of a good movie. This woman had to have been completely out of her mind. As many times as I'd lain on that floor unconscious, that damn snake could have killed easily lashed out and killed me. Yet she thought she was helping.

"The snake?" I whispered.

Her eyes were bright with joy and triumph as I stared at her with so much rage and pent-up anger that I shook from head to toe. The smile slowly began to fade from her face. For the first time since I'd entered her house I smiled a toothy ear-to-ear "Joker crushes the Batman" kind of smile.

"Yes, what about the snake?" she asked quietly, tilting her head to the side in question.

"I am the snake!" I hissed back at her, before firing two shots center mass. They dotted her chest like snake eyes, the silencer doing its job perfectly. Tia screamed in terror and I tried to feel bad for her but I couldn't find it in me. Carlos and Jin ran inside just as I shot Chief Reid once in the forehead.

"Nigga, I told you she was gonna kill some-damn-body if you left her evil ass alone," Jin whispered super loud from the doorway.

Carlos quickly put his boy in check. "Shut up, Jin." He grabbed me by my shoulders. "Tajah, look at me. Are you okay?"

Smiling, I pulled my daddy's medallion from underneath my hoodie and picked up Lorenzo's briefcase. "I'm good now. The Law of Talion is my operation and things are about to be real fuckin' different. I need a list of every member, ally, and all of our assets. Tia, you are my sister and everything but you are practically a stranger to me. You've seen what I'd do to my own mother. So, whose team are you on? You too, Shoni." They looked up from my mother's side; tears were streaming down her and Shoni's faces. They were both sniffling loudly, and puffy eyed they responded in unison, "Yours."

"Carlos, I'm going to need a king to help me reorganize this secret ball of shit society back into what it should be. Would you do me the honor?"

He puffed out his chest and gave me a huge, bright smile before pulling me in for a long, deep kiss. You'd have thought I'd just asked him to marry me and we weren't standing there surrounded by three dead bodies.

"Wait," Jin said, sliding his hand in between our bodies, separating us. "Why everybody getting jobs in this secret thing except for me? Can I be a secretary? I'll answer the secret society lines and shit. I ain't too proud to answer phones and fax secret society messages. Do y'all fax messages? Matter of fact, you think your momma have any other thick-hipped chocolate childrens we need to go rescue because I'm feeling kind of left out. Can I have a kiss too?"

He needed to be the house comedian was what he needed to do.

"Damn, Jin, listen, you are an honorary member. Your first job is to shut up and help dispose of these bodies." I bit my lip to keep from smiling as I addressed him.

"You got a sword? Ain't I supposed to get knighted or tapped on the shoulder or something like that? You can't just say the words and that's it. There has to be some kind of ritual."

I looked at him sternly. "How about I've got this pistol, and I'm going to tap this trigger a couple times in your honor if you don't let me get back to kissin' my man."

He saluted me or something close to it, and walked over to Tia and Shoni. I stared up at Carlos, amazed that with my momma and Manny officially gone life seemed so much clearer again.

"You know, I don't think Alicia is going to come back after this," I told Carlos.

"That's fine," he replied, looking down at the briefcase in my hand and then around at my momma's house before whispering in my ear, "Not that it mattered but Alicia was kind of broke anyway. I'd stay Tajah if I were you too. Besides, she's the one I've always been in love with."

Our lips met to the soundtrack of Shoni knocking Jin upside the head and cursing him out for touching or looking at something on her body or booty. I was a little too preoccupied to pay attention to the fine details. Yes, our lives were definitely going to be interesting from this moment forward.

Notes